THE VILLAGE OF SUSPECTS

AN INSPECTOR RUPERT MYSTERY

BY

PETER SAMUEL

TABLE OF CONTENTS

CHAPTER

Inspector Rupert travelled to London in preparation for starting his new job with the London Metropolitan Police.

It was a wet and windy Sunday morning as he travelled down the A1. A journey he had made many times before, when he was first married to Deborah, who would eventually persuade him to follow her dream of becoming a teacher in the village of Welwyn in Hertfordshire.

When doing that, he would have to leave his beloved Metropolitan Police in London and the city he loved so much.

There were those ghosts again when he remembered the London subway that clattered, banged, and swayed as it thundered towards his drop-off point, where he would alight and join the throng of marchers who seemed to walk in step like an army platoon on the parade ground. The early commuters, heads bobbing up and down in unison, some with bowler hats and carnations in their jacket lapels.

When they reached the escalator, that is when the courtesy and manners disappeared, as they pushed, shoved, and jostled for the next available space on the moving steps that would lift them up to street level.

He was over the moon at being drafted back into Scotland Yard, Serious Crime in London. However, this came at a cost. Demotion from Chief Inspector back to Inspector, a rank he had fast-tracked, attained and held in 1937. With a promotion on the horizon. He was only 23 years old back then. One of the youngest Inspectors to gain a senior rank so soon.

A Chief Inspector Frank Skinner met him when he arrived at Scotland Yard on Monday, when he reported for duty.

He led him to a small office from which Inspector Rupert would work until his bigger office on the first floor became available after it had been decorated and refurbished.

Inspector Rupert couldn't care less about its size, an office at last, that's when he realized something was happening at last, but it was not the welcome he expected. Things in the Metropolitan Police had changed.

The Chief Inspector was not the friendliest of types as he barked out the information and orders. "Listen, Rupert, you are going to be thrown in at the deep end. We're having problems with a murder case in the village of Tringford, which lies close to the B1019 and B1818 junction. We, in the top brass, have spoken amongst ourselves, and your name was mentioned and put forward to handle this awkward case". The DCI threw the case notes onto the desk.

"The Commissioner has given me your orders and agrees you are the man to take up the case. The village is a bit awkward to get to. I suppose the best way would be through Chelmsford, along the A12 until you pick up the sign for the A414 that takes you to an unlisted C road that links you with the B1019 to Tringford. There's a small hotel where lodgings have already been arranged for you. It's nothing fancy, but comfortable and good food". He paused. "There's one thing you should know, Inspector, and that is you will hit a brick wall as far as information gathering is concerned. The locals tend to clam up when they find that the police are in the village. What information we do have is here in the report sheet, along with your case note orders".

Inspector Rupert knew about Chief Inspector Skinner. A leech and a parasite who claimed and gained promotion through the successful work of other officers.

Inspector Rupert smiled. "I've come across brick walls in Hertfordshire, sir, part of the reason why I'm here. If this case turns out to be as tricky as getting to the village, then I think I've got a bit of a problem on my hands; however, never say die, eh?".

Chief Inspector Skinner had little sympathy, and his response was short.

"Be quiet, Inspector, but you'll manage".

"How long has this case been on the go, sir? Why can't one of the county police take it on? To bring in Scotland Yard seems like a waste of resources to me."

"Just get yourself out to Tringford, Inspector".

Skinner hadn't answered how long this unsolved murder case had been open. Inspector Rupert suspected it had been open and closed, then reopened for some reason. However, this was not the right time to rock the boat, so he sat and listened to the Chief Inspector waffle on, something he himself had probably done as a Chief Inspector in the past.

After a lengthy briefing, he telephoned the Tringford hotel to confirm that he would be arriving tomorrow and that his room was in fact booked.

He still had his luxury flat in Waterloo Mansions in Mayfair, expecting to get another good night's sleep before taking up his assignment the next morning. That was not about to happen. He was ordered to get out to the village without delay. "No rest for the wicked, eh"? He said in a calm tone of voice. "One thing, Rupert, protocol and procedure have changed since you were last at the Yard. We know your reputation for doing things your way, however, we at the Yard do things our way nowadays, and I hope you understand that from the outset, that way we'll get along just fine, but if you don't, then me and my superiors will come down on you like a ton of bricks, is that perfectly clear Inspector."?

"Clear as day sir, I think you'll find by my past record, that I've never had an unsolved case, not ever, and that is because I did things my way, nobody else's, apart from a good team of officers behind me, I hope that is clear to you sir, and of course your superiors". He smiled.

"I suspected this of you, Rupert. You think because you have massive wealth behind you, that you can march into the Met. and do as you please. Well, let me inform you that your money will not make any difference to your standing in the Metropolitan Police, or at Scotland Yard".

"Frankly, sir, I didn't expect the flags and banners to be flying when I returned to the Met.

However, I did expect a friendly welcome. I can see now that things have changed. The transfer of an officer coming from another force was always given a smile at the very least. But just to finish, before this conversation gets out of control," he paused.

"I've never used my wealth to enhance my career prospects, certainly not in policing. I inherited my wealth due to the death of a dear friend and his family, so please don't mention this subject again, Chief Inspector. I think that should be clear enough to you, sir".

"If you disrespect my rank and fail me, Rupert, so help me, I'll crucify you. You're a marked man in my book".

"Yes, yes, DCI. Skinner, but believe me, I've been through worse instances than this, so if you don't mind, I'll get on with the job to which the Commissioner has assigned me".

He pushed past the Chief Inspector without any words of "Excuse me" and made his way to the front desk, where he received the keys to the allocated police car. He couldn't believe that his first day on his return to duty with the Met had started with a confrontation.

Inspector Rupert took his allocated orders to the front desk. Chief Inspector Skinner had followed him and continued to give his verbal opinions of Inspector Rupert's wealth and failed marriage.

Inspector Rupert knew the D.C.I was looking for an aggressive response. That is why this was said in the presence of a witness. The bar officer, who was behind the desk, kept writing.

His time would come, so he ignored the jibes. After a final altercation, he walked calmly out of Scotland Yard to the police car compound.

He started the drive out of London, which seemed to take forever. Every traffic light he came to showed amber or red. "What a bloody start to the day". He thought as the traffic lights moved from red to amber, then eventually turned green.

He reached the north circular and headed east towards Chelmsford, where he picked up the A12. Driving through the town, he followed the Chief Inspector's directions to the letter, occasionally having to stop and look at the road map before he turned onto the A414.

The drive got slower and steadily worse when he reached the B 1819. There were farm tractors and combine harvesters making their way from the fields; some had trailers attached, with children sitting on the piles of potatoes, freshly picked by them, to earn a few shillings. They waved enthusiastically as Inspector Rupert sounded his horn, which was totally disregarded by the tractor driver, who eventually turned into the farm gate entrance.

If he thought that was bad, then a bigger delay was to follow when he reached the unlisted C road. Flocks of sheep came towards him, controlled by the collie dogs and whistles from the shepherd. After the road was cleared, he knew it had to come, and he was right. A herd of cattle was coming towards him, the drover tapping the rear end of the last cow and shouting. He had to reverse yet again until a passing place could be found. He sat waiting until the herd had passed. He wondered if this was a set-up. Did the surrounding farms and villagers know he was coming? After all, he was booked into the hotel, and word would surely have spread like wildfire. He smiled at the thought and dismissed it as paranoia.

He looked at his watch when he arrived at the hotel. "Five bloody hours", he said angrily as he collected his bags from the back seat and made his way to the reception. He rang the desk bell three times, then banged on it when there was no one answering. He heard a door creak in the back of the reception behind the curtain.

The weather-beaten face seemed to say it all. "Yes"? The small woman with a couldn't care less attitude asked abruptly.

"Inspector Rupert, Scotland Yard, I've a reservation already booked". He said in a friendly voice.

"Sign here," she said in another couldn't care less attitude, handing him a nibbed pen and a bottle of ink.

Inspector Rupert had to smile as he took out his gold Parker pen that had been given to him as a going-away present from the team at the Welwyn Garden City police station in Hertfordshire.

He tried to make light of the conversation. "When is the village expecting to move into the twentieth century"? His smile had no effect and was treated with contempt.

"You're in room nine, located at the rear of the hotel in the converted stables, breakfast is at 08:00 am sharp, and dinner is at 18:00 pm. until 19:00 pm". She handed him the room key.

"There is no room service. If you require a drink, then the bar is open from 11:00 am until 14:00 pm, then 18:00 pm until 22:00 pm". She shut the registration ledger loudly after he had signed it.

Inspector Rupert noticed her name on the lapel badge.

"Just two things before you disappear, Nancy". He paused. "I'll be wanting to speak to you in due course regarding a murder that took place in the village a while back, so don't leave the village without informing me".

He saw the disgusted look on her face. "I live in the village of Maldon, Inspector, and that is four miles away, so do I stay here until you're ready to question me"?

Inspector Rupert rephrased the request. "Only until I've taken a statement from you, which we can do later when I've unpacked and freshened up". He had to have the last word.

"Tell me, Nancy, have you finished your course?" He leaned towards her on the reception desk. "What course"? She asked indignantly.

"The charm school course, if so, you could sue them". He laughed as he lifted his bags, wondering what to expect when he got to his room, but he was surprised at the spacious, well-furnished room with a toilet, wash basin, and shower facilities.

He threw his bags onto the case rack, removed his shoes and lay down on the comfortable double bed to relax. It had been some morning, right from the outset.

It wasn't long before he drifted into a light sleep, coming awake with the sound of a car door slamming shut. He looked at his watch before jumping up and stripping off to shower before dinner. He took a statement from Nancy, the unhelpful troll, before entering the dining room.

The meal itself was very good, then he remembered that he needed towels, so he went to the reception, prepared for the Troll to appear; however, it was a well-mannered young woman who was behind the reception. "Can I help you, sir"? She asked in a pleasant voice.

"I had a shower earlier, only to discover a hand towel was the only one available".

"I apologise on behalf of the hotel, sir; I'll have that attended to immediately". She gave a radiant smile. "Is there anything else"?

"I would prefer to have a room in the hotel." He said in the hope she would move him.

"There is room three, sir, but it is below the stairs and across from the bar, which can get very noisy when other residents decide to have a late-night drink, but I can arrange to have you moved if you wish".

He looked at her lapel badge. "No thanks, Julie, if Mary and Joseph can sleep in a stable with their son, then so can I". He paused. "I'll need to speak to you on another matter concerning the murder of a young girl here in the village last year, so if you could write down your address and telephone number where I can contact you, when you're away from your work at the hotel".

"I just work part-time at the hotel, Mr. Rupert. My day job is at the village chemist shop, so you can find me there nine to five, six days a week. I live with my husband in a shepherd's cottage, which is three miles outside the village, it can be a bit awkward getting home if I work late, the last bus is 19.00 pm and that is when I need to rely on the hotel owner, Mr. Farlow who is only too keen to give me a lift". He noticed the hesitancy in her voice and the disgusted look on her face.

"This Mr Farlow, does he behave himself when he drives you to your home, Julie"?

"He has tried his luck on several occasions, thinking it's his God given right, with him being the boss, then it usually turns into a wrestling match, with him insisting that he drives me up to the cottage, especially every time my husband is away at the sheep and lamb sales. That's when Farlow is at his most persuasive, he seems to know everything that goes on in the village, and I'm not the only one he has tried it on with". She paused, "Talk to the vicar's wife". She gave a smile.

"I still have work to do stocking the bar, so you will have to excuse me, I need to get on and hopefully catch the last bus, or it's shanks pony I'm afraid because Farlow is in London on business".

"Fear not, Julie, I'm going out to do a recce on some of the roads and farm names, so I'll drop you off at the cottage gate, as long as this does not become a regular habit".

He followed her into the snug bar where she served him coffee, and when she had finished her chores, they headed out towards the shepherds' cottage.

The rain had started, so he offered to drive her up the track. It was a bumpy ride when the darkness fell; the track was full of potholes. He pulled the car up to the door, and Julie reached across and kissed him on the cheek.

This was the ideal place to question her, for names and addresses of prominent people in the village, working part-time in the hotel, and full-time in a chemist's shop, had their benefits. He took out his notebook and began to question her.

He compared the chemist shop to any village post office where the gossip mongers gathered to swap juicy titbits of scandal, whether it was true or not. He wrote down the names of shop owners in the village and businessmen who worked in Chelmsford. This would save a lot of time when he came to interview each person. He closed his notebook and thanked her.

She put her hand on his thigh. "Come in and have a drink, Inspector, tea, coffee, or something stronger. Don't worry, my husband is away at the lamb sales".

"Better not, Julie, I still have a lot of work to do, so perhaps some other time".

She reached over and kissed him on the cheek again. "That's something I can look forward to, Inspector, so I bid you good night and thanks for taking me home".

He watched her get out of the car before driving away down the potholed track.

He shone his torch on the road map before getting out to open the gate, deciding to visit the old churchyard marked as a place of importance and historical interest.

He got out of the car at the ruined church, walking into the graveyard, and between the gravestones. Some of which were made of sandstone and eroded so bad that they were unreadable; however, there were ones dating back to the eighteenth and nineteenth centuries that could be read, with the light of the torch beam.

One consolation was that the rain had stopped, and the clouds raced across the sky, allowing the full moon to illuminate the gravestones and the silent graveyard.

There was one thing that intrigued him as he walked around the ruined building.

Someone had been here recently, the remains of ash where a large bonfire had been used, but for what purpose, he mused while studying the charred remains of the burnt-out tyres and tree trunks that made up the charred remains. He thought about Guy Fawkes night, but at one of those bonfires, there were rockets, Catherine wheels, sparklers and squibs, but as he looked around, there was no evidence of that.

He stepped inside the remains of the old church and noticed a name on a wall grave, the owner obviously cremated. A name was readable: Edward Linton, vicar of this parish.

"1784-1847"

It seemed ironic as he studied another gravestone that lay horizontal. Farlow, 1835–1898, husband of Annie Linton, 1837–1858; some of the inscription was unreadable; however, he did a quick calculation in his head. She died at the tender age of twenty-one, but it was the name Farlow that set his mind racing. Could this be a forefather of the hotel owner? Someone he would need to question when Jack Farlow returned from his business trip to London.

He looked at another horizontal gravestone that had no markings, but it did look as if the colouring of red looked like dried blood. Had some ritual taken place here recently?

There was nothing else he wanted to see, so he made his way back to the hotel before the rain started again. A quick nightcap and then an early night.

The snug bar was reasonably quiet as he pulled his barstool closer to the bar. He positioned himself against the end of the bar wall, where he could watch who was coming and going, refusing a refill of brandy and soda that was offered frequently.

He was amazed at the attentive service he was getting from the buxom barmaid, with a fine facial bone structure and figure to match. Her long blond hair was tied back in a ponytail.

She introduced herself as Mrs. Angela Farlow, wife of the hotel owner.

"We've an Inspector from Scotland Yard, ladies and gentlemen, who has come to investigate a murder. How glad we are that he has decided to grace us with his company tonight". This was said loudly for the benefit of the local drinkers.

She turned to ask, "Why are you sitting here at the bar, Inspector? I could have brought this drink to your room".

She gave him a wink and a broad smile before going off to serve another resident. When she returned, Inspector Rupert came to the point.

"I was told there was no room service". He said quickly.

She laid her hand on his.

"For you, I could make an exception". She rushed off again to serve another customer.

After the lady had been served and attended to, she returned to her stool leaning forward, she whispered, "if you ever need a little company Inspector, I'll be only too glad to oblige, I get fed up with my own company when my husband is away on business, and Jack is such a boring lover, I need a little fun to pass the time".

"Talking of Mr. Farlow, I understand he has gone to London. When will he be back? Because I need to speak to him urgently".

"Please, Inspector, forget Jack for now; besides, he comes and goes as he pleases. Why should I not do likewise"?

She passed the time talking. "So, you've been out and about already, Inspector, so what do you make of our charming moonlit village"?

He dodged the question by putting on his policeman's helmet. "I must interview several people, Mrs. Farlow, so I'll start with you tomorrow morning after breakfast if you don't mind". He finished his drink and stood up.

"One thing that intrigues me is the fact that the few people I've had the pleasure of meeting have never mentioned the young girl who was murdered". He raised his voice slightly so the locals who were drinking in the snug bar could hear. "Her name was Janice Calderwood; she was murdered last October". He looked at Angela Farlow. "Therefore, I'll be taking down your particulars at our meeting tomorrow".

He knew he had phrased it badly when she said quietly, "You can take down my particulars any time you're ready, Mr. Rupert and tonight would be a good time while my husband Jack is in London".

"Sorry, Angela, what would my boss say if I were to shack up with you during this murder investigation, and what if your husband, Jack, found out? So, I'll meet you at the reception tomorrow at 10 am, and don't be late".

He turned and walked out of the bar, across the courtyard to the stables and his room.

He took out the old statements taken at the time of the girls' murder. Laying them neatly on the bed, he began to sift through them, reading each one carefully.

Janice Calderwood celebrated her sixteenth birthday on the date she was murdered. The pathology report said it had been a vicious attack in the park by the river. She had multiple stab wounds on her body, her throat had been cut, and her wrists had been slashed before being tossed into the river. The killer would be hoping the blood would be washed away in the rain, and the swollen river current would wash her body downstream, over the weir and out to sea.

The Chelmsford police found no clues, not even the murder weapon.

He studied the coroner's report that failed to mention that there were bruises on her arms and legs, as he read on, 'a vicious attack' because the young girl's throat had been cut from ear to ear. A Mr. Godfrey Teddington had performed the autopsy and made his report to the Prosecution, Crown Office, and the Coroners' Court. Those were important clues caused by an attacker or attackers. He was not at this stage ruling anything out.

There were other questions to be asked about the police report. When no blood was found at the apparent scene of the crime, was she killed in the park? Or perhaps upstream, the old church sprang into his mind. Was it some kind of ritual carried out in that area?

He decided to bring in a forensic team from London. How he wished Andy Thomson, who had served him so well in the past with the Hertfordshire constabulary, could be drafted in, but that was not possible. He studied again all the old statements and reports of the police, the pathologist, and the findings of the coroners' court.

Those people who gave statements in the past would need to be questioned again, using their own methods.

One thing that became clear to him was the fact that each statement and report was brief, almost as if the people who had been questioned were glad to be rid of this murdered girl.

One other thing he noticed was that each statement sounded just like the previous one, almost as if they had rehearsed their story concerning their alibis. Did they all have something to hide?

Those documents were not safe left in his room, so after taking down the list of names to be questioned again, he gathered them together and walked out to the police car, where he locked them safely in the car boot for protection.

There were two names on the list he had highlighted. Mrs. Linton and Jack Farlow. Why did Julie fail to mention that she and her husband had been questioned by the Chelmsford police? She had an ideal opportunity to do so when he drove her home earlier. Perhaps the reason was that the statements were practically identical, word for word; the defining factor that kept them apart was their signatures at the bottom of the page.

Jack Farlow would have had the opportunity when Janice worked at the hotel, but there was no motive, unless they were having an affair, and she was threatening to blackmail him.

There were many questions to be asked, and he would ask them, beginning with Angela Farlow tomorrow morning, but now it was time for bed.

After a comfortable night's sleep, he went refreshed to breakfast, then went to the reception area to meet with Mrs. Angela Farlow, the co-owner of the hotel. 10 am was arranged the night before in the snug bar, and she had made it clear she was available in more ways than one.

She was attending to another guest, as he sat flicking through the magazines that were carefully laid out on the coffee table in the foyer. Angela Farlow was dealing with a complaint by a resident, who was given room three, and was complaining about the noise when the snug bar closed, and the last resident had staggered up the stairs.

Having been offered room three and refusing it. Inspector Rupert gave a wry smile as the complaint reached a new level of shouting, then went on to other complaints.

Eventually, Nancy the troll appeared, the obnoxious woman who had signed him in yesterday.

Mrs Farlow used her position and handed the irate resident to the troll to sort out.

He had got little information from the sour-faced troll; she gave little more than what was on her statement taken by the Chelmsford police at the time of the girls' murder.

He sat back as Angela Farlow came over to give him a warm smile.

"Sorry about that", she said, standing in front of him, so close that he could smell her expensive perfume.

"If you could be as brief as possible, Inspector, mornings are generally busy in the hotel, besides which, I've a busy day of interviewing applications for bar work ahead of me".

"We all have a busy day ahead, Mrs. Farlow, so cut out the playful stuff; we need a quiet place to ask some delicate questions".

She signalled with her head for him to follow her. She took him into the hotel office at the rear, away from eavesdroppers. "This should be quiet enough for you, Inspector Rupert, so let's get on".

Inspector Rupert had to admit that she looked as good from behind as she did from the front, her buttocks swaying with her movement. Her cleavage showed as she sat down, letting her pearl necklace drop into the valley of temptation. He could smell her expensive perfume and caught a whiff of her scented breath.

"Before we get down to business and the technical stuff, Amadeus, I want you to remember the offer I made to you last night. Hubby will be in London for the rest of the week, so why waste time"?

Her offer and smile would've attracted any male predator. He had to gather his wits quickly, before things got out of hand.

"This is a formal police inquiry, Mrs. Farlow, so I would be obliged if you call me Inspector throughout the proceedings. Now let's get started, please". He paused.

"You remember the young girl called Janice Calderwood, who worked at the hotel before she was murdered"?

"Yes, I remember her, Inspector. How could we villagers forget such a tragedy, a sweet kid, who was good at her work, flirted with my husband occasionally, but that is what young girls do. She could be classed as a prick teaser". She drew breath before continuing.

"A good young chambermaid who knew when to keep quiet, especially when the Mr. Smiths and Mr. Browns appeared with their young niece. There was a regular who had so many nieces that I wondered how many brothers and sisters he had, you know what I mean, Inspector"?

"Perfectly, Mrs. Farlow, they were using the hotel as a knocking shop. And with the murdered girl flirting with your husband, that gives you a very strong motive for murder".

He said it loudly so that Angela Farlow got the message.

"Not quite, Inspector, this is a respectable run hotel, and you could never prove otherwise". She paused.

"Yes, Janice was a flirt, Inspector, but never asked questions. She had lots of admirers in the village, especially among the married men. She did have a so-called steady boyfriend who blew hot and cold from time to time as far as I'm aware".

"I've a name that I'm following up on, Mrs. Farlow". He stood up. "Do you have a record of her parents, any family or a home address, because I know she was not a local girl"?

Angela Farlow sat back, "They're in a filing cabinet in the cellar, Inspector, but you will have to wait until my husband gets back, because you would not have me going down into that dark, damp hole, for all the tea in China, not even for you, now if that's all".

"That won't be a problem, Mrs. Farlow. I'm not afraid of the dark. I'll fetch my torch".

She gave that enigmatic smile. "You certainly are thorough, Inspector. Why do we not drive out into the country this afternoon, and you can ask me more questions? I'll give you anything you want".

He stood up. "Sorry, Mrs. Farlow, you have a busy day ahead of you". He paused.

"So, still no word of your husband returning". He paused again.

"Do you have a contact number where he can be reached"?

"No, he has several business acquaintances in the city. He could be anywhere".

"Just one more question, if you please". He looked down at her.

"Can you remember the last time you saw Janice Calderwood alive? When did you realize the girl was missing"? He had hit a nerve when she lost her patience.

"How in hell's name am I supposed to remember that? It's been a year since her murder, and let me remind you, it's a hotel I'm running, not a childcare practice or orphanage".

"Hardly an expression I would use, while talking about a dead girl, Mrs. Farlow".

The D.I said softly, trying to encourage her to reveal more about Janice Calderwood.

He leaned forward. So, no boyfriend, except the one who visited occasionally, and she has been dead for over a year. I would've thought that in a small village such as this, her killer would've been locked up long ago, hence my reason for being here. "He had her attention".

What about your husband, Mrs. Farlow? Was it simply flirtation? Was it just friendly terms with her boss, and with Janice being an employee? "Was it something more"? He paused.

Out of curiosity, did you know the part-time lovers' name? I have it already, but just to ensure it is the same person"?

"That is two questions, Inspector," she said, standing up.

"No, I don't know the boyfriends' name, and you can ask my husband personally about his relationship with Janice Calderwood, when he returns from London, now if you don't mind, I've work to do Inspector, and if you need to question me again then make it slightly earlier or in the evening, because mornings can get a bit hectic".

She didn't wait for a response, but walked casually out of the office, saying, "Close the door behind you. Make sure it's locked".

Inspector Rupert stood for a while, thinking about the interview with Angela Farlow, who was clearly flustered and annoyed when he asked her about the dead girl and her husband's friendship with her. That was something he would put to her husband on his return.

There were other questions he could have asked, but that could wait, because he had her scant statement to fall back on, so he closed the office door and made his way to the churchyard to find Janice Calderwood's grave.

That was a stumbling block. With no headstone and no permanent cemetery warden, he would have to get the plot number from the registrar in Chelmsford, unless perhaps the grave diggers could help, if they were working in the cemetery.

He began to have an uneasy feeling about this case. He wondered if he was getting into something he knew little about.

The subject of witchcraft crossed his mind. What little he did know about the craft was something you could read about in any public library.

Witchcraft was one thing; devil worship was another. Was this the reason the Chelmsford police had hit a wall of silence?

The setting was right for witchcraft. A small tributary stream that flowed into the large river. Fire and water, with the main river close by.

A large bonfire to dance around, an old, ruined church and graveyard with gravestone slabs, ideal for performing sacrificial rites; however, witchcraft should not be confused with Devil worship, which was far more dangerous, but regarding the covens of witches, he believed that someday they would just jump on their broomsticks and simply fly away.

He tried to put it into perspective. The girl could have been used as a sacrificial lamb to the slaughter if Devil worship was involved with whoever, and whatever. There was still a lot of investigating to be done, but it was time he called in the forensics team, who could determine whether the red stains on the burial stone slab were human or otherwise. He could talk to his boss, but decided to leave it for a week until more questions could be asked, and a forensic report could be received. He made up his mind to drive over to Chelmsford the next morning with two departments to visit. The births, deaths and marriages at the town hall, then the mortuary and pathologist who carried out the autopsy on the dead girl.

Something struck him like a sledgehammer blow. He left the cemetery and walked swiftly to his car in the hotel car park. He took the statement documents from the car boot and counted them. Thirteen in total, now that was strange, had the names on the statements anything to do with the dead girl? This was a conundrum as to whom he would question first. Had he or she diverted the police investigation to each member of a coven? There were so many conundrums relating to this murder. He decided to visit the chemist's shop first, then the village post office.

It was a man in a white coat who came to serve him. "What can I get you, sir"? He asked politely.

"I would like to speak to Julie Linton if she is available." Inspector Rupert looked around the shop, hoping to catch a glimpse of her.

"Sorry, Mrs. Linton has phoned in with the excuse that she is unwell. Is there anything I can help you with, sir"?

"Yes, perhaps there is," Inspector Rupert watched the chemist's reaction.

"A young girl was murdered here in the village last year; her name was Janice Calderwood. Perhaps you can tell me what she was like as a person? Did she visit the shop often? Perhaps to purchase condoms or sanitary towels, also, if you have any idea of her grave number position in the local cemetery"? He smiled. "I would be obliged if you could help me".

The chemist continued to go through his prescription list.

"Was that her name? I heard about the murder, but after that, I never paid much attention. I didn't even go to the funeral or church service". He started to write something down in the prescription book before looking up.

Inspector Rupert knew he was lying because his name appeared on the statement list, which had stated that he was fond of the promiscuous girl and had laid a wreath at her burial plot, so the chemist knew much more than he was telling. Inspector Rupert nodded, knowing he now had someone who could point to the young girls' unmarked grave. He took out his notebook and pencil. "If you could just confirm your name and address, I'd be much obliged, sir". He already knew John Merrick's name. He had it in the statement's report. The chemist gave his name, insisting that Inspector Rupert show him his warrant card.

"Ah, so you're the policeman everyone is talking about"?

Another person entered the chemist's shop, so the conversation ended abruptly.

"Thank you, give my regards to Mrs. Linton," he tipped his hat, said, "Good morning," then left. It was strange that Julie Linton had reported sick, because when he left her last night, she seemed to be in fine health. It was also strange that after arriving in the village yesterday, he had little contact with anybody except Julie Linton, Angela Farlow, and the Troll, who signed him in.

It was Angela Farlow who had broadcast his name and rank across the bar, as if sending out a warning to the other locals who used the premises "Regularly", according to Julie Linton.

There would come a time to question Angela Farlow again.

Now it was time to drive to Chelmsford to get some answers, then tomorrow he would question the names on the statement list again. As for today, if he had time, he might call into the local Chelmsford nick to talk with the police who were involved in the case; however, it was more important to question the pathologist, to ask why so many important factors had been left out of the pathology report and the inquest hearing.

He made that his first port of call. The reception area was deserted, so he entered a door that said no entry. There were heavy plastic slats hanging from the ceiling, so he pushed them aside and entered the mortuary room, brightly lit by overhead strip lights. The stainless-steel cutting table had been cleaned until it sparkled.

"Hello, is anybody here"? He laughed at the unintended pun.?

An older man appeared.

"What in hell's name are you doing in here? Get out immediately before I call the police".

"I'm from Scotland Yard, Mr Teddington, investigating the murder of a chambermaid called Janice Calderwood who worked at the local hotel, in the village of Tringford, where she was murdered and ended her days".

Inspector Rupert watched the pathologist while reaching for his warrant card.

"Sorry to barge in on you unannounced, but there are some questions I must ask concerning her murder that took place in the village last year. I'm hoping you can throw some light on the subject".

The pathologist studied the warrant card.

"Scotland Yard, you're a bit outside of your patch, Inspector".

"Indeed, we've been called in to investigate this unsolved crime. The girl was murdered, her throat cut from ear to ear, her wrists slashed, and stabbed repeatedly, before being dumped into the river, according to your report. I'll repeat, her name was Janice Calderwood, aged sixteen, who that day apparently had just celebrated her sixteenth birthday".

He retrieved the warrant card from the pathologist.

"Do you people never think of phoning first? I can give you ten minutes because I've a crash victim coming in, follow me". He said bluntly, leading the Inspector into his office.

He opened a filing cabinet.

"Calderwood, Calderwood, Janice, yes, here we are". He withdrew the file. "Yes, a nasty one, as I recall. Body drained of blood, because of her injuries, lacerations and bruising to her arms and ankles. Signs of sexual assault, but not a virgin before her recent penetration. Semen samples were taken from the vagina. That's about it, really. One thing more, she had a crescent moon silver necklace still attached to her naked body when she was found and pulled from the river". He paused, "All this would've been in my report that went to the coroner's court, Inspector, and a carbon copy to the Crown Prosecution Service, perhaps if you bothered to get a copy from them, then you would not be wasting my time".

Inspector Rupert rubbed his chin. "That is strange because there was no mention of the crescent moon necklace in the coroner's report. There was nothing mentioned about sexual intercourse or semen specimens. Why was that, Mr. Teddington? Important clues were missing concerning the girl's death". He paused. "I've got it on good authority that she was a flighty girl, promiscuous is the word used, which would explain her willingness when sexual penetration took place". The pathologist ignored him and studied the pages of his report.

"Note, Inspector, that Janice Calderwood did not. I repeat, not, give herself easily to the male; on this occasion she struggled, hence the bruise on her arms and legs". He studied the file.

Here we are, a full report of other findings. He touched on blood loss, but the report failed to say that the body was drained of blood when she was found floating in the river.

"There are things in the reports, including yours, Mr Teddington, that simply do not add up". The Inspector paused.

"In your opinion, would you say that Janice was murdered elsewhere? And when you were called to the crime scene, had the blood drained from her body at the spot when she was pulled from the river? Where did you work on the body"? He raised his voice. "So, I ask again, is it just possible that she was murdered somewhere else? And her body was then dumped into the river upstream, before becoming entangled in the river reeds, where it was then dragged out, and up onto the riverbank at the park where you carried out your examination".

"That's your job, Inspector Rupert. I go to the locus where the body is found," he smiled.

"Is it the actual place and the scene of the crime? I don't know. I ascertain how she died, what weapon was used and the approximate time of death, her state of dress, her stomach content and her organ weights. After that, it is up to you lot to find the killer, he or she might reveal where the crime was committed, now if you don't mind, Inspector".

"Please, Teddington, don't do a Ponsonby on me, I thought I had left all that behind in Hertfordshire". He never explained the outburst as he got up to leave.

"Ah, good old Wilfred, is he still above ground? Well, well". He hesitated. "Off the record, Inspector, this is only a guess, but I would say your victim died close to where she was taken onto the riverbank. There was no pebble damage. Have you considered the weather and the steep riverbank? This river that flows through the park would be an ideal way for blood to be washed away into the river over a period. And one more thing, a lot of rain had fallen before, and on the day she was discovered. Was she killed and thrown into the river at that spot? I would say it was. Very handy to dispose of a body". He started to prepare for the other body that would be arriving shortly.

He finished by saying.

"When the police recovered her body from the river, a search was made for the weapon, which is all in my report that went to the Crown Prosecution Service and the Coroner's hearing. Take the time to read it, Inspector. However, I would imagine the weapon would have been washed downstream".

"Thank you, Teddington, you've been very helpful, now I'll leave you to your incoming accident victim".

Inspector Rupert had considered that Janice had been thrown into the river elsewhere. However, there was no evidence to support that thought, and as the pathologist guessed, it was too handy a spot. Just rolling the body down into the river was the most likely explanation. Still no mention of clothes. He pressed the pathologist.

"There was no mention in the police report of clothing taken from the river or the crime scene. The dead girl's clothing, Mr Teddington, I take it from your report that no clothing was found in the vicinity where you worked on her body".

"Please, Inspector, stop wasting my time. If there was clothing found, then surely your lot would've mentioned it in the police report. When I did a quick examination of Janice Calderwood, she was naked as a jaybird except for the crescent moon necklace".

Inspector Rupert was determined to get as much out of the pathologist while he had him on the hook. "According to your report, Mr. Teddington, there was no mention of her body being immersed in water for a considerable length of time, where there would've been traces of river water in her lungs and stomach content, and there is the question of her clothing".

The pathologist ignored him and walked out of the mortuary office.

CHAPTER

Two

The more Inspector Rupert thought about it, the more it became clear to him that the killer had murdered Janice in the park, then simply disposed of her naked body in the river, but the clothing still posed a conundrum. Had the killer taken them as a keepsake, a trophy, in some perverted form of revenge? Or was there a possibility that she was murdered in a vehicle, after being stripped in preparation for a sexual encounter, and her clothes were still in the vehicle when the killer drove off.?

His next visit was to the town hall. The receptionist studied him while chewing gum.

He showed his warrant card. "I wish to trace a grave in Tringford church cemetery that has no gravestone or marker. Who would I talk to regarding this request?"

The receptionist said nothing, but pressed a button, then spoke. "An Inspector Rupert, wanting details of an unmarked grave, Tony". She waited while blowing a bubble of the gum.

"Okay, I'll send him up". She looked at the Inspector through blue-rimmed spectacles.

"First floor, second door on the left. Mr Saunders will see you now".

Inspector Rupert couldn't help using his favourite saying to uncooperative or rude people, like this receptionist.

"Did you sue them"? He asked with a smile. "Who?" She asked indignantly.

Inspector Rupert's face and manner changed. "The charm school". He strode off towards the stairs. He didn't knock on the door but walked in to find a clerk sitting patiently, waiting while sharpening his pencil. He didn't bother getting up but merely pointed to a hard chair, placing the pencil behind his ear, then lifted a pen.

"Name"? He asked quickly, going through the procedure.

Inspector Rupert of Scotland Yard, now get off your fat arse and go to your filing cabinet, where hopefully you'll find a record of a burial in Tringford cemetery. The name is Janice Calderwood, who was buried in Tringford cemetery, in early November or perhaps later in November last year.

He watched the expression on the clerk's face change to one of surprise as he got up quickly and went to the filing cabinet.

He opened the drawer with each folder listed under C. and found nothing that related to Janice Calderwood's details or grave.

"Nothing, Inspector, no name, date or grave number. It's strange that there is no record of her. I don't know how it hasn't been listed for some reason". He paused.

"There's a map of the cemetery that shows where she was buried, that at present is out with the foreman grave digger. Some lairs are not listed in the old part of the cemetery, but just ask old

Ted the foreman grave digger, who is out on three burials today, a very busy time, Inspector. But I'll tell him to get in touch".

"Busy or not, I need to talk to him now, Mr. Saunders, so tell me where he is, and I'll drive out to where he is working".

"That's impossible, Inspector, he could be at any one of the cemetery locations. Besides, the grave diggers finish when all work is completed by five". He shut the filing cabinet drawer loudly.

"Where is he working, Mr. Saunders?". Inspector Rupert asked harshly, determined and demanded an answer.

"Please, Inspector, they could be anywhere in the county, as I've just said, winter is a busy time".

"I know perfectly well", Inspector Rupert said coldly. "Do you not keep track of your workforce in the county? They could be sitting with their feet up in a pub as we speak". He paused. "I'll expect you, or your grave digger, to meet with me at the Tringford hotel tomorrow morning, 09:00 am, and don't be late".

He stood up and pointed at the clerk.

"Don't have me coming back here to fetch you; otherwise, you could find yourself arrested for wasting police time. I'll also be asking questions later about your file on Janice Calderwood, which seems to have gone missing. I've never heard of files going missing from council offices before. Grave diggers, yes, but not files. Just be sure you have that information for me at the hotel tomorrow".

He made his way out while the clerk arranged himself onto his comfortable leather chair.

Inspector Rupert turned around when he was halfway down the stairs, and made his way back to the births, deaths and marriages office where Saunders was sitting with his feet up on the desk.

The clerk was already on the phone with his own boss. He put down the phone when Inspector Rupert appeared.

"It might be a long shot, Mr. Saunders, but I want you to look through other files in your cabinet, just in case it got placed elsewhere by mistake". He smiled at the clerk's reaction.

"We close in an hour; do you not realise the amount of paperwork I have in those file listings for the past year"? The clerk was obviously upset.

"The sooner you get started, the sooner you'll satisfy my curiosity, Mr. Saunders; besides, I've all the time in the world". He sat down to wait.

The time passed quickly, and the security guard tapped the door. "You're still busy, Mr. Saunders. Any idea when you'll be finished"?

Inspector Rupert interrupted before the clerk could answer, "We'll let you know. Now, please close the door on the way out, because we must get on".

The door closed gently as the security guard took the hint. The Inspector checked his watch and was about to head back to the hotel for dinner. "Can I suggest to you, Mr. Saunders?" Why not look in the drawer and files under J? The clerk opened the file drawer. "Damn it, the junior clerk must have filed it under her Christian Name J, instead of her surname C. An easy mistake to make, I suppose". He handed the file to the Inspector. "There, problem solved," the clerk said, relieved. "Hang on, I'll photocopy that so you can take it away with you". He left the office and then returned, eagerly handing Inspector Rupert the photocopy of Janice Calderwood's file of her grave position and number.

"Sorry about that, Inspector". He sounded genuinely upset, so the Inspector thanked him for his time and walked out of the office. He was pleased with the way things had gone that day, but now it was a choice between the local police station and his dinner. He made his way to the police station, where the desk sergeant was trying to pacify an upset woman, whose cat had gone missing.

"Be with you in a moment," he said to the impatient Inspector, who did not like to be kept waiting. Eventually, the woman left after several reassurances that her moggie would be found.

"You'd better find that cat sergeant, or it could be cat-astrophic". Inspector Rupert said, smiling.

"Alright, smart arse, what can I do for you"? The Sergeant said with ire, ignoring the intended pun. "Bloody cats, whatever next"? the disgruntled bar officer said, before gasping.

The apology was fast in coming when Inspector Rupert showed his warrant card.

"It might not be convenient, Sergeant, but I need to speak to the senior officer who was involved in a murder case in Tringford, over a year ago, almost to the day".

The Sergeant looked bemused". A year ago, yes, I remember that incident quite clearly. Halloween night". He went into a cupboard and took out a thick ledger.

"This will tell us who attended the incident". He thumbed through the pages. "Here we are, An Inspector Strickland and W.P.C. Cartland, I know Cartland is on the night shift starting at 22:00 pm. but Inspector Strickland is the senior officer covering the early shift duty, 06:00 if that's any help, sir". Inspector Rupert nodded. I'm staying at the Tringford hotel in the village of Tringford, while investigating this murder, so I need the Inspector to get in touch by telephoning me. I'm sure you can arrange that, Sergeant. He paused and rubbed his chin. "Perhaps it might be better if I spoke to them face to face, so if one or both could come to the hotel when he or she is available. That would be a better idea". He thought for a moment. "It might be better to allocate Cartland to the case before she starts her duty here in Chelmsford, because I need another officer to assist me with my inquiries, however, I still need to speak to Inspector Strickland, he can phone me at 14:00 pm at the Tringford hotel tomorrow, with any details he might remember". He paused. "If they could gather any information regarding the investigation they made at the time, it could help and have all the factual statements and reports sent with W.P.C. Cartland, that would be appreciated".

The Sergeant smiled, "All in the course of duty, sir, anything else"? There was a hint of sarcasm in his voice.

"No, that will be all for now, Sergeant," The Inspector said with the same tone.

"Until tomorrow, then". He turned and walked out of the station.

Finding a fish and chip shop, he sat in the car to have his dinner. Fish and chips with a bottle of Coke to wash them down. He hadn't realised he had stopped to eat his dinner in the red-light district of the town. A knock on the window made him stop eating. "Looking for business, sir"? The young girl in red leather gear asked politely.

"Police, now bugger off before I arrest you for prostitution". He heard her voice talking to another girl.

"Another perverted pig looking for a freebie, fucking wanker". Inspector Rupert started the car and drove to another location, where he sat and enjoyed his fish and chips. He washed it down with the bottle of Coca-Cola, then made his way back to Tringford.

He decided on a nightcap before turning in. There was no sign of Angela Farlow. It was Julie Linton who was serving.

"Large gin and tonic, Julie," he paused as she turned away from him. He had spotted the bruise on her cheek.

"Feeling better"? He asked as she handed him the drink and got him to sign the room tab. She didn't answer but just started to wash and dry the used beer and spirit glasses. She had tried desperately to conceal her bruises with makeup and use her good side to face him when he asked.

"How are you getting home tonight? Can I offer you a lift before I drink this"? He wanted to get as much information about her boss at the Chemist's shop.

"No, thank you, I've other arrangements, besides you got me into enough trouble when you drove me home the last time. My husband came back early from the sales and was watching us from the darkness of the cottage. He gave me a severe slap when I got inside, after you drove off". She continued with her chores.

"You could have him arrested for assault and causing grievous bodily harm," he said softly, with a stern look on his face.

"Is that a fact, Inspector, and where would that leave me, with no money, and no place to go"? She smiled as a customer demanded attention. "Bobbie never hit me before until you came on the scene, so please stay away from me in the future. I was quite happy the way things were, but now I've a jealous husband to contend with". She continued to keep busy before serving the other customer.

Amadeus gave up, finished his drink, and then left the lounge bar quickly. He made his way back to his room and studied the pathology report, along with the coroner's court findings, again. There was no mention of the body being immersed in water. This was only a suggestion by the pathologist that it would've been an ideal place to let the blood flow away in the current, but no mention of it in either report. There was no mention of the dead girls' clothes. She had been pulled from the river naked, so what happened to them?

Tomorrow would surely answer his question, where the young girl was killed and buried.

When he had that information, he could start questioning the names on the statements given by the villagers. Starting at the top of the list. But realised that four names were absent from the village. Jack Farlow, Cyril and Marjorie Hornby, who were still in London, then there was the vicar, who would probably divulge more than what was on his statement taken by the Chelmsford police at the time of the murder.

They would have to wait; there was more than enough to be getting on with.

He would start with the butcher Arthur Moorcroft. He sat pondering over the police reports from both officers that were again practically identical, give or take a few differences, but not the slightest mention of clothing. He would grill them tomorrow. The forensics could carry on at the old church. If he had time, he would drive out there tomorrow afternoon, after he received the phone call from Inspector Strickland.

With a busy day ahead, he took the paperwork from the bed and put it into his briefcase. He switched on the bedside lamp, then switched off the overhead light, preparing for bed. He stood naked, about to put on his pyjamas, when a soft knock startled him. The knock got louder.

"Hold on a moment", he shouted, reaching for his dressing gown. He opened the door slightly, then opened it wide.

"I'm lonely, Inspector", the voice said huskily. Angela Farlow stood with a bottle of champagne in one hand and two flute glasses in her other.

She brushed past him and entered the bedroom, uncorked the champagne bottle, letting the froth spill onto the carpet. Pouring the bubbly liquid with expert hands, she handed him a glass.

"This is not a good idea, Angela; I think you should leave before I have to throw you out," he said angrily.

"Oh, don't be a spoil sport, Rupert, I've seen the way you look at my arse when I walk by you, I've seen you admire my tits, so sit down and relax, have a drink, and a chat, that's all I ask".

She held the filled champagne flute in front of him. He reached for it and watched her beautiful figure pour herself one. She sat beside him on the bed. "There, now what shall we talk about"?

Amadeus began to relax as Angela poured another helping of the champagne.

They had talked quite amicably for a while before the champagne was finished. He hesitated for a minute, then reached into the holdall and produced a bottle of brandy. "No diluter, I'm afraid," he said, pouring her a drink and then topping her up each time she finished her drink.

He kept pace with her, and the conversation paused when Angela reached for him and kissed him gently. He responded in a drunken manner as they fell back onto the bed in each other's arms. They hugged and kissed before Angela put her hand into his dressing gown and began to fondle his erection.

He pushed her away from him with some force. Her attempt to seduce him had failed. He immediately began to secure his dressing gown tier. It had been so long since this had happened to him, he found it very hard to resist the temptation, but resist he did.

She quickly picked herself up off the floor and collapsed onto the bed, cursing him, before falling into a deep sleep.

It was not practical for him to carry her back to the hotel, so he left her where she grunted and snored. He pulled the sheets over her, then lay down on top of the sheets beside her, keeping his dressing gown tied tightly. He turned away from her just in case she got any ideas during the night.

Amadeus woke up with a throbbing hangover. Angela Farlow had left. He looked at his watch. Quickly dressing in yesterday's attire that lay crumpled on the floor, he crossed swiftly to the hotel dining room for breakfast.

A woman police officer in uniform sat down beside him and handed him a Polo mint, "The sweet with the hole, sir". She poured his coffee. Then went to fetch his full English breakfast.

On her return, she introduced herself. "W.P.C. Cartland, sir. I understand you wish to talk to me about an incident last year, so I jumped at the chance to become involved. Forgive me for my early intrusion".

She held out her hand for him to shake before starting to explain.

"Inspector Strickland won't make a phone call today, court duty". She helped herself to the coffee and toast on offer.

"Hard night, sir"? She smiled.

"We need to talk somewhere less intrusive, Constable," he said in a low husky voice. "We'll take a walk around the graveyard when I've finished eating".

"Well, I've heard of some romantic places to go walking, sir, but a graveyard"?

"There's nothing romantic about this meeting, Constable". His head hurt as he raised his voice, which invited tables close by to listen in on their conversation.

"You take this photocopy of a grave number and do a recce, try to find the grave diggers who hopefully will be at the cemetery. They can help show you where the grave of Janice Calderwood is situated. I'll join you shortly after breakfast". He looked into her beautiful brown eyes. Her auburn hair tied in a ponytail made his heartbeat beat faster.

She finished her coffee and then made her way out of the dining room. Inspector Rupert cringed at his thought and the depleted memory of last night. Had he satisfied a long-lost urge that made him wonder if anything had happened when he had slept with the beautiful woman, even though Angela Farlow, at this stage, was not a prime suspect, the cloud would always hang over him until the case was solved.

He had foolishly let his heart rule his head. He had overlooked the fact that if there was a witches' coven, she could be part of it, then what? He would be in serious trouble with his superiors, who did not like investigating officers getting emotionally involved while working on any investigation. The threat from Chief Inspector Skinner played on his mind.

His head was throbbing as he walked towards the churchyard cemetery. He stopped at the chemist's shop to purchase aspirin and a bottle of still water.

"Feeling a bit hungover after your champagne party, Inspector"?

He looked at his watch, wondering how Julie Linton could possibly know about his tryst with Angela Farlow. The shop had hardly been open for morning business and prescriptions.

She smiled at his reaction. "Take my advice and drink plenty of water, it stops your body getting dehydrated". She took his money, then handed him his purchase and change.

"You should go back to bed, or have you had enough of bed for one night"? She giggled loudly as he left the chemist's shop in a hurry. It was a short walk to the church yard, the light breeze and fresh air made him feel better, also the fact that Julie Linton had been doing early work at the hotel and had wrongly picked up the gossip from the hotel staff. He felt a little better after he had washed down the aspirin with a small bottle of water. W.P.C. Cartland met him at the cemetery gate. "An old gravedigger arrived with his boss and showed me the grave location before they had to rush off to fill in a grave after a graveside service in Chelmsford, sir. There was no need for the map in my possession".

"Right, Cartland, show me where the girl is buried."?

They walked past the war graves until they reached a small block of concrete with a number etched on one side. No name, just the number, that would surely be listed in the church burial records. "You would've thought that the hotel where she worked would've had a whip round to erect a stone in her memory, sir, instead of this block of concrete". W.P.C. Cartland shook her head. "This is supposed to be a Christian community," she said, looking at the concrete block. "They could have clubbed together, sir, if only to put up a small headstone," she said with a raised voice. "They make enough from the collection plate every Sunday, where does that money go, I wonder"?

Her voice had reached a high pitch. "Indeed, Cartland, but have you considered church repairs? Perhaps the community wanted her to disappear quietly without a trace". He paused. "I wonder if her parents or relatives attended the funeral. Which reminds me, I must talk to the vicar, who has given little away, in his statement". He looked along the retaining wall at the old, faded gravestones; some of the names and dates of the lettering were totally unreadable. "This must be part of the old cemetery; I can see spaces where there are probably more unmarked graves". He paused. "People just couldn't afford headstones in those days".

He remarked on the uncut grass that grew over the spaces. "They, too, will be just a number in the parish records of yesteryear". He changed the subject.

"I was studying your report, W.P.C. Cartland, also Inspector Strickland's, there was no mention of Janice Calderwood having been put into the water naked, which would've been the murderer's first reaction, getting rid of the body and her clothes quickly, then letting the current carry the body downstream". Cartland shook her head. "I'm sorry sir, but that's simply not true. We read and discussed each other's reports. The truth is sir, we had just begun to walk downstream, when we spotted the body entangled in the weeds and froth of the river, I personally waded in and pulled her upstream, because there was brambles and nettles on the bank, it was impossible to get her onto the bank at that place, I pulled her body upstream to a point where Inspector Strickland managed to pull Janice Calderwood out of the river and onto the bank, that's where she lay until the pathologist arrived and examined her, before taking her to the mortuary sir". She gave a sigh. "The reason I remember it so clearly it was heavy rain, and the current was getting stronger, the wind was blowing, giving it a chill factor, it was bloody freezing my tits off, not to mention every other part of me below the waistline. I was just glad when other officers arrived with the forensic team and taped the area off. "Inspector Rupert rubbed his chin". You're positive you put all this in your report, Constable. There is no mention of the girls' clothes, nor whether she was naked when pulled from the river. Could they have been discarded into the river? Although they would have become entangled in the weed, just like the body.

"Of course, I'm sure sir, I keep all my diaries and notebooks, which I can dig out if you require them, they'll confirm my report. And there was no sign of any clothes in the river weed".

They walked to the cemetery. It gave Inspector Rupert time to think about his tryst with Angela Farlow, even though Angela was not a suspect. The cloud of doubt would always hang over him until the case was solved. He had foolishly let his heart rule his head. He thought again of the consequences, that if there was some form of a witch's coven and she was involved, then what?

Again, he thought about how he would be in serious trouble with his superiors, who did not like investigating officers getting emotionally involved while working on any case.

His head was throbbing, so he stopped at the chemist's shop to purchase aspirin.

"Feeling a bit hungover after your champagne party, Inspector"?

He looked at his watch, wondering how in the devil's name Julie Linton knew about his tryst with Angela Farlow.

The shop had hardly opened for business and for prescriptions. She smiled at his reaction.

"Take my advice and drink plenty of water, it stops your body getting dehydrated". She took his money, then handed him his purchase and change.

"You should go back to bed, or have you had enough bed for one night"? She giggled loudly as he left the chemist shop in a hurry was a short walk to the church yard, and the light breeze and fresh air made him feel better after he had washed down the aspirin with a small bottle of water.

W.P.C. Cartland met him at the cemetery gates. "The grave digger has been and gone sir, he has a filling in job to do at a graveside service in Chelmsford. However, he showed me where Janice Calderwood's burial plot is situated".

"Right, Cartland, show me where the girl is buried. Then we'll go to question the vicar". They walked past the war graves until they reached a small block of concrete with a number etched on its side, partially hidden by the overgrown grass.

"That number should be listed in the church burial records, sir". She hesitated.

"You would've thought that the hotel where she worked would've had a whip round to put some flowers on her grave".

Inspector Rupert shook his head. "I know this is supposed to be a Christian community Cartland, but not all communities contribute to burials and head stones, that could open up a floodgate of applications, surely that would've been up to the girl's family to raise a headstone, and don't forget, it is over a year since she was murdered".

She continued to look at the meagre concrete marker block.

Inspector Rupert changed the subject.

"The vicar gave little away in his statement to the Chelmsford police".

He looked along the retaining wall at the old, faded gravestones; some of the names and dates of the lettering were totally unreadable. "This must be part of the old cemetery; I can see spaces where there are probably more unmarked graves". He paused. "People just couldn't afford headstones in those days," he remarked on the uncut grass that covered over the concrete spaces.

They, too, will be just a number in the parish records of yesteryear. He changed the subject again. "I was studying Inspector Strickland's report. It gave no mention of Janice Calderwood's naked body having been put in the water, which would've been the murderer's first reaction, getting rid of the body quickly, then letting the current carry the body downstream, but what about her clothes"? Cartland shook her head. "I'm sorry, sir, there were no clothes on the riverbank. We both assumed she had been killed elsewhere and disposed of at that point. We read and discussed each other's reports. The truth is, sir, we walked downstream and discovered the body entangled in the weeds and froth of the river. I personally waded in and pulled her upstream because there were brambles and nettles on both banks, so it was impossible to get her onto the bank at that place. I pulled her body a little upstream to a point where Inspector Strickland managed to pull Janice Calderwood out of the river, and onto the riverbank, that's where she lay until the pathologist arrived and examined her, before taking her to the Chelmsford mortuary, sir". She gave a sigh. "The reason I remember it so clearly it was raining heavily, and the current was getting stronger, the wind was blowing, giving it a chill factor, it was freezing my tits off, not to mention every other part of me below the water line. I was just glad when other officers arrived with the forensic team and taped the area off".

Inspector Rupert rubbed his chin.

"You're positive you put all this in your report, W.P.C. Cartland"?

"Of course, I'm sure sir, I keep all my diaries and notebooks, which I can dig out if you require them. Inspector Strickland will confirm my report".

They walked over to the vicarage after taking note of the number on the concrete block that marked Janice Calderwood's unkempt grave.

A woman opened the door with flour on her face; she managed to push some loose strands of blond hair behind her ears.

Her blond hair strands dropped again and hung loosely against her cheeks. She pushed them back behind her ears, then wiped her forehead that leaving another white streak. She had a radiant smile despite her floury face.

"I'm sorry, I never heard the front door; what can I do for you"?

She wiped her forehead as the strands dropped forward again.

"Inspector Rupert, Scotland Yard, and W.P.C. Cartland from the Chelmsford Constabulary. I wish to speak to the vicar if he's available".

He made a mistake, thinking she was a kitchen maid. The woman introduced herself as Amanda Chapman, the vicar's wife. "I'm sorry, but my husband is in York at a Church of

England seminar and won't be home until Saturday, can I be of any help"? She said with a friendly smile.

"Bugger", he said to himself. Everyone he wanted to speak to was unavailable.

"Nothing that can't wait for the moment, Mrs. Chapman, it's regarding the young girl who was murdered in the village last year, so it's just a routine enquiry again".

They stood on the doorstep before she invited them in, after they showed their warrant cards. "While we're here, perhaps you could answer a few questions regarding the girl's death".

"Poor kid, why would anybody want to harm an innocent girl"? She paused. "We had really just arrived in the village at the time of the girl's demise, unpacking boxes, arranging the furniture, and curtains along with everything else that goes with a move to this God forsaken place". She suddenly realised what she had just said.

"Sorry Inspector, I hate this place of sanctimonious hypocrites". She reached for the kettle and filled it. "I'm about to have a cup of tea Inspector. Would you and the W.P.C. care for one?"

"Yes, I would Mrs. Chapman, I'm parched, although I can't answer for W.P.C. Cartland".

The W.P.C. just nodded with a smile and a "thank you".

"Good, as you can see, I've just been baking, so you can test my pancakes and scones and let me know what you think."? She put the kettle on the stove, before laying out the freshly made home baking of scones and pancakes. She put the butter in a dish, then put a crystal holder of homemade blackberry jam on the table.

He sat down after removing his coat and hat. She scooped some cream from a bowl, then rubbed her finger around the edges. This is home-made Inspector as well has a taste". She put her finger towards his mouth and let him take the cream onto his lips as she slowly let him lick her finger before she let her finger enter his mouth, moving it in and out.

"What do you think Inspector"? Her tongue was moving back and forth on her lips.

"Very sweet, Mrs. Chapman, I'll have some of that on a scone, and that will remind me of my first cream tea in Devon, many years ago". There was also Mrs. Bunty Harley's magnificent spread, he recalled with fondness at the marvellous banquette of baking she had laid out in the Tilsberry estate cottage in Hertfordshire that day, like the one he was facing now.

It reminded him how it was Mrs. Bunty Harley who had pointed him in the right direction, which ended up with the solving of the Tilsberry manor murders. He moved his leg quickly when he felt the vicar's wife attempt to touch his leg with hers, under the table. She gave him a wicked smile.

"Down to business, Mrs. Chapman". He swallowed the lovely soft pancake.

"Do you get many visitors coming to the vicarage, Mrs. Chapman, perhaps when your husband is away giving a sermon or any other business concerning the church"? He took a sip of tea before continuing.

"When he is away on church business, do you visit the friends you have made after arriving here, a courtesy visit to their own homes, especially if their wives are away shopping or visiting relatives. I'm sure you know what I'm driving at, Mrs. Chapman".

He watched her reaction as she became uneasy. "I rebuke that insinuation Inspector, of course I've lots of male friends, I'm the vicars' wife in case you've forgotten, I'm active in organising Church Fetes, Easter Parades, Pantomimes, and Christmas parties on top of that I also play tennis and badminton, I'm involved with a Mothers and Toddler group, I play darts and dominoes for the hotel teams, as well as taking part in their quiz nights". She smiled nervously. "What do you do with your spare time, Inspector? Apart from a quick evening rendezvous with the hotel owner's wife? She had regained her confidence.

The Inspector dodged the question. "You're certainly a very busy lady, Mrs Chapman, where do you find the time for the church and your husband's needs"? He smiled to soften the question before continuing. "Personally, I like all kinds of crosswords and puzzles. I suppose that's what makes me good at my job, solving murders, is my best achievement, and I'll solve this one, Mrs Chapman". He continued quickly. "I've been doing a little digging and in the time I've been here Mrs. Chapman, I know you have been unfaithful to your husband on several occasions, but let's leave that for the moment, because with all your activity an memberships of different organisations, tell me, have you ever heard of any rituals that have taken place in the old church yard out in the countryside, I mean satanic rituals, or witches covens, anything connected to Devil worship.? You, being the vicar's wife, just might have heard a whisper going around the village or from the outlying farms."

"Don't be ridiculous Inspector, this is England, the last burning of witches, and witch hunts and trials died out in the seventeenth century, I'm very glad to say".

"The burning of witches might have stopped, but there are still covens that exist today, Mrs Chapman, witches' covens and Devil worship, believe me, those covens are practised, and are as strong nowadays, as they were back then".

He took out his notebook. "Your husband returns on Saturday, perhaps you could tell me something about the hotel manager and his wife, they seem to be going abroad quite often, then there is the owner, Jack Farlow, who is a frequent visitor to London, any idea why"?

"Why ask me, Inspector? I think Angela Farlow is the one to ask, especially when you and she get together for secret trysts". She gave a loud giggle.

He was angry that his night with Angela Farlow had leaked out and had become the talk of the village so quickly. He knew that the gossip mongers in the village would have a field day, and he would be lucky if the word did not filter back to his bosses. He tried to take the sting out of the accusation with a smile.

"We talked about residents, staff, and her shared ownership of the hotel. We also talked about her relations with villagers, and her workload, nothing more, she serves the drinks, I drink them down, you could call it a working business relationship".

He always remembered an old Inspector at the Yard in his early days in the Met in London. "Deny everything Rupert, until the cards are stacked against you". He sat back in the chair, changing the subject again.

"One thing that does puzzle me is why there is no gravestone erected in Janice Calderwood's memory; after all, this is a close-knit Christian community."

"That's for her family to arrange Inspector. The church did offer, but her family wouldn't accept our charity and said they would attend to it; sadly, they have not".

Inspector Rupert nodded as the vicar's wife stood up. "I've a dental appointment this morning Inspector; however, I'm free this afternoon, should you find yourself with free time, away from Angela Farlow". She gave him an enigmatic smile as she watched him put on his coat and hat. He turned towards her before he and W.P.C. Cartland were about to leave.

"I'll need to talk to you again, regarding Janice Calderwood; however, we can kill two birds with one stone when your husband returns".

He watched her grimace, but before he left, he pointed his finger at her.

"Don't leave the village without informing me, Mrs Chapman".

The police officers made their way to the park to study the area where the body had been trapped. The place where she had been dragged up onto the bank was a sensible place because of the thick bramble bushes that lined the banks. A fast-flowing river now, he could see how the body had got tangled in the swirling vortex that had froth today. It probably had the vortex and froth back then.

The murderer had probably assumed that the river would do its job when the rain came. The river would obviously swell and pull the corpse out of the vortex and wash it downstream towards the area where the river gets deeper and becomes a raging torrent that would carry the body over the weir, then out to sea. That sounded like a more practical method of disposing of the body, instead of coven gravestone rituals a mile away upstream at the old church, although it was possible that the body had been put in the river at the ruined church, where it was an isolated spot. He questioned the fact that the body had been put into the river at the picnic park, where there was always the chance of a courting couple or a dog walker who might stumble upon the act of disposal. He shook his head and began to walk upstream towards the footbridge. The walk would do him good and help clear his headache, which beat like a Cherokee war drum.

The walk up the riverbank did just that. He began to feel slightly better as he walked across the bridge, looking for scuff marks, where the young girl could have been put into the river at this point, although he found it highly unlikely that the murderer would've carried the body from the road or the park, which was some distance away.

He stood watching the fast-flowing river before returning to the village.

Thinking about her injuries, and her throat being cut from ear to ear, he surmised it would take a very sharp instrument to penetrate so deep; that's when he decided it was time to visit the barbers' shop.

He walked along the main street until he saw the red and white pole. Noticing the open sign on the door, he walked in and introduced himself.

The attentive barber rubbed his hands, springing from his seat at the thought of a potential customer. A stranger in the village.

"Take a seat sir, I'm Tommy, a professional stylist, trained in ladies and gents hairdressing".

Inspector Rupert sat in the cutting chair. "I need a trim Tommy, but I also need to ask some questions about a young girl's murder when you begin to snip".

The barber put a protective cover over his head, letting it fall to his shoulders to protect his clothes.

"Short back and sides sir"? He asked his customer in a polite voice.

"Yes, that will do Tommy". Inspector Rupert waited until the barber had started before he asked his questions.

"You must get a fair amount of people through your door. Tommy, people who are prepared to give you intimate details of their family life, and extramarital activities in work or elsewhere"?

The barber laughed. "At one time, I considered opening a psychology clinic. Inspector, you have no idea what people talk about when they come in for a haircut or a hairdo. If only that chair could talk, it could tell a few home truths about this village and the surrounding areas".

Inspector Rupert was very interested. "You probably know why I'm here Tommy; it concerns the murder that took place in the park on Halloween night last year, almost a year to the day". He paused.

"Janice Calderwood worked at the hotel, but what I'm interested in is whether she had any close boyfriends or girlfriends, if the hat fits. I understand she was a pretty girl who flirted but got on well with the men of the village."?

"Yes, she was pretty in her own way, but not stunningly beautiful like the vicar's wife Amanda, now there is a beauty". Tommy stopped cutting.

Talking of flirts. How did you manage to get into Angela Farlow's knickers? Now there's another I'd give my back teeth to get into?

Inspector Rupert looked at the barber in the mirror.

"I didn't get into Angela Farlow's knickers as you so crudely put it, but regarding the vicar's wife, I've got to agree with you Tommy".

He didn't go into the details of his tryst with Mrs. Farlow but moved on quickly.

"Has Amanda had any extramarital relationships that you can think of, even a special friend"? Come now, Inspector, a vicar's wife having a bit on the side, definitely not, that's simply gossip and wishful thinking on some members of her husband's parish who would love to get her into bed, a story for the news of the world, who would have a field day making up a story like that.

The barber lifted a mirror so that the Inspector could check the outcome of the cut. "You're heading down the wrong road, Inspector. There was tittle tattle when they first arrived, but that was just village gossip".

The barber held up a mirror again, to let Inspector Rupert scrutinise his haircut at the back.

"Perfect Tommy, please tell me more about Amanda. What was the gossip about"?

He waited until the barber removed the clothing protection.

"Oh, it was something to do with the vicar who had a congregational post in Letchford Garden City, and it was while he and his wife were there, an overzealous stalker persisted in following his wife about. I think that is part of the reason they moved to this god forsaken hole".

Inspector Rupert stood up to pay the barber. "Have that on me Inspector, I was just closing anyway".

The Inspector thrust the coins into his hand. "That could be construed as a bribe Tommy, so take the money".

Inspector Rupert was adamant but still interested in what Tommy had said.

"There is one thing Tommy, this is the reason I came in here, although I would've paid you a visit anyway". He paused. "You in your profession use shaving razors; what do you do with the disposables"?

"There are no disposables, Inspector. This thick leather belt keeps the blade sharp. The razor is only used for close shaves, which I can do for you now if you wish".

"Another time Tommy". He was about to leave. "Something has just sprung to mind, Inspector. There was an incident here in the shop when a razor went missing over a year ago; they are not the cheapest or easiest equipment to get hold of". The barber hesitated.

It's probably nothing". He began to fold the gown.

"Tell me Tommy, it could be very important".

Inspector Rupert knew instinctively he had made a breakthrough. This was what he was looking for. The barber tossed the gown into the corner with the other used laundry.

"Let me think".

He did think, and it took a little while before he spoke.

"I believe it was a year past September. I could get my accountant to give you an exact date, because it was marked into the accounts book and put down as an overhead cost". He paused.

"I'm trying to remember the day the razor went missing, because I thought about it when it happened, being an important tool that helped make me money. There were only a few regulars that month, also two men from Maldon who used me occasionally for a shave, then there was a stranger, a tall, well-built, blond-haired character, young around twenty, perhaps a little older. He didn't talk much, but he did say he was on a buying spree involving the stables a few miles from the village. Basically, that's all, Inspector. However, if you ask around the stable yards, I'm sure they could give you a name."

"I was coming to that Tommy, so he didn't give a name, but did he mention where he had come from, or where he was staying"?

The barber just shook his head. "Perhaps the hotel, but as I said, he hardly spoke, I don't know, sometimes the farms and stables put people up if there is a sale of horses or cattle in the offing". He went to the till to give the Inspector his change. "Keep it, Tommy. However, there is another question." Somebody was holding a party out at the old, ruined church; any ideas who that might be? There was a slight hesitation before the barber showed any emotion.

The barber laughed. "That'll be the Royalist Brigade Inspector. They've held it every year since Oliver Cromwell died, to commemorate the battle of Maldon, which the Duke of Essex won during the English Civil War. I would've been a round head if the truth be known, but please keep that to yourself, Inspector, passions run high in this area of the Royalists, and it could affect my business". The barber jangled the door keys, which was a hint to Inspector Rupert to sod off.

"Thanks, Tommy, if you think of anything else, I'm at the hotel most nights, and if you get that date from your accountant, I'd be most grateful". He let the barber show him out into the street, bathed in the moonlight that gave the village church graveyard an eerie appearance.

CHAPTER

Three

There were no streetlights, only the houses that had their lights on and their curtains open. He stood thinking about the barber's hesitancy when asked about the area where a large bonfire had been used for pleasure. However, with no link to the murder, it bothered him.

Inspector Rupert took the torch from his coat pocket and made his way back to the hotel for dinner. As he walked, he went over in his mind what the barber had said: Two men from Malden. Why travel to Tringford for a haircut and shave when there would be a barber closer to home? Perhaps the Troll could answer that question.

A stranger here to buy horses. He stopped and scribbled down a note to visit the surrounding stables and farms again. They would surely have the name of a horse buyer for future business references. He was convinced that the blond stranger and the stolen razor were the key to solving the case. If he could find the stranger, his troubles would be over.

He didn't discard the locals who were at the barbershop that day; there was always a chance that one of them held a grudge against the young girl. He would have to wait for the dive unit to get back to him, and also the barber's accountant's information on the income and expenditure book, hoping that a name would be placed against an account. It had occurred to him before that this case was to do with jealousy, revenge or both, the most common of excuses for murder known to police force detectives. He was convinced that two people were involved, one to hold the struggling victim while her wrists were being slashed, then the marked bruises on her upper arms and ankles would've been when the two perpetrators lifted the body, rolled it down the steep bank and tossed it into the river. Now he had a lead to work on. A stranger who was a horse buyer in the village, albeit not on the exact month or day that Janice Calderwood was murdered.

However, he was ruling nothing out. There would be a busy day ahead tomorrow, so after his dinner, he went to his room to shower. It was early to bed. He lay in the darkness and heard a slight tap at the door. He ignored it, guessing that Angela was on the prowl again. Eventually, the tapping stopped, and the next thing he knew, it was morning when the dreaded alarm went off. He got out of bed quickly and dressed in his pressed suit that had been laundered by the hotel. He was first in the dining room where Julie Linton was laying out the buffet, before she went to her day job. He helped himself to a large English breakfast.

It had occurred to him before that this case was to do with jealousy and revenge, but a most frenzied attack to commit murder. This was unheard of. A killer normally did the business and scarpered. But this killer or killers took time to dispose of her body.

There would be another busy day ahead tomorrow, so after his dinner, he went to his room to shower. It was early to bed. He lay in the darkness and heard a slight tap at the door. He ignored it, guessing that Angela was on the prowl again. Eventually, the tapping stopped, and the next thing he knew was the dreaded alarm going off. He got out of bed quickly and dressed in his pressed suit that had been laundered by the hotel. He was first in the dining room where Julie Linton was laying out the buffet before she went to her day job at the village pharmacy.

She approached his table. "I hope you don't mind me interrupting you Inspector, but I wanted to ask you for a lift home last night, but unfortunately you must have been working since there was no sign of you, I did tap your bedroom door, I know what I said before about you giving me a lift and my husband's rash outburst. However, one of the farmhands gave me a lift, but I just wish I had waited for you".

"Why was that Julie? Did you have a problem with the farmhand"?

"Just the usual wrestling match, but I escaped Virgo intact". She smiled. "Tea or coffee"?

"Tea, please, Julie". He gave it a stir. "Do you want me to have a word with this farmhand, Julie"?

"No, that will not be necessary, but his testicles will throb for a day or two, and he will be lucky to find the keys to his Land Rover after I tossed them into the field". She smiled again.

"I noticed the vehicle was still there this morning when I came to work by bus".

"I'm not sure you should be working late at night, especially when you must rely on a lift home, and the farmhand could file a charge of aggravated assault against you. If you want my advice, get the hotel to alter your hours in order that you can catch the last bus home. Is the extra job or money worth it"?

"Of course, it is, Inspector. I need the money, and it keeps me away from the cottage for a while. I could get my husband to collect me, but he is part of the reason I've taken this extra job. He has his own work and job to consider and frankly is a bore".

"Nevertheless, Julie, I don't think you should be hitch-hiking home at night, it only takes one oddball to watch out for you, and then what? "He let her pour him another cup of tea.

He sat thinking about the day ahead. He would visit the divers first, just to see if they had uncovered anything from the river. Then he would visit the surrounding farms in the area. He took out his map and studied which one he would visit first.

"Robbie is away to the winter cattle sales in Derbyshire, so perhaps you could give me a lift home tonight, Inspector". She waited for a reply.

"Sorry, Julie, that's not a good idea. I might end up with swollen testicles and an abandoned police car, besides, what would the neighbours think"? He watched her storm off back to the kitchen.

Amadeus had now been propositioned by three separate women, and one had succeeded in trapping him. This was something that must not happen again, especially when he was close to solving the case, and heaven knows what his superiors would say, so he would have to tread carefully in the future. He finished his breakfast, then made his way across the park in the wind and rain to the river. The divers were busy snorkelling against the current. The team leader scrambled onto the bank". Nothing to report, sir, we're nearly finished in this area, so we will split the team and search upstream and downstream later, after a warm cup of coffee". He blew the excess water out of the snorkel tube. "Personally, I would prefer to search downstream, because of the access from the opposite riverbank, which is not so overgrown. However, we'll

make up our minds after a coffee break". He paused. "There is also
the fact that the river has risen overnight, and the current is getting
stronger, so we might need to use a safety harness and line, also
revert back to weights, with oxygen masks and bottles to allow us to
stay submerged longer".

"You're in charge here, Drew. Ignore me and do it your way",

The team leader put on his mask and waded into the fast-
flowing river.

Inspector Rupert shivered as he made his way back to the
hotel stables and the shelter of the police car. He let it heat up
before driving out to the first farm that looked as if it could do with
a lick of paint and some tender loving care. The geese scattered as
he approached the farmhouse door. "Inspector Rupert from
Scotland Yard," he said to the farmer's wife. He took out the
warrant card from his pocket and showed it to the woman standing
in the doorway in her muddy Wellington boots. Her hair reminded
him of the musical and film, The Wizard of Oz. Her hair matched
that of the scarecrow". What do you want? The road tax is in the
post". Inspector Rupert smiled. "That's not my department. I want
your name and wish to know if you're married, also, how many
male and female employees you have on the farm. Most important,
do you buy and sell horses"?

"By Eck, you're a nosey blighter". She paused. "I work the
farm on my own, ever since my husband passed over to the other
side, ducks, and I don't deal with horses. Anything else"?

Inspector Rupert knew this was futile. "No, that will be all,
thank you", he turned and walked back through the mud to the car.
"Mrs. Lavender," she shouted as he retrieved his shoe from the cow
manure in the farmyard. "Bugger" was his reaction.

"Mrs Lavender, what a joke". He said in an exasperated voice.
He reversed the car quickly in case it sank into the cow manure and

mud. "What a bloody start to the day," he said, narrowly missing a parked tractor as he exited the farm track, before joining the main road.

He drove with caution out to the next farm. It came as no surprise to see the farmer leaning on the entrance gate with the Land Rover parked across the farm track. He parked on the verge and walked to the smirking farmer. "I need to ask a few questions, sir. If you don't mind". The farmer folded his arms as the rain and wind soaked his shirt.

"I do mind, Inspector. Why do you want to ask questions about a murder that happened over a year ago is beyond me"?

Inspector Rupert nodded as he approached the gate. "To be perfectly frank with you, Dobson, I'm getting sick and tired of people in this area telling me what to do". He paused. "Now we can do this here or at the Chelmsford police station. If you don't co-operate, I'll take you into Chelmsford and hold you in custody, how does that sound"?

The farmer stood erect but did not open the gate. "Get on with it, I'm not refusing to talk to you, but you'll not set foot on my land without a warrant".

He leaned on the gate. Inspector Rupert fastened his coat, which was flapping in the wind.

"It's obvious your neighbour gave you fair warning I was in the district, and understand that's country life, war drums and all that. However, I'm questioning everyone about the murder of Janice Calderwood, so it is nothing personal".

He watched the farmer, expecting him to find shelter in the Land Rover, but that didn't happen. He stood defiantly in the wind and rain.

"How well did you know the murdered girl"? It was a direct question.

"I didn't know her," came the terse reply. "We country folk keep ourselves to ourselves".

Inspector Rupert nodded. "It's a small community, Mr. Dobson, lots of rumours and backstabbing going on, that's why I decided to pay you a visit, you farmers know everything that happens in the surrounding area, I know that from experience. If you didn't hear about the murder, then you must have read about it in the local rag".

"I don't read newspapers, but I did hear about it in church. Sometime last September," he paused," no, last October it was, around Halloween time, that's it. Yes, around that time, Inspector". He continued to stand erect. "I've work to do, Inspector, just like you, and you'll not solve your murder gossiping to me or any other neighbour in the vicinity, so if you don't mind".

"Just one more thing, Dobson, I believe that's the Land Rover that was parked close to the gate of the shepherd's cottage, and passing place, last night and this morning, it was still there. A vehicle connected to an assault case, of a sexual nature, although no charges have been brought so far, but I might need to talk to your farm hand about the incident, so tell him not to leave the area, or else you could find yourself in serious trouble, aiding and abetting".

Farmer Dobson laughed, "You could never make that stick, Inspector". He hesitated. "I take it you've been talking to Julie Linton, the shepherd's wife".

The farmer shook his head. "Would it surprise you to know that the incident happened exactly opposite to what that little tart told you? Inspector Roddy told me what happened after she fondled him and forced him to stop driving. He got out of the Land Rover to cool off and urinate, due to the pint he had in the snug bar. When he ordered her out of the vehicle, she flew into a rage slapping him hard across the face, however when he tried to start the vehicle, he found that the ignition key was missing, she jumped out laughing teasing him with the key, then threw it into the long grass, laughing as she ran away up the track towards the shepherds' cottage". He paused. "Robbie the shepherd should have got rid of her after she had an affair with a young boy from the village. There were others whom she very cleverly manipulated, but that's unfounded rumour, Inspector. However, let me give you a sound piece of advice: investigate Julie Linton, she is bad news, and will stop at nothing to achieve her conquests and demands".

Inspector Rupert was slightly shocked. He had never seen Julie Linton in that light before. "Thanks, Mr. Dobson, I'll bear that in mind when I talk to her again. Just one more thing, can you remember a blond-haired stranger in the area around the time of Janice Calderwood's death, apparently here to do some horse trading"?

"I doubt it Inspector, any time the stables are selling, they give us the first option to buy before they're put out on the open market, and there has not been a sale for nigh on three years, otherwise I would've known about it, so I doubt very much that your blond-haired stranger was in the region for horse trading, you can drive five miles to the nearest stable, I'm sure they will confirm what I've said, I'll pass on your message to Roddy, I'm sure he will be pleased". The farmer turned and was about to walk towards the police car.

"Just one more thing, Mr. Dobson. Is it true that the Royalists still celebrate the victory of the battle of Maldon at the old church on a yearly basis? Apparently, a lot of people attend".

The farmers' attitude changed. "I don't know who has been feeding you all that guff but let me give you a little bit of advice". He paused". Stay away from the old church, it has a curse put on it, that is why it fell into disrepair". He turned and walked away. Inspector Rupert sat with the heater on full blast as he took notes.

He now had a contradicting story about the so-called Royalist gathering from the barber. It was the sound of the farmers' voices that sounded more like a threat than a piece of advice. He now suspected some form of witchcraft had been carried out at the old church but had to admit he knew nothing about the old beliefs and the rituals they carried out, some witch's brews still form part of the medical world today, but apart from seeing films which exaggerated Witchcraft beyond belief, he was oblivious to what went on. Besides, he had much more important matters to attend to than start an investigation into witchcraft, which he doubted had any bearing on the present murder investigation, but he was intrigued and knew he would pay a visit to the old churchyard again, perhaps in the brightness of the full moon.

The visit to the other stable was a complete waste of time as they confirmed what farmer Dobson had said, and when he mentioned the old churchyard, he was met with the same warning to stay away.

The most important question now remained. Why was this blond stranger in the district posing as a horse trader? That was a big question that would need to be answered. He drove steadily back to the hotel for a heat at the large log fire, accompanied by a brandy and soda.

Inspector Rupert finished his drink, and his clothes had dried, so he went to the public phone booth in the reception area.

"I need to speak to Inspector Buckingham. This is Inspector Rupert, Scotland Yard. I need her to do me a favour and do a little digging for me". It took a little while before the voice said.

"This is Inspector Buckingham. What is it you need, sir"?

Inspector Rupert explained what was required. "I remember you visiting an occultist, and wonder if you still have his name and address on file? His name and address would be most appreciated".

After the initial surprise, Inspector Buckingham said quickly, "I remember the very person that you need, sir. However, I think he changed his address. Give me a little time and I'll get back to you".

"You can drop the sir, Victoria, we're of the same rank now, remember".

"Rubbish," came the reply. "You'll always be Detective Chief Inspector to me, sir". He heard her opening and shutting drawers. The line went dead.

Inspector Rupert arranged for another large brandy and soda to be brought to his room, even though there was a lack of room service. The hotel was making plenty out of the police budget; he insisted they had to work for it. Plenty of staff were available to carry out his request.

There was something in a statement he wanted to check, so what better time than the present? After reading through two statements, he nodded, rubbing his chin.

There was a tap at the door, "My, that's good service. "He said loudly, expecting the drink to appear as if by magic.

It was the dive leader holding a forensic bag. "This was found downstream against the weir, sir. I thought you should see it right away". Inspector Rupert held the forensics bag up to the lightbulb and studied it.

The leader had a fair idea of what he was holding and what had happened that fateful Halloween night. The razor looked new, considering it had been dragged over sand and pebbles of the river. He thanked the diving unit leader for his tenacity in finding the razor and suggested that now their job was complete, they could stand down, and celebratory drinks for the diving team would be available in the snug bar.

The next morning, he was up early. Lots to do now that the murder weapon has been found.

The Chelmsford police had responded swiftly to his request, sending two constables in civvies. No uniforms required at this stage. They would be doing the legwork, knocking on doors, trying to revive people's memories. They would make a nuisance of themselves by questioning the shop traders in the village, just to see if their statements changed.

W.P.C. Cartland handed him a large brown envelope containing photographs.

"Inspector Strickland thought you should see this sir; he dug it out of the files from last year".

He took the envelope with excitement, pulling it open like a child on Christmas morning opening presents. He also got the news that Jack Farlow had returned from London.

That was his priority this morning, so without any hesitation, he walked to the reception desk. I want to speak to Mr. Farlow now, please, so please inform him I am at reception". Inspector Rupert browsed through a magazine as he sat waiting for the hotel owner to appear.

Eventually, Jack Farlow appeared from behind the door of the reception.

"Inspector, I understand you want to speak to me regarding the death of Janice Calderwood last year. Please come through to the office, where we will have some privacy".

They made their way to the hotel office.

"I'll come to the point quickly, Mr. Farlow. You are top of my suspect list, since you were having an affair with Janice Calderwood at the time she was murdered".

"That is a very serious allegation you're making Inspector, and I hope you can substantiate it with proof. Had I known this was to be an accusation so serious and unfounded, I would have had my lawyer present, now, if there is nothing else, please arrest me or bugger off in order I can get on with running a hotel".

"All in good time, Mr. Farlow. However, there are more questions that need to be answered. So, I'll put it to you in another way". He paused. "Were you having sexual relations with Janice Calderwood, a member of your staff"?

"Certainly not, and anyone who makes that allegation against me will find themselves in court. This is a bloody village of secrets and gossip mongers who have no life; their prime aim is to destroy successful businessmen and women. They have even attempted to blacklist the vicar and his wife". The Inspector tilted his head.

"Not without foundation, Mr. Farlow. However, let's move on. You seem to visit London on a regular basis. You disappeared the very day I was travelling to the village to begin my investigation, that makes me suspicious, Mr. Farlow".

"Coincidence Inspector, Cyril and Margo Hornby, my employees or I should say ex-employees, managed the hotel until they decided to move abroad. I'm sure you know they accompanied me when I left the village, simply because they were flying off to a new life in the Spanish sun. I took them to Heathrow for their flight and saw them off. As for the rest of my disappearing act, I visited the fruit market and I visited the fish and meat markets, buying produce for the hotel. It might seem strange to you Inspector, but guests must eat, and like fresh food on their plates".

He stood up. I have stock-taking and consignment delivery notes to attend to. God knows what Angela, my wife, was doing in the time I was away; if it was left to her, this hotel would shut permanently within a month, the good-for-nothing bitch".

Inspector Rupert wondered what Jack Farlow knew about his wife's clandestine visit, now common knowledge among the gossip mongers in the village of suspects.

"Don't leave the village again without informing me Mr. Farlow". Inspector Rupert stood up. "One more thing while I'm here, you as a businessman must hear what goes on in the surrounding areas, and I was wondering about some celebration held in the old church on the outskirts of the village, some kind of battle celebration dating back to the civil war".

The hotel owner shook his head. There was a story going around about a witch's curse, mumbo jumbo. Inspector, is this to do with the murder of Janice Calderwood"? Inspector Rupert ignored the prying question.

"Take my advice Inspector, do what you are paid to do, and refrain from intruding into things you know nothing about". This was another warning fired across the bow of Inspector Rupert. He took a mental note before continuing.

"One thing more, Mr. Farlow, apparently there was a horse trader who frequented the village on a regular basis and was seen in the village the night young Janice Calderwood was murdered. I've checked the register at reception with no results. I've questioned various members of staff, but there is no record of him ever staying at the hotel. Can you throw any light on that subject? Perhaps he was a company rep"?

"We are a busy hotel with patrons escaping from city life. We run a good establishment here Inspector, and if he did stay as a guest, then it would have been recorded. Besides being a businessman, I would have remembered this so-called horse trader had he been here".

Inspector Rupert was satisfied with the reason Jack Farlow had left the village in a hurry. His alibi could be easily checked with flight departures and purchase dates of produce. "Remember my warning Mr. Farlow, about leaving the village; meanwhile, thanks for your time". He exited the stuffy office to search for the police constables who were still in the dining room awaiting their instructions. He addressed them in an authoritative tone.

"There has been too much flummery going on in this village, and yesterday I called a halt to it, so when you go knocking on doors, use your initiative and power of the law to get those buggers talking".

After he had dished out the daily orders, he and Cartland made their way to the rear of the hotel, where the police car was parked. He took the forensics bag from the glove compartment. "Your task for today, Cartland, is to get this razor, which was recovered from the river late yesterday afternoon, off to the forensics laboratories. I'm sure this is the murder weapon used to kill Janice Calderwood, but I need confirmation. Hopefully, there will still be traces of skin and blood on the weapon, despite its time immersed in the water".

He hesitated, "Ask if they could treat it as a priority, because I'm sure by the end of play today, we will be able to make an arrest". He sat for a moment, giving a lot of thought to his next questions. "What do you know about witchcraft, Cartland? I seem to be getting warned about activities in the old church of the village. That makes me inquisitive". She gave him a quizzical look. "I did some thesis work on the occult at university, sir. Nothing in-depth, but enough to know the difference between good and evil".

There was a silence before Inspector Rupert urged her to tell what she knew. "Witchcraft is a group of people who delve into remedies and potions taken from Mother Nature's garden, in days of yore. Witchcraft has been a form of pagan worship for centuries sir, even before the purges of the 17th century when witches were hung and burned at the stake. These women accused of witchcraft had a problem. They were intellects of their time, wise and able to come up with potion remedies, nothing more than that. They had healing power, back then".

She paused. "It was a catch-22 situation sir, when called to a sick person's bedside, if that person survived, then everything was hunky-dory, but if the patient died, the healer was classed as a fraudulent witch and thrown into a pond. If she survived and floated, she was deemed as being a witch. However, if she had drowned, then her body would have been given a Christian burial. There is another twist: if she sank and was pulled from the water after a time, but still alive, she was put on trial for witchcraft and hung. I'm sure you can draw your own conclusions on the justice of it all sir".

Inspector Rupert was about to speak when W.P.C. Cartland held up her finger, indicating she was not finished yet.

"Another thing connected to witchcraft is midwifery. The hags, as they were called, were summoned to a woman or girl in labour. Again, if the patients survived the birth, everything was fine, but the same scenario applied if the pregnant mother or baby died in childbirth".

Cartland wasn't quite finished. "Most witch hunts were carried out in Essex, the home county of Mathew Hopkins. This took place from 1648, perhaps a little earlier; it was during the English Civil War, so nobody paid much attention when Mathew Hopkins proclaimed himself Witch Hunter General and proceeded with his evil persecution. Most targeted were the poor, the old and people who could not defend themselves, and of course, the herbalists and midwives who were accused of being in league with the Devil. It's still unclear today what his motive was, whether it was financial gain or simply a common hatred of women. One thing is certain: he himself was deemed to possess witchcraft and was thrown into a pond where he swam to the opposite bank and escaped the punishment that he had inflicted on so many innocent people, which also destroyed family life in those isolated villages of the time. Mathew Hopkins disappeared into the mists of time. However, it's common knowledge among our professors and surgeons today that the herbalists and midwives in those days saved more lives than what was recorded or talked about sir".

Inspector Rupert had heard enough and wanted to be on his way, but W.P.C. Rosalyn Cartland was not easily dismissed.

"Witchcraft has changed over the millennium, they believe in the full moon where Diana, the Moon Goddess, traverses across the heavens, and to reach her bountiful lover, Lucifer the rising sun God. Today, initiates must go through a trial of endurance by walking naked across hot embers of a fire, then follow a priestess who immerses the naked initiate in a stream of cold running water, then she entices the initiate forward into the darkness calling their name softly, then into the firelight, across rough terrain with the voice of the priestess urging the initiate on until they finally reach the fire where they started their journey. Congratulations are placed upon the new member of the coven by the high priest". W.P.C. Cartland continued quickly. "This form of witchcraft has spread throughout the U.K., but must not be confused with devil worship sir, which I know little about. I got quite a scare when, as a student went to a party which got out of hand. Somebody produced an Ouija board, and we partook in this so-called harmless game, but things changed in the room sir. The large log fire went down to dim embers; the candles flickered and went out. The room became ice-cold. Somebody screamed. The electric light refused to come on. Somebody lit the candles and went to the fuse box to find them all intact before trying the light switch again, which now worked, the log fire in the grate burst into flames".

W.P.C. Cartland took a firm grip on the forensics bag. "They tried to knock all those fears out of us at the police training college, but that incident will stay with me forever sir," She paused.

" I suppose a little sleuthing into the witchcraft activities would be a bit of harmless fun, but please heed my advice and do not dabble in devil worship, that is very dangerous sir".

Inspector Rupert could see W.P.C. Cartland was visibly shaken when talking about the devil, so he did not lecture her on her tuition lectures at the police college, where he himself had gone through the lectures of the living and the dead.

"I'll take heed of your advice, Cartland, now it's back to business. I've an arrest to make in Chelmsford before I can continue with the next stage of the murder investigation". Cartland got out of the car and made her way over to the hotel to collect her car. Inspector Rupert collected his briefcase from his room when the expected telephone call from Inspector Buckingham arrived. He took a note of the name and address of the occultist. A Señor Phillipe de Santos, of Spanish origin. Albeit the occultist lived in St. Albans, which would mean a journey north, he was grateful Inspector Victoria Buckingham had taken the time to do the research. Her end of the telephone conversation was a question. "Is there something you're not telling me, Amadeus Rupert you cunning devil"?

He wondered if she was fishing for an answer, so he simply replied," Nothing you need concern yourself with Inspector, but thanks again for your tenacity". He replaced the receiver before she could gather her wits and start to ask direct questions. But he did have something in mind; there was no time like the present, strike while the iron is hot was always his motto. So, he wrote down the name, address and telephone number with area code. He left the hotel in an optimistic mood. He drove out of the rough hotel car park and joined the village street that had become alive.

Inspector Rupert was pleased to see the constables had started at the bus stop as he drove past, where the public waited patiently for the early service bus into Chelmsford. There were a lot of flailing arms as the public tried to make their point. He gave a wry smile as he drove past unobserved by the mob and the two police officers. He put out a message on the police car radio as he joined the A12 heading for Chelmsford. "Bring him in, "he said in an order to the switchboard, who would pass his message on to the Chief Superintendent. The road was busy due to the early morning traffic, as people were heading to work. The journey took a little longer; however, he didn't mind, stopping at a petrol station to fill up and to purchase a packet of mints, which was always kept in the glove compartment and used when the need arose to help irradiate the smell of alcohol.

Today was not one of those days. He parked the car in the compound, then made his way to the front desk, met by an over-enthusiastic officer.

"Chief Superintendent Sorley is waiting for you sir, in interview room four".

Inspector Rupert nodded his acknowledgement, then walked smartly along the corridor. Everything had been arranged and set up.

The sergeant sat by the recorder, ready to switch it on when ordered, and a constable stood guard at the door. It was all common procedure.

Chief Superintendent Sorley made a gesture towards the prisoner. "He's all yours Inspector. Let me know when you've finished". He left the interview room.

Inspector Rupert was in no hurry. He removed his coat, hat and scarf. Sitting down, making himself comfortable, he tossed the brown envelope onto the table. He signalled for the recording machine to be switched on, giving the prisoner a brief welcome to proceedings that were about to take place.

"Good morning, Mr. Shipley, Mr. Morgan Shipley. I'm Detective Inspector Rupert of Scotland Yard. I'm here to question you regarding a murder that took place in Tringford village just over a year ago. Last Halloween's eve, to be precise. It has come to my attention that you were in the vicinity of the village that night and that week, posing as a horse trader, apparently there to buy, with lots of money on his hip, which enticed the women of the village to drop their knickers when their husbands were at work. It wasn't the first time you had paid the village a visit, was it, Morgan? In fact, you had visited the place on numerous occasions, depending on circumstances, and a call from the public telephone box on the village green can verify that. However, on the night and the week in question, you booked and stayed in the hotel. Yet there is no signature, and certainly no record of you ever being there. Why, I asked myself, should you do that? However, after checking back in the register from the hotel cellar, I found that you had stayed there a couple of times before. You registered under a false name, having dyed your hair dark brown. However, there was a different reason for you being there, and that was to visit the vicarage. Now I ask myself why all this subterfuge, all this skullduggery, so I did a little digging and discovered why". Inspector Rupert paused. "We've a copy of your signature on a statement you made to this very station when arrested on another charge". He paused, then took the photographs from the brown envelope. He spread them carefully on the table facing the prisoner. "Let's talk about the case where you were found guilty of stalking this woman, whose naked body is a blatant example of her willingness to pose for you, Morgan. You're the man who was given a two year suspended sentence and a court order to stop stalking and harassing this woman in the photograph, however those points are the least of your worries Mr. Shipley, because in a moment you'll be charged with participating in the murder of Janice Calderwood, the hotel chambermaid who flirted with you, promising herself to you. But let's stay with the stalking case for a moment, because frankly I don't think you were the stalker, I think it was the other way about, I think you took the blame because you were also besotted with an older woman who posed for you and had sex with you, and the younger man, they called the village stud. Promising that she would leave her husband and go off with you," He paused. "That, Morgan was never going to happen, is that why you were persistent, trying to win her affections"? The Inspector paused.

"Then disaster struck, Cupid fired his arrow, and you fell head over heels in love with Janice Calderwood, who told you she was a virgin, working as a young chambermaid at the hotel where you befriended her, courted her, giving her hope of a better future away from the village where she found herself trapped. But despite all your gifts and promises, she never relented or gave up her so-called virginity. Sadly, that was her downfall, because she gave herself to you willingly in your car that Halloween night, and that is when you discovered that Janice Calderwood was not a virgin and had been stringing you along all that time. She had refused point-blank to have sex in the hotel where you were caught in an embrace by a very angry Mr. Farlow, the owner, who, incidentally, had lied to me about his affair with the young chambermaid Janice Calderwood. He threatened to sack her if it happened again. So, there it is, Morgan, after a steamy session in your car, with Janice Calderwood goading you and teasing you about her affair with her boss, a starry night, the moon shining bright, you killed her, Morgan, is that the way it was before the heavy rain came down?

He watched the young man wince. "Let's return and let me mention the hotel again. It was so easy to smuggle someone in and out of her room, but that wasn't you, Morgan. However, let us go back a bit, a little bit further, before you met Janice. You were bedding the vicar's wife while the vicar was away on church business. Later in the game and being a stranger in the village with money to spend, telling those who wanted to hear that you had a stable of your own in Hertfordshire, you became quite a celebrity in these parts of England, posing as a horse trader. The women fell at your feet, and you became quite adept at bedding them while their husbands were at work. The reason I mention this charade again is the fact that it didn't suit this old lover from another place and another time, did it, Morgan? This was the pick of the crop until Janice Calderwood turned up. I'll make it clear to you, Morgan, you'll face charges relating to the death of Janice, but right now I'm interested in this woman who betrayed you time and time again".

He tapped the photograph of the nude woman. "It was not her husband's vocation or misgivings that made them leave the parish here in Chelmsford, was it, Morgan"?

It was the first time he got a reaction from the accused, who was now looking worried.

"You're right Inspector, I did take the wrap for Amanda, how stupid of me until I realised what was going on. It was Amanda's affair with a young fourteen-year-old choir boy that forced them to leave the parish here in Chelmsford and seek a quieter vocation. That choir boy was my younger brother, Inspector. I planned my revenge while continuing our affair, which took place in the rectory when the vicar was away. There were other places, where we had sex, Amanda was insatiable, she didn't know the meaning of word stop or rest, that's why it was so easy for me to persuade her to strip and pose for the camera, I had intended to blackmail her but that never happened, she did however invite me to a sex session with two other men and told me to bring my camera. I had intended to film her in action with the pair from Maldon, but that never took place due to timing and the vicar returning early". He paused. I've done some stupid things in my life Inspector, but I've never killed anyone. I'm glad you've brought this case to a head, because I've so much to tell you".

"That can be made in a moment, Mr. Shipley. I've carried out more investigations, but for the present, Morgan Shipley, you're being held on suspicion of murdering Janice Calderwood. You have the right to remain silent; however, anything you do say will be taken down and may be used in evidence against you. Do you understand"? The accused answered "Yes".

It was only now that his solicitor intervened. "I think at this point, Inspector, my client would like to confess as to exactly what happened that night".

There was a deathly hush as Morgan Shipley nodded.

"For the recorder Morgan, do you wish to confess? Please say yes or no".

"No, I'm not taking the blame for this Inspector, because I killed no one, I was present when Janice was murdered, but not by me".

The Inspector nodded. "Tell me who did, Morgan, because I know there were two people involved, and you were one of them".

"No, Inspector, the only way I was involved was because I was in love with Janice Calderwood. We were making love in the car when the attacker pounced".

"So, I take it you and Janice were naked in the car, which will explain the fact that we found no clothing of the victim, either on the bank or in the river. What did you do with them Morgan"?

"I panicked after the attack; all I wanted to do was get out of there. I never gave her clothes another thought as I dressed quickly". Inspector Rupert nodded and rubbed his chin.

"But you didn't drive away Morgan, you assisted in disposing of her naked body into the river". Morgan Shipley nodded.

"It was stupid of me, I know, but the killer threatened to slice me open if I refused to help".

The interview conversation ended five minutes later. He got the information he wanted, and now was the time to return to Tringford to question the vicar's wife and the other woman who was involved in the killing of Janice Calderwood.

The drive back to Tringford was filled with an air of contentment. He went over in his mind how he would approach Amanda Chapman. There were so many things going on in his mind that he found it hard to concentrate on the driving and was glad when he slipped off the busy A12 onto the B1019. There were the occasional tractor and flocks of sheep on the road.

He parked the car at the hotel car park, then walked across the village to the vicarage.

He was surprised when the vicar answered the front door.

"Good afternoon, sir, I would like to speak to your wife if she's at home".

"And you are? "The question was asked softly.

"Sorry, vicar," he searched his pocket for his warrant card.

"Inspector Rupert Scotland Yard, Mr. Chapman". He spotted the dog collar below the jacket. "Come in Inspector. I'll fetch my wife. Is it important"? He asked again in a gentler manner.

"Very important sir". He stepped into the hallway of the vicarage.

"Please take a seat in the lounge. I'll fetch her from the kitchen downstairs. Can I offer you some tea or coffee"? He was about to walk away to fetch his wife.

"No thanks vicar, busy afternoon ahead". Inspector Rupert entered the lounge as instructed and awaited Mrs. Chapman.

Eventually, she made an appearance. Inspector Rupert stood up as she walked towards him.

"What is it this time Inspector"? She sat down on the comfy chair opposite,

Inspector Rupert knew it was done on purpose as she crossed her legs slowly, giving him an eyeful of her cream thighs above her stocking tops.

Inspector Rupert looked at the vicar who had sat down beside his wife.

"You don't have to see or hear this vicar, so I would advise you to take a walk in the garden,"

"Anything you have to say to my wife, you can say to me Inspector, we've no secrets from each other".

He leaned back in the chair. "Really vicar, I wish for your sake this was true". There was a silence for a moment before Inspector Rupert spoke.

"It is your prerogative vicar, but what you're about to see and hear might not be palatable for your eyes or ears, so I give you the opportunity to step out of the lounge before I begin, however, if you do stay then I must warn you not to interrupt the proceedings when it gets underway, that could be construed as wasting police time".

He waited to see the vicar's reaction.

"Okay, let's begin. Amanda. I've now concluded that you lied to me over the death of Janice Calderwood. You held back vital information that was vital to solving her murder.

I have in custody a young man who knows you very well. His name is Morgan Shipley, does that name ring any church bells"? The vicar sat forward in his chair intrigued.

"The Chelmsford police have reopened the case of stalking when you brought charges against this young man called Morgan Shipley, but that isn't strictly true, is it Mrs. Chapman? The truth is, it was you who was the stalker, it was you who encouraged Morgan Shipley to carry on your affair here in Tringford while your husband was away on church business, you had sex in the vicarage, sex in his hotel room sex in his car, even a quick romp in the garden shed while your husband the vicar was at home in his study preparing a sermon for the coming Sunday". He paused,

"Frankly, I couldn't care less how often you've done it, or where, but it did annoy me when you lied to me, telling me you hardly knew Janice Calderwood, the young temptress who your lover Shipley fell in love with. That really did upset you. The thought of a young teenager, who looked older than her years, a young teenager who refused to participate in your sex trysts with two men from Malden, every Saturday before your husband returned on the six o'clock bus". He paused.

"It was Morgan Shipley who was protecting young Janice, determined to keep her so-called virginity intact until she turned sixteen, A virginity she had lost two years before. How was he to know when she would not let him near her until they celebrated her sixteenth birthday on Halloween's eve? You were livid with Morgan Shipley, who had become a celebrity in the village, splashing money around as if it was going out of fashion, reaping the benefits of the married women who were more than keen to spice up their dreary lives. This also had a lasting effect on you".

The vicar was shaking and holding his hands over his face.

"You're talking absolute rubbish Inspector. I don't know who has been planting those seeds in your head, probably Shipley the weirdo, the stalker, but if this ever went to court, I would deny every last part of it, his word against mine Inspector". Inspector Rupert rubbed his chin,

"You had revenge in mind Mrs. Chapman. Perhaps you didn't have murder in mind, but that's how it turned out". He took the brown envelope from his jacket pocket.

"These are proof that link you and Morgan Shipley as an item. They were taken in happier times". He tossed the photographs onto the table.

The vicar peeked through his hands and gasped. "Oh God," was all he said before covering his eyes again.

"What you didn't know Mrs. Chapman, is that Morgan Shipley was snap happy with a brownie camera in his pocket, yes, you had posed for him when you were both alone, but it was during one of your sex games that he photographed this while the camera was on a timer". He removed another envelope from his pocket.

"This was another threesome, only this time it was you, Shipley, and another woman who had sex in different positions that day. Another woman who was also infatuated by the good-looking Morgan Shipley, the so-called horse trader who had bedded her on numerous occasions, a woman who was also so besotted with him. Unfortunately, she told you of her love for Morgan Shipley. You were so angry that you revealed at this point and told her about Morgan Shipley's infatuation with the young chambermaid, making her promises he could not keep. He showered her with gifts you gave him for services rendered".

The vicar stood up quickly and walked out of the lounge with a disgusted look on his face.

"I've said it before; I'll say it again. I couldn't care less about your sexual activities, there is nothing wrong with a roll in the hay if it is legal, which brings me to another point, that having sex with a fourteen-year-old altar boy called Leonard Shipley is illegal, and you will be questioned again by the Chelmsford police and could face charges relating to that after I've brought other charges".

He gathered the photographs together, then pointed at the woman, who was kissing Amanda Chapman's erect pink nipple.

"This is the woman you enticed to go along with your plan, who got out of hand that Halloween night in the park".

Inspector Rupert dropped a hint about the stolen razor.

Amanda Chapman nodded as tears filled her eyes.

"It was never supposed to go that far; it was only to show her what Morgan Shipley was up to, shagging all and sundry in the village. I had no idea that she had stolen the razor from the barber's shop while the barber went across to the baker's for a cake, something he did every day at the same time, because he was a creature of habit".

"If you had told me this before Mrs. Chapman, which I know is the truth, then all this would never have seen the light of day, certainly not in the vicar's presence, but you didn't and that's why your husband, the unfortunate vicar had to witness this pornography".

He stood up. "I'm going to leave you to sort out the mess with your husband. However, you'll receive a visit from the Chelmsford police regarding the stalking incident, and the perjury in court will play a big part in your court verdict. They will add wasting police time, etc., etc. and any other charges they wish to bring against you, which will include unlawful sex with a choir boy minor."

He paused. "Don't leave the neighbourhood without informing me, and my advice to you is to get yourself a good lawyer. "He paused. "The reason I'm not arresting you right now is because I've a much bigger fish to catch and fry. I'll leave that to the Chelmsford police".

CHAPTER

Four

He left Amanda Chapman sobbing as her husband returned to the lounge, attempting to comfort her, while trying to make sense of the sordid affair she had got herself involved in.

It took a bit of time to find the constables who were busy knocking on doors.

"Come with me, Cartland". He ordered, "We're about to make an arrest. I'll explain as we walk".

W.P.C. Cartland could hardly keep up as they hurried to fetch the police car.

Inspector Rupert wanted to arrest the murderer before any warning telephone calls could be made. He opened the shop door and approached the counter. He lifted the hatch and stood facing the culprit.

"Julie Linton, I'm arresting you on suspicion of murder. You have the right to remain silent. Anything you do say will be taken down and may be used in evidence against you".

The bewildered chemist stood with his mouth open.

"Get your coat, Mrs. Linton". Inspector Rupert said loudly.

She was handcuffed and led out of the chemist's shop. It had only taken a few minutes to arrest her, but as she was led out to the waiting police car, a small angry crowd had gathered, probably the vicar's wife had taken her revenge by making a few rapid phone calls.

Julie Linton was taken to the Chelmsford police station and placed in interview room two. Inspector Rupert entered the room.

"You've been read your rights, Mrs Linton; you can instruct your lawyer to be here at 10:00 am tomorrow morning. If you have no solicitor, we can arrange one to represent you, although I recommend you get your own brief, as some of the lawyers that are appointed to represent suspects," He hesitated. "Well, what can I say? It's just that they lack experience".

Julie Linton attempted to speak, although her throat was hoarse.

"Save it for tomorrow, Mrs. Linton, that's when you'll be formally charged, you'll have every opportunity to express yourself then, meanwhile you'll be held in the cells here at Chelmsford, then after the charge interview tomorrow, you'll be moved to a more secure prison". He paused, "You'll be allowed one telephone call to your solicitor. You'll not be allowed any visitors until you have been formally charged and transported to a secure prison to await your trial. I would suggest you try and get a good night's sleep, although I can imagine that will not be easy due to the predicament you find yourself in; however, that's your problem, they will be serving a hot meal shortly, so make the most of it, because it might help you sleep". He got up quickly and walked out of the room.

The drive back to Tringford was filled with mixed emotions. When he had started the investigation, he was quite taken by Julie Linton's gentle manner, and there were so many twists and turns in the investigation that it took longer than expected. The prime factor was the lies, the deceit, and the typical village attitude of bringing the shutters down against a stranger, especially a policeman.

The aroma from the hotel dining room smelled good, so he went straight to dinner. He gave his usual nightcap in the bar a miss, because he knew there would be a barrow load of questions fired at him by the press, so he poured himself a brandy in his room from the half empty bottle in his bag, a snifter before he turned in, intent on keeping a clear head for tomorrow's charge briefing.

It was strange how the alarm clock always seemed to tick louder when trying to get to sleep. Perhaps he would've been better off going to the bar and easing the tension that had built up over the last few days. Eventually, he dropped off into an uneasy sleep. He woke up to the alarm ringing loudly, and in a cold sweat, he got out of bed.

He showered before putting on a cleanly, laundered shirt. He decided to skip breakfast in the hotel and use the canteen at the Chelmsford police station. It was just as well he had made that decision, because a crowd of reporters and photographers were moving about in the foyer, ready to pounce at the hotel entrance on the suspicious police officer who didn't expect them quite so early. Inspector Rupert tooted his horn and, with a smile, gave them a wave as he drove past the baying mob. He drove carefully along the single-track C road, then the B road, until he reached the A12. He headed for Chelmsford, where he ate a hearty breakfast in the police canteen prior to the interview. The coffee went down a treat as he stifled a yawn.

"Hard night sir"? The voice said from behind him. W.P.C. Cartland did not wait for a reply.

"I thought Julie Linton was going to pass out on us on our way to the Chelmsford police station, she was as white as a sheet and crying, asking for her husband".

"She should have thought about her husband before she got mixed in with the fake blond horse buyer and the mare he was shagging, to be honest, I really don't know where Amanda Chapman, the vicar's wife, got her time and energy from.? She was at it day and night, like a bitch in heat".

"Good old country air, sir, do you know that when cows fart, they create a chemical in the air that's a stimulant to the Bull, and it's the female hormones that trigger a reaction in the testicles of the bull, and make the cows more randy". She smiled.

"You're having me on, constable, just concentrate on your scrambled egg, that will give you all the hormone treatment you need". He wiped the plate with his toast.

"By gum, I enjoyed that. Okay, constable, time to go to work". He said in a happy voice.

He was seated in the interview room, awaiting Julie Linton and her lawyer. The Sergeant sat at the ready to operate the recorder. Inspector Rupert took the photocopied statements from his briefcase and laid them out where the solicitor would be sitting. The door opened, and the solicitor followed the accused, who was held by a constable and would eventually take his place at the door as backup.

"Sit down, please," Inspector Rupert said amiably, directing each to their seats "Thank you for being on time", he didn't mean it. Julie Linton and her solicitor would've been taken up from the cells anyway.

Inspector Rupert Spoke softly; it was a good way to help the prisoner relax.

"Okay, Julie, let's get started".

She had dark shadows under her eyes due to the lack of sleep.

The solicitor placed her briefcase on the floor and sat down with a poker face.

"Before we begin, Inspector, it has come to my attention that you held my client in an interview room without legal representation being present. I hope you'll make that clear when you start recording".

An interview did take place when she was brought here under caution. So, I can say she was taken here under arrest; it is our right to question the prisoner for up to thirty-six hours.

However, I didn't question her at the time because Julie Linton was under no obligation to talk to me; she was advised about her rights when arrested and told she would be held in Chelmsford overnight, and after she is formally charged, which is now about to take place, she will be taken to a secure prison to await her trial. I'll put that on record if you so wish, you'll also note that the two statements of witnesses who are prepared to act for the Crown Prosecution Service are laid out in front of you for inspection".

The lawyer began to write while asking, "You say the prisoner was under stress when you brought her into this intimidating room". She hesitated.

"Did you seek medical advice for my client"?

"What"? Inspector Rupert was getting agitated at the senseless question.

"I'll make it clear, Inspector, in case you misunderstood me, did you call a doctor for my client. Was she taken to a hospital for her respiratory condition"?

The Inspector shifted in his seat and replied "No, I believed your client, if that's the term you wish to use for her, was brought here under severe restraint in handcuffs as a matter of fact, while she was finding it difficult to breathe as you say, she still had enough breath to curse, swear, and spit at the arresting officers".

"Was she attempting to escape"? The young solicitor waited as the Inspector moved the charge sheet papers around the table.

"Well, I'm waiting, Inspector Rupert," this was said in a forceful manner.

Inspector Rupert did not answer; he might have been mistaken, thinking this was a young rookie just out of law school, but he noted immediately that this young lawyer was not one to be meddled with.

"I was not given your name, miss"? He said with eyebrows raised.

"Peabody, Alice Peabody of Peabody and Peabody, Chelmsford office". She continued to write, not lifting her head until she was finished.

The name hit him like a sledgehammer blow. How many times had he crossed swords with Peabody and Peabody, the London Barristers, who in the past had virtually destroyed his evidence when they got him into the court witness box, along with his career?

He was physically shaken for a moment but recovered in time when the solicitor stopped writing. She looked at her watch.

"I want those points I have made put in typed format, Inspector. Now, if you don't mind, I've a business meeting this morning, so please let's begin". The recorder was switched on.

Inspector Rupert started the proceedings with the usual jargon of time, date and those in attendance. "Julie Linton, you've been arrested on suspicion of murdering Janice Calderwood, whose address was given as the Tringford hotel in the village of Tringford. We've witnesses to prove that you deliberately cut both her wrists and her throat, helped by your accomplice, Morgan

Shipley, who has admitted to being part of the murder and has been formally charged. It was then that you both acted together and threw the girl's naked body into the river as the blood spurted from her veins. He looked at the statements. This was also witnessed by a bystander, Amanda Chapman, who was not directly a participant in the murder, but was sexually involved with Morgan Shipley, just as you were, Mrs. Linton. Then, after rinsing your hands in the river, you wanted to have sex in his car, where just ten minutes before, Morgan Shipley had taken the young girl's so-called virginity. This was the last straw for you when the bystander, Mrs. Chapman, teased you about Janice and Morgan having it off an hour before. But you knew about Shipley and Janice from Amanda Chapman on a previous occasion. She was only rubbing salt into the wound. Your wounded heart. Mrs. Linton" He paused. "It's a simple case of murder, so before I charge you, I want to remind you that you're still under caution, and you have admitted that you understood your rights when first arrested. You still have that right to remain silent; however, courts tend to look on that as a sign of guilt".

The solicitor interrupted him. "My client wishes to remain silent, and it is wrong of you to suggest that the courts find the accused guilty, just because she refuses to speak in this, or any other interrogation, Inspector".

"This is not an interrogation, Miss Peabody, but a formal charge briefing". He tried to correct the outburst from the angry solicitor.

"Alright, now that she is not under interrogation, Inspector. I might suggest that we bring this charge briefing to a close".

The lawyer gave a wry smile as Julie Linton began to speak. She had found that proud and defiant self-confidence which she displayed before and during her arrest.

"You have it all wrong Inspector Rupert, it was the other way about, it was Morgan Shipley who lost control that night, when he discovered that she was not a virgin, and that the hotel owner, Jack Farlow had been banging her regular, while she played miss goodie two shoes, egging Shipley on with a promise she would remain forever his, and would give herself to him on her sixteenth birthday, but Shipley was not prepared to wait any longer, he took her, forcibly in the back seat of his car. I would call that rape". She drew a long breath and sighed. "That is when he discovered the truth about Janice Calderwood". She paused for breath.

"When I arrived in the park, there was a ferocious argument going on between Janice Calderwood, Amanda Chapman and Morgan Shipley. Amanda Chapman was holding the young girl firmly in the back seat of the car. That is when all hell broke loose. I tried to separate them and threatened Morgan Shipley with a razor I had stolen from the barber's shop to shave my legs. He wrestled the razor from me and began to cut Janice Calderwood's throat, but as he tried to slash her, she put up her hands to defend herself, and that's when her wrist was cut. Seeing she was severely injured, he grabbed her other wrist and slashed it open. He threatened to kill me if I didn't help put her body in the river". She paused, "I admit stealing the razor was wrong, I admit throwing her body into the river was wrong, but I did not strike the fatal blows that killed her".

Inspector Rupert considered her explanation of the events that happened on the night of the murder.

"There you have it, all, Inspector, you have arrested the wrong person again. If I might add, I checked you out before I took on this case. It was during the Serial killer murders in Hertfordshire, if my memory serves me correctly". The solicitor paused.

"However, you seem to be pretty good at wrongful arrest, don't you"? The solicitor leaned back, folding her arms.

"If you have nothing more to add, Miss Peabody, I'll charge your client with murder".

There was an uneasy silence in the room. He turned to the prisoner.

"Julie Linton, you have been arrested on suspicion of murder. I now charge you with being an accomplice in the murder of Janice Calderwood on the 31st of October 1950 in Tringford public park". It was short and to the point. But things had changed. Accusations made. The prisoner was led away as the solicitor put her notes carefully into her briefcase. Inspector Rupert stepped towards her.

"Yes, Inspector, I'm of that breed, the Peabodys that you know so well, only it is another generation from my aunt and uncle who gave you so much grief over the years".

She lifted her briefcase. "I understand your son Colin has reached the rank of Inspector in the Brighton and Hove force. I do hope we clash at some stage in our career, I'm sure we would be just as energetic in our quest for victory as you past dinosaurs have been".

She shook his hand and walked out of the stuffy interview room.

Inspector Rupert was speechless for a moment. He was about to call her back, but decided she was right, there was a new type of breed coming through in the legal profession, and indeed in the police force. He gathered the papers together and took the recorded tape from the sergeant. He sat back to consider what had been said by Julie Linton, apart from another jealous woman's statement, which any reasonable defence team would destroy in court; it was her word against the unreliable Morgan Shipley. Who was lying? And who was telling the truth? That was the question. There was something that bothered him; had he slipped up like before in charging the wrong person, however, that would be for the Crown Prosecution Service and the court to decide.

He reminisced about the old days. Back then, his run-in with complaints officers could have resulted in a much more serious internal investigation by the complaints division, but for a crafty Chief Superintendent, he would have been long gone.

Inspector Rupert was glad that the Tringford murder had been solved. "The village of suspects" was the way Superintendent Sorley had described it; how right he was.

Inspector Rupert knew he was in for a lecture on police behaviour, procedure, and etiquette. It wasn't that long ago that he had a run-in with this ill-tempered Chief Inspector Skinner.

Inspector Rupert tried his best to pacify the irate Chief Inspector Frank Skinner, who wanted to know about his late-night tryst with Angela Farlow.

"Nothing happened that night, sir. She wasn't a suspect; I had already satisfied myself that Angela Farlow was no more than a lonely woman who needed a bit of love and attention, which I refused to give her".

Inspector Rupert tried to explain again that nothing had happened that night.

Chief Inspector Skinner exploded. "You sat in the bar drinking with her, Rupert, you allowed her to enter your room, while you were in a state of undress, apparently ready for bed, the bed which you and Angela Farlow slept in together" He was foaming at the mouth.

"The bloody press doesn't care about love or emotions, Rupert. Christ, man, you've been in the job long enough to know how things work".

The Chief Inspector's voice was angry. "This puts a different reflection on your success, Rupert. You do realise that I need to go upstairs with this, and it could draw a line under your promotion prospects. If not, your career. You could be dismissed for this dereliction of duty, Rupert, which will be in my report, and believe me when I say that I'll be more than happy to see the back of you, now get out".

Inspector Rupert did not care about promotion; over the years, he felt that he had been side-lined, despite his successes, even when he had solved the biggest murder cases in the Hertfordshire constabulary's history, where he was promoted to Chief Inspector, which was due anyway. Then a slap in the face when he was demoted to obtain a place back at Scotland Yard, after which he found that an Inspector who had cooperated with the crime bosses at a masonic lodge, leapfrogged into the vacant slot of Chief Inspector that he, with his experience and success, had been overlooked. The silence in the room was unbearable; however, he kept his cool before walking to the office door.

"You must do what you think is right, sir. Personally, my time is my own time. You might want to work twenty-four hours a day, seven days a week, but I don't. I try to separate work from pleasure, but I do realise that can be difficult. Now, if there is nothing else, I'll go and write my report for the Crown Prosecution Service, excluding my so-called fling with Angels Farlow, sir". He turned quickly, only to continue with his defence.

"One thing I don't approve of is officers who are in the Metropolitan Police or any police force having conversations with known criminals, like a cancer, it will eat away at the very fabric we stand for. Eventually, it will ruin the reputation of a good, harmonious lodge, and it also has grave consequences for officers of the Metropolitan Police, who are out there doing their best to prevent crime, while the crime bosses are one step ahead due to leaked information. It's time something was done about it, and with me getting close to retirement, it might be something to content myself with when I do retire".

The Chief Inspector's attitude changed. "Come off it, Rupert, what good would that do you? You could find yourself buried up to your neck at the low water's edge in the Thames". The Chief Inspector was about to continue but refrained from divulging any more.

"You get that report off to the Crown Prosecution Service and take care, Rupert".

The last words spoken sounded like a warning to him. He walked to the door and turned. "It's sad when it gets to this stage, sir, but I'm not easily frightened or warned off". He opened the door. "There will be other investigations made before I retire, sir".

He smiled at the thought, knowing he still had another few years to serve, with no time off for good behaviour. However, the thought of signing on for another five years had been eroded from his thoughts; it was time for a new generation to take the reins, hoping that one day his son Colin would join the respected Metropolitan Police, perhaps get into the Scotland Yard Serious Crime squad.

With the Tringford murder now practically cleared up, he and W.P.C. Cartland had some spare time on their hands. "I've been thinking about the witch's coven that is held out in the old churchyard. I have no doubt that some form of ritual has taken place, and I'm keen to find out what it's about, which could prove useful in some future investigation". He hesitated.

"It's a full moon tonight, the weather is fine, so why don't we do a recce on them, just to see what all the fuss is about"?

"You can cut out the 'We,' sir. It's not part of my duty to become involved in this spying game you call a recce. If you want my advice, I will let sleeping dogs lie, because your interference could cause problems. Besides, what if a bunch of so-called witches want to dance naked around a bonfire? What harm are they doing, sir"?

"You're missing the point, Constable. All I want to do is satisfy my curiosity, nothing more".

"I'm missing nothing, sir; be careful because curiosity killed the cat".

"And satisfaction brought it back". He answered quickly. "I agree this does not come under any police jurisdiction, and do not hold you in any way to participate with this little game, which is also to pass the time more than anything, if only to keep me from spending another boring night in this god forsaken place, which is driving me mad, therefore you finish for the day, and I'll meet you in the dining room tomorrow at the usual time".

"Take care, sir, you don't know what you might be getting yourself into, so until tomorrow". W.P.C. Cartland walked to her car and drove off.

After his dinner, Inspector Rupert checked the torch batteries and replaced them. He lay on top of the bed until the clock struck midnight. He grabbed his hat, coat and scarf before exiting the bedroom and stepping out into the bright moonlit night. He decided to leave the car and used the moonlight and his torch to walk up the riverbank path, which led to the derelict church. Approximately two miles upriver, he could see the outline of the bonfire. As the sparks flew into the night sky, he heard the chanting and verses being spoken by the High Priest, whom he recognised as being Jack Farlow, the hotel owner.

He stood against the corner of the derelict church wall, out of sight from the naked coven. Watching intently as the coven performed the ritual of undressing. Caressing each other's bodies before a halt was ordered. Everything stopped, and an easy silence filled the air as more wood was thrown onto the bonfire, and again the sparks flew into the moonlight night.

Amadeus watched with awe as a male was brought from the darkness into the bonfire light.

The High Priest began to chant. "This initiate has come forward of his own free will and requests that he may discover the love and bounty of our Moon Goddess Diana, who will bestow upon him the bounties should he pass the initiation tests that have been prepared for him".

Amadeus watched as the initiate was disrobed and stood facing the High Priest, who lifted both hands to summon a priestess from the coven whom he recognised as Amanda Chapman, the vicar's wife. She took the initiate's hand and led him through the hot charcoal raked from the bonfire. The bonfire. To and fro he walked without a wince of pain.

When that part of the initiation ceremony was over, it was just as W.P.C. Carter had said. The Priestess led the initiate away from the coven to a pond by the stream, where he was immersed in cold water without flinching.

Amadeus took a risk by following the initiate at a distance by the light of the moon, who, in turn, was enticed by the priestess to follow. He was flabbergasted as he watched the initiation ceremony. He thought of John the Baptist baptizing the believers of Christ in the river Jordan. The moonlight had given him enough light to observe without using his torch. He was tempted to follow the pair away from the pond into the pale-yellow light but decided to go back to the safety of his hiding place and await the return of the initiate and the Priestess. He listened as chants filled the night. The coven circled the bonfire, humming and chanting until the pair returned.

The High Priest lifted his hands before embracing the new member of the coven.

"You have been initiated into the secret world of witchcraft and will reap the benefits of our Goddess Diana". He paused. "However, let me give you a stern warning". The High Priest took the new member by the shoulders and whispered into his ear.

The new member of the coven spoke. "I hereby solemnly swear I shall lock away in my heart and soul the memory of what I have been taught, forfeiting my life to our Goddess Dianna, should I ever divulge the secrets of the coven and my witchcraft".

The High Priest released him. "Enjoy some of the fruits we have bestowed upon you".

He raised his hands and chanted. The coven began to circle the fire as the new member was given a partner.

It came as a surprise to Inspector Amadeus Rupert. Each coven member fell to the ground and began to cavort into sexual relations with their partner until the male was spent and had ejaculated. He had seen enough and was prepared to leave when a couple of coven members came close to his corner, sat on the horizontal gravestone. Now he had a full view of the Priestess who had initiated the man. He couldn't believe it when Amanda Chapman sat down naked and spoke to the new coven member about Lammas night. Put it in your diary, because it'll take you higher into the degrees of witchcraft. I'll certainly be there, promise me you'll come"?

The initiated member promised. Amanda embraced the man; she came on top of him, and they had sex on the horizontal gravestone that the forensics team had previously examined.

Amadeus wanted to get away as quickly as possible but had to wait until they had finished their sex encounter, afraid that any movement might give him away. When the pair re-joined the coven, he took one last look at the cavorting members still engaged in sexual behaviour before hurrying down the river path to his hotel room.

The first thing he did when he reached the safety of his room was to pour a very large brandy.

He then noted in his diary the place and date Amanda Chapman had revealed.

His night's sleep was interrupted by dreams of what he had witnessed. He didn't have nightmares and sweats like that since he returned from the German prisoner of war camp after his burning Lancaster bomber had plunged into a German lake. This was something Deborah, his ex-wife, had nursed him through.

The alarm clock sounded. He got out of bed feeling slightly tired. However, after a shower, he sprang into action, ready to face the day.

He considered approaching Jack Farlow, then Amanda Chapman, about the events that had taken place the night before, but thought against it as he ate his breakfast.

What did he have apart from an explicit sexual performance by willing, consenting adults? "Nothing", he said to himself, before a hand was placed on his shoulder by W. P. C. Cartland.

"Good morning, sir, and how are you this fine morning"? She poured herself a cup of coffee.

"Fine, Cartland, just a little bit of tidying up to do this morning, then we can both go back to our normal duties".

"I've been thinking about that, sir and want you to know I'll miss you and all the excitement of solving a murder. You certainly have opened my eyes to the way people carry on".

"You should consider applying to join the Criminal Investigation Department, Cartland. I'll certainly back your application if you do wish to join the C.I.D".

"Thank you, sir, it certainly is worth considering". There was a moment's silence. Inspector Rupert knew there was something she wanted to ask, so he gave her an opening.

"It was a beautiful moonlit night last night, Cartland. I had a walk up the riverbank before I turned in. It got a response to my inquisitive nature, but not one he was expecting".

"You did, didn't you. How could you be so stupid as to ignore my warnings? Did it satisfy your needs to encroach on a harmless crowd of witches, sir? Did you learn anything from the incantations and mumbo jumbo that was spoken? Personally, I don't think so".

"I don't have to remind you, W.P.C. Cartland, that you're speaking to a senior officer, but if you want an answer, then yes, it did satisfy my curiosity. I found out about two very important members of this village and their coven, something that I might follow up later and charge them with having unlawful sex in a public place, something you failed to tell me about when we discussed it".

Cartland put down her cup. She began to go into fits of laughter. "Were any of the participants raped or held against their will? I don't think that is the case, sir. How do you know if their meeting or sex acts were carried out in a public place"? She laughed again. "Probably the land belongs to a member of the coven; it might even still belong to the Church of England, like so many old churches". She refilled her coffee cup. "I don't suppose you're willing to divulge the names of the High Priest and Priestess, who I know would be important participants at the ritual. Did you have a witness with you to back up your story"?

"You're right, W.P.C. Cartland, and I have no intention of disclosing their names just yet; however, there is something I must ask you, with you being a local girl". He gave a wry smile.

"What do you know about Lammas night, and a place called Dentary Manor"?

She looked surprised. "The name Lammas is synonymous with the Devil's birthday on the 23rd of May; however, it is believed by Horologists and students of the occult that Halloween is the true date of the Devil's birthday, alias Satan, when people dress up in scary clothes and masks. When evil is portrayed, and in the air. However, Llamas Day, now known as Lammas, is a custom of fertility, much like Easter, when church altars are decorated with fruit and grain to celebrate the harvest and the rolling of the boulder that sealed the tomb of Christ".

Cartland shrugged her shoulders. "Simply an old pagan tradition of which there are many".

She sipped her hot coffee. A dark look spread across her brow. "You mentioned a Manor house called Dentary". She hesitated. "This is a large estate which lies in the heart of the Essex countryside. Surrounded by sprawling meadows and woodland. Not a place I would visit on my own sir, it has a reputation of Devil worship that took place there in the mid seventeenth century, before the family who owned the estate were taken out and hung on a large Oak tree which still exists today, and if I can give you some extra sound advice sir, stay away from this cursed estate where apparently Devil worship still goes on".

"But if there was any crime committed, then why have the authorities like us never investigated such occurrences"? Inspector Rupert asked with a hint of anger.

She hesitated. "Frankly, sir, I think members of our establishments who have a very high rank are involved in Devil worship and attend such gatherings, hence the lack of prosecution, and I return to the witchcraft question. What could we prosecute"?

"Be sensible, Carland, if I want to carry out an investigation, then I would go through the normal procedure of getting the go-ahead from the boss".

W.P.C. Cartland wiped her mouth. "And if the boss is part of a coven, do you think you would get the permission you requested, sir? I doubt that very much".

"Well, I can inform you that I have a date of their next meeting, which will be held at Dentary Manor, and I have every intention of attending the fancy dress ball complete with costume and mask". He smiled at her uneasiness.

"As far as I know, you would need to be a member of a coven to obtain an entrance ticket; otherwise, you won't get past the front gate, sir".

"You seem to be very well informed about those events, Cartland". He said softly.

She interrupted him. "Snippets, sir, that's all, and pieces I picked up at university".

She wiped her lips. "So, what is on today's agenda, sir? There can't be much left to do".?

"I think we should pay the barber a visit just to give him Instructions on how to keep dangerous equipment locked away. There is the fact that he fed me false information regarding the Royalist celebration at the old church. I want to talk to him about that, it won't take long, so you can stay in the car".

Cartland just wanted word that she could return to her home station, now that the murder investigation had closed. She didn't like this dangerous village where suspects roamed the narrow, unlit streets.

Inspector Rupert walked into an empty barbers' shop.

"My, my, Inspector, another trim so soon". He said to prepare an over-gown to be placed over the Inspector's head.

"That's not the reason I'm here, Tommy, so please take heed of what I have to say. Firstly, you lied to me during the murder investigation, telling me it was Royalist sympathizers who held an annual meeting at the old church, which we now know was a downright lie, Tommy.

You could be charged with wasting police time. However, there are more important points you should heed. One, get your razor and other dangerous equipment under lock and key. The other point is, get yourself a life instead of partaking in witchcraft mumbo jumbo. Please don't deny it because you were seen taking part in an initiation ceremony last night in the old churchyard. On that score, I cannot charge you, but take my advice and find another hobby to occupy your time".

"Who told you all this, Inspector? Give me a name and I'll have them in court". Tommy was upset that his secret had been discovered.

Inspector Rupert pointed his finger. "Just do as I ask, Tommy, and you'll be left in peace".

The Inspector reached for the door handle. "Remember to get your razor under lock and key".

He walked out to the waiting police car.

"Right, W.P.C. Cartland, I think we can round the day off by getting some flowers from the florist and pay our last respects with a visit to Janice Calderwood's grave".

Cartland was quite taken aback at the Inspector's turn of showing sympathy. Much as she liked him and appreciated how good he was at his job, she had always thought him a cold-hearted, hard-hearted bugger with no thought for anyone but himself. Now she looked at him in a different light.

They stood looking over the concrete block when Inspector Rupert spoke softly.

"Perhaps someday someone will erect a proper headstone in her memory".

"Yes, I hope so too, and I just want to say it has been a pleasure working with you, sir; you have taught me a lot". Her police training had taught her to hide her emotions.

Inspector Rupert shook her hand. "Remember to consider a position in the C.I.D. Cartland, I think you could forge out a very worthwhile career for yourself. Meantime, I think we can call it a day. He fastened his coat and then walked away, leaving her with her thoughts.

He collected his belongings from the hotel room. Then signed out of the hotel, clearing his tab bill. With nobody about but the Troll, he left a tip and a message of thanks with her to be passed on to the staff and Angela Farlow.

Now that he had a free weekend ahead, he decided to kill two birds with one stone. He could travel to St. Albans to speak to the occultist tomorrow morning, then continue to Watford to watch Watford F.C. get trounced again. He smiled; there was always the unexpected.

After telephoning the occultist to make an appointment, he made his way back to London to pack fresh clothes for an overnight stay after the football.

The drive back to London was a tedious affair, with the usual traffic. He had a welcome drink in the Old Queen Vic. before heading home to his luxury apartment, glad to be back in the city and his own bed.

CHAPTER

Five

He left the city early, hoping to avoid the rush hour and any unforeseen delays on the route. The journey up the A1 was surprisingly pleasant, reaching St. Albans in plenty of time for his appointment. He drove to Chestnut Grove to be sure of his appointment time for the meeting. Punctuality was always an important factor with him. He hated people who turned up late for appointments with him, so he was always sure he paid people the same courtesy.

Number 4, Chestnut Grove, was a grand, granite-built Victorian Villa with private parking.

He approached the main door, but before he could knock or ring the bell, a cross-eyed woman opened the door, almost as if she had been waiting for him.

"Name"? she asked sternly.

"Is that necessary? Señor De Santos is expecting me". Inspector Rupert said, showing his warrant card, which she studied intently.

"I have to announce to you, Inspector, it's the way we do things here".

"Rupert," he said in a boring reply. "Inspector Rupert Scotland Yard".

"Follow me, please," she said, inviting him in. She tapped on a door on the ground floor.

"An Inspector Rupert, Phillipe, will you see him now"?

"Yes, Annabella, show him in, and bring some tea with the marshmallows".

Amadeus was shown into the spacious morning room where skulls, African pictures and memorabilia hung on every wall. Shrunken heads with hair still attached. Spears and shields from African tribes of the Dark Continent filled what little space remained.

The occultist spoke firmly. "Excuse me, my manners if I don't rise, Inspector, my eyesight is not what it used to be; however, take a seat, then we can discuss your problem".

Amadeus was shocked at the sight that confronted him. The occultist was obviously blind, but instead of having two coloured eyeballs inserted into the sockets, it was two white marble eyeballs that stared across the desk at him.

"Ah I can see my appearance has come as a shock to you Inspector, this is what becomes of interfering in something I should've stayed well away from, Devil worship, and black magic was the result of me losing my sight by Satanists who seared my eyes out with a red-hot poker, because of what I had witnessed". He clasped his hands. "Forget me and tell me what has brought you here"?

Amadeus explained about the witch's ritual he had encountered, explaining how the rituals were carried out, while paying their respects to the moon Goddess Diana.

"Harmless fun except for the sexual content, Señor De Santos". He said with a smile.

"No form of witchcraft is harmless fun, Inspector Rupert; each coven is involved in Satanic worship". He paused. "Perhaps not all members are Satanists, but it only needs one rotten apple to taint the rest of the fruit in the barrel, I'm sure you will have come across that in your line of work, however, with the information you have given me it is perfectly clear that you witnessed a white witch's coven, simply because of the initiation ceremony and where it was held". He hesitated". A black witch initiation does not involve water, fire, yes, but not water. Devil worshippers detest running water like a river; even a small, burbling stream terrifies them. It is written in some Satanic writings that the Devil himself, with all that power, can't swim. Personally, I take that with a pinch of salt, and let's not forget, Satanists at every level must cross the river Styx on their way to hell, to be by the side of the Master".

The Occultist laid his hands flat on the desk. "However, I can tell that there is something more dangerous you wish to discuss with me". He pushed his palms forward in a gesture for Inspector Rupert to begin.

"When this initiation was over, two witches came close to my hiding place, the man who had just gone through the initiation, and the Priestess who took him through the rituals. They sat close to me, enabling me to hear their conversation". He paused. "The Priestess informed the Initiate of a masquerade ball to take place at some manor called Dentary, where he would be elevated in the degrees of witchcraft".

The occultist held up his hand to silence the Inspector. The tea and chocolate marshmallows were brought in by squinting Annabella.

Phillipe thanked her and waited until she left before continuing to describe the witch at work with the initiate.

"There is your rotten apple in the barrel. She is obviously a black witch who worships the Devil. She is a dangerous person, Inspector, and you would do well to give this masquerade ball a wide berth, have nothing to do with it, I beg you; this so-called ball will be a front for Satanists from all over the world to attend a High Black Mass. It will attract hundreds because a figure masquerading as the Devil will put in a quick appearance, then later in the Mass, a female virgin will be places on the alter, the Devil will re-appear naked in his Goat mask, he will have sex with her, taking her virginity in front of the masked Satanists, I witnessed such a masquerade ball, and the whole Black Mass, but with the knowledge I have, I was lucky to escape undetected when the ball broke up in the early hours of the morning". He waved his forefinger "How they found out I was not a Satanist will remain a mystery until the day I die. I was well versed in Devil worship and their signs, but I was at another Satanic meeting, much smaller with thirteen hooded Satanists, there appeared to be no danger until I was grabbed and suffered what you see in front of you today". His face remained sombre.

"They leave me alone, because I know too much about them, who they are, what position in government they hold, and other important people of the Realm who walk past you in the street every day". He smiled.

"Knowledge is power, Inspector, that takes decades to cultivate". He stood up, indicating the advice session was over.

"Come with me to the attic, there is something I must show you". Amadeus followed the blind man upstairs to the attic. The door creaked open, and the room was filled with natural light from the glass dome above. The first thing he noticed was the circle on the floor, which had signs of the zodiac on the rim of the circle. Different shapes and hieroglyphs. Points of the compass were marked on the tiled floor. Four tall candle holders marked the North, South, East and West. Each slow-burning candle flickered in the draught.

Amadeus looked at the large leather armchair that was bolted to the floor, with wrist and ankle shackles that could be quickly attached to the arms and limbs. Amadeus cast his eyes up towards a platform that housed a very large telescope. The Occultist read his thoughts.

"Those were the days when life was simple, Mr Rupert. I was a simple Astrologer who studied the vast Universe. I read people's horoscopes based on their star sign. I also read palms, which gave predictions. "He paused. "Do you know the vastness of the Universe, Mr. Rupert"? He smiled. "Some stars that you see in the night sky tonight have since burned out and died long ago. Think of the speed of light. This twinkle of light that travelled through the vastness of space and shines on us millions of years later".

Amadeus was trying to comprehend what point the Occultist was trying to make.

He turned to the Occultist. "What purpose does this serve, Señor De Santos"? He asked softly.

"This is my bolt hole, Inspector. There are dates in the Satanic calendar that demand revenge on the non-believers who have tricked them and learned their secrets. There is one approaching shortly on the 23rd of May, some call it the Devil's birthday, but I'll settle for Halloween, which is more likely. Those demons that are sent on that date to destroy me will not dare enter the circle, or they will be destroyed; however, they do try to entice me out of the circle, hence the shackles on the chair that stop me from being enticed to my death. Notice the oblong bar with a gold crucifix hung over the chair. This protects me and stops me from undoing the shackles that would mean certain death, cast down to Hell for eternity. I also have holy water that I can use in an emergency. Take my advice, Mr. Rupert. Stay away from any form of ritual, unless you are prepared to give them your soul". He stepped out onto the stairway. "Annabella, who is an Astrologer and Palmist, understands my need to be harnessed to the chair and releases me in the morning light when the ordeal is over. She will show you out".

Amadeus walked slowly down the stairs in front of the Occultist.

When they reached the vestibule, Annabella was waiting. He turned to thank Señor Phillipe De Santos, but he had crept slowly and furtively back to his desk in the museum of skulls.

Having received the knowledge, he came for, he jumped enthusiastically into the car and drove up to Watford, hoping to catch the kick-off. The final whistle sounded, 3-0 Watford FC.

He had intended to stay the night but had second thoughts and drove back to London.

Sunday morning seemed strange as he got out of bed, slightly disoriented as to where he was after a few celebration sherbets in the Queen Vic. However, the smell of his housekeeper's cooking breakfast soon put things right in his head. He relaxed in his dressing gown with the Sunday papers spread on the floor. He didn't bother to dress but spent the day in his pyjamas, going over his notes and what the Occultist had said.

There would be time for an investigation into the Satanic affair.

Monday morning came round. Now it was time for other work.

Showered, shaved, and wearing fresh clothing made him feel good as he travelled into work at Scotland Yard.

He barely had time to take off his coat and hat when his office telephone rang. It was the Assistant Chief Commissioner who demanded his presence immediately. Inspector Rupert knew that DCI. Skinner would have taken his report upstairs. But there was little time for Chief Inspector Skinner to alter his report regarding the night spent with Angela Farlow, let alone the Assistant Commissioner. being in this early. But he knew there would be repercussions to come.

Inspector Rupert was intrigued, so he took the lift and approached the Assistant Commissioners' office.

"Come in, Rupert, take a seat, I'm so glad I caught you before you disappeared into the sticks again".

The welcome was polite, so he dismissed the fact that it had anything to do with his tryst with the lovely Angela Farlow in Tringford village, which seemed like a decade ago.

The Assistant Commissioner sat back and put his hands behind his head. "I've an important job for you, Rupert. You seem to have a special knack for being able to solve crimes reasonably quickly, so after a talk with the Commissioner, we've decided you're the best man for the job".

Inspector Rupert sat and listened attentively. "It must be important and dirty when I've been chosen and summoned here, sir. I'm sure there are other higher-ranking officers who could carry out your request".

"This is not a request, Rupert, although you'll be doing the Commissioner and me a personal favour when you take this on board".

The Assistant Commissioner gave his well-known crocodile smile, before he rolled you over and took your body down to tenderize you, before chewing you to pieces. It resembled his old advisory, the solicitor Jennifer Peabody.

"We've got a big problem in the city with drugs, Rupert. Apparently, coming into the country by a means I will explain shortly. You've handled drug cases before and came out with a satisfactory result; that's another reason we've selected you".

Inspector Rupert noticed it wasn't "if you take on the job", but "when", and that little word made all the difference. He knew it was an order given in the nicest possible way.

"You should have joined the diplomatic service, you scheming bastard", he thought, giving the Assistant Commissioner his own enigmatic smile.

"You do realise, sir, that I've just finished investigating a murder and still have a bit of tidying up to do, sir. "How easy it was to lie to this pompous git. "Oh, you've finished with the Tringford murder case, nobody informed me, excellent, that'll save me arranging someone else to take over. Which reminds me, I haven't received your report from Chief Inspector Skinner. Have you kept him up to speed, Rupert, because I know what you're like?".

"I'm surprised you haven't received my report, sir, "he smiled.

"I wouldn't worry; you'll get Chief Inspector Skinner's report eventually".

He paused and tried one last time to get the Assistant Commissioner to give it to the Drugs or Vice squad.

"You have departments to deal with those crimes sir, my personal dealings with drugs were the result of an ongoing case or cases in Hertfordshire, but the drugs involvement was all part and parcel of that investigation, the drugs just happened to link with the fountain murder case, and that was the real reason we were investigating the murders of the aristocratic family, not the drugs sir. Not the drugs"

"Yes, yes Rupert, but this is different," He paused". What do you know about a circus"? The Assistant Commissioner was deadly serious when his facial features changed.

"A circus sir"? Inspector Rupert screwed up his nose. "The only thing I know about a circus is they have clowns, a bit like the Met. in many ways sir, they have trapeze artists and stunt performers, they also have a lion tamer who risks his life putting his head in the lion's mouth and should not be surprised if one day the lion sneezes and bites his bloody head off. That's the feeling I get with this question, sir, as if I'm about to do a Daniel act and thrown into the Lion's den".

"Rupert, Rupert, this is not a proposition or request, this is a direct order from the top, so stop acting the fool, and go down to Chief Inspector Skinner's office, and he will give you the information you require". He waved his hand in dismissal.

The Assistant Commissioner gave the crocodile smile again as Inspector Rupert stood up. He did not salute but simply turned and walked away in a pensive mood. What were the (High Heid Yins) up to?

After receiving instructions from DCI, Skinner, on where to start, he had enough for one day and would visit the big top tomorrow. A Russian state circus, which should be interesting.

What the "High Heid Yins" had failed to mention was the fact that the Russian state circus was doing a summer season in Blackpool.

He became aware of this as he sat in his office, and after clearing his in-tray, decided to read his orders that had been sealed in an envelope. He could not believe its content as he read through the pages.

Inspector Rupert realised immediately he was being shafted and sent north out of the way. He raced upstairs, taking them two at a time until he reached the fifth floor. There was no sign of the secretary; the Assistant Commissioners' door was locked. He stood and listened for a moment, just in case the fly sod was lurking inside behind a cabinet. He tapped the Commissioner's office door, waited, then tried the handle. It was locked. The fly sods had scarpered, knowing Inspector Rupert was not going to take this lying down. He shook his head, then descended the stairs to Chief Inspector Skinner's office, which he found locked.

He sat in his car contemplating what was happening, then, after giving it a great deal of thought, he decided to play along with their game, just to find out exactly what was going on. He drove home, then caught a west coast train from London Euston to Preston, where he changed trains for Blackpool. A taxi from the railway station dropped him at the Grand Metropole hotel close to the tower. After settling into a fine spacious room with a sea view, which looked directly down the promenade, He took his binoculars from his bag and scanned the seafront, and a fine view of the tower where the circus was carrying out a nightly performance. He had eaten on the train, so he decided to take a walk down the promenade onto the north pier. He would begin by visiting the police station in the town and start to ask questions.

The police station wasn't too far away; he enjoyed the walk after his breakfast. Showing his warrant card to the duty sergeant, he was shown upstairs to another Inspector's office. The pair shook hands as introductions were made. "Inspector John Semple, take a seat".

Inspector Semple remained standing, looking out of the window.

"Looks like we're in for a squall of rain, Inspector Rupert".

It was said amiably to start the conversation. "Perhaps you can enlighten me as to why you have travelled all the way from

London, was it to see the Blackpool illuminations"? He smiled.
"Not quite, John. I was given strict orders to come here to
investigate the Russian state circus".

He handed the local Inspector the paperwork. "As you can see,
there is a problem here in Blackpool and London with drugs,
which they think is being brought in from abroad, by this travelling
circus. "He watched the Inspector's face light up.

"We certainly have a drug problem, but no more than any
other town or city in England. If you're looking for drug
trafficking, you should be targeting the ports and airports, not a
circus". He paused.

"If you want my advice, look closer to home, London, Dover,
even Liverpool, but the state circus? I don't need a ticket to get a
laugh, Inspector; I'm getting one right here. I'm sorry for being
flippant, but I cannot for the life of me understand why you have
been sent here when our own drug squad have our drug situation
under control. I should add that the circus manager and owners
allowed us to do a drugs sweeps of all the animal cages, their
caravans and trailers. We had our sniffer dogs do a thorough search
and found nothing, not even a hint of any illegal substances. I feel
sorry that you've made this journey for nothing, and you should be
asking questions in London why they've wasted resources and
money the way they have, when a simple telephone call would've
answered your question". Inspector Rupert nodded. "I'll make the
most of the time allowed John. I'll do a little sleuthing of my own.
The means justify the end, John. "The Inspector walked towards
him, "I've been authorised to tell you, Inspector, we don't want
your crowd from London stepping on anyone's toes up here. The
Russian state circus is a big attraction for the people of the town,
and brings in thousands of tourists, who spend lots of money, so
take my advice from one officer to another, catch the first train out

of Blackpool to Preston today, and head back south, where you'll find an answer to your problem".

Inspector Rupert was not happy with the advice given to him by a fellow ranking officer.

"I'm just obeying orders, Inspector Semple, so don't try to threaten me with your advice. There are powers greater than you lot up here who are out of harm's way and have an easy life, who want this problem solved"

There was little more to be gained by talking to this officer.

Inspector Rupert was about to demand that a more senior officer listen to his problem and why he was sent so far from London, but it was obvious the conversation was over, so he walked out of the police station into the warm spring sunshine. The stroll along the seafront was exhilarating despite the strong wind. He walked onto the north pier and tried a few slot machines without much luck, so he about turned and crossed the road to the Blackpool tower, taking the lift to the viewing platform at the top. The panoramic view was magnificent; however, it was cold, so he went down to street level and booked a seat at the circus for the afternoon performance.

The screaming children were filled with awe as they watched the trapeze artists go through their performance, which turned to laughter as the clowns pushed cake into each other's faces. There was nothing to be gained here, so he decided to go to the lorry and caravan park where the trailers were unhooked from the cab tractors. He certainly could not fault the transport. Each vehicle and articulated trailer parked in the watery sun that shone periodically through the clouds, creating a large rainbow as he walked between the tractors and trailers, he was stopped by a large security guard. "What are you doing here? You have no right to be anywhere near those vehicles. Now clear off before I get angry". The words were said in broken English.

"Police", Inspector Rupert said quickly, showing his warrant card as the hulk guard approached, uttering what Inspector Rupert assumed was a warning in Russian. Suddenly, a female figure approached.

"Ivan does not speak good English well; however, I'm fluent in English, so what is your problem? And why are you in this restricted area"? Inspector Rupert reached for his card again. The female studied it intently.

"You're wasting your time, Inspector. We have our own security, who deal very harshly with intruders and anyone attempting to steal or damage our property. Ivan is one of our guards who walks around the lorry and the caravan park, patrolling twenty-four hours a day, on different shift patterns. They also have Rottweiler dogs patrolling the outer fences. So, we don't need any police protection, we're capable of looking after ourselves".

Inspector Rupert nodded, "And your name is"?

The woman looked slightly taken aback by the question. "My name is Olga Romanovsky, a trapeze artist. Now I must go and rest before my next performance". She smiled, then walked away. Inspector Rupert folded his arms while scrutinizing the surrounding caravan trailers. He decided that there was nothing to be gained by hanging around. Ivan made sure he was off the premises; he made his way back onto the seafront and strolled towards the central pier where a live band were performing in a pub called Legends. He spent the rest of the afternoon there before walking back to the hotel for dinner. The visit to Blackpool was a complete waste of time.

The Lancashire Constabulary had the Russian state circus checked out when they arrived in the town, and Inspector John

Semple was right. If any drugs had been brought into the country by this route, they would've been dispersed long before now. There was also the fact that there was no trace of any illegal substance was found in any of the caravans or articulated vehicles. He decided that tomorrow, he would take a trip to the village of Cleveleys on the tram, then catch the midday train to Preston to catch the London-bound west coastline. However, this scenario was far from over. Questions would be asked back at Scotland Yard.

The journey back to London gave him plenty of time to think. He wondered why the Russian state circus was targeted as drug smugglers, when there were so many drug runners that were on the Metropolitan Police radar, and who had links with the coastguard stations around the coast of Britain, although it was nigh impossible to cover every nook and cranny of the rugged western coastline, especially in the northwest of Scotland. There had to be a reason why he had been sent on a wild goose chase, with no chance of an arrest or even an interview with the circus management.

The steam train shuddered to a halt in Euston railway station, and it blew off steam as if in an angry gesture of the tiresome journey undertaken all the way from Glasgow, calling at Preston, where he had boarded. He took a taxi to his Mayfair apartment, which had been cleaned, and dinner had been prepared for him. He unpacked his travel bag. One thing that struck him immediately was that the toilet bag was open. It was a part of his nature to close buttons and zips that held toiletries, so why was this item left wide open? He remembered quite distinctly closing it and packing it before he went down to breakfast that morning.

He wasn't quite gaga yet, as he went back over the day's events. That was the only time the travel bag was out of his sight for the entire day was when he went to breakfast. There was a possibility that the maid had spotted something left in the bathroom and had placed the item in the toilet bag, but that seemed absurd, because all she would have to do was leave whatever it was on top of the bag, and it was most irregular for housemaids to interfere or tamper with residents' luggage. He scratched his head and began to put the dirty laundry in the basket. The Blackpool tea towel was hung in the kitchen, and the toilet bag was in the bathroom. His suit needed to be dry-cleaned and pressed, so he put that aside before opening the wardrobe to hang up his clean, unused shirts. The toilet bag was making him feel uneasy, so he went through to the bathroom and opened it. He removed the razor and the shaving stick, then the au de cologne that had obviously been tampered with as it smelled to high heaven because the bottle had obviously been opened and carelessly closed. He made sure the top was screwed on properly, then placed it by the wash hand basin. The hand cream lid was not replaced tightly, so he undid the lid, just to be sure it was properly attached again. This was something else that he was sure had been tampered with. He would never have left the tub of hand cream like that; besides, he hadn't used the cream since he left London.

"What in hell's name is going on? "He said loudly to his reflection in the mirror.

"This has definitely been opened by someone". He noticed that the best part of the hand cream in the container had been removed. There could only be one explanation for that. Something had been placed in the container tub, then removed along with some hand cream. There were four questions on Inspector Rupert's mind. What was in the hand cream? Who had put it there? But more important, who had been in his room? Who had removed something and why? Now he was interested in revisiting the Lancashire town of Blackpool.

It was a damp and windswept London as he made his way to Scotland Yard.

He never informed Chief Inspector Skinner or the Assistant Commissioner of his return to the city. When he entered Scotland Yard discreetly, he remembered the locked doors from when he was given the assignment. This would be a surprise for the "High Heid Yins".

He smiled as he took the lift to the fourth floor, entering DCI. Skinner's office with a slight tap on the door. He noticed the name and rank plate had been removed.

"You're back, Rupert. Why did you not make your return and presence known to us"?

"The weekend is my leisure time, sir. And let me say, you crowd were quick off the mark the day I left for Blackpool, sir" was his opening line, without the normal handshake and small talk before his superior was over the shock and realised who was standing in front of him.

"You're supposed to knock loudly before entering my office, Rupert. Have you no manners? And from now on, you'll address me as Chief Superintendent. Don't bother congratulating me. It was a quick promotion made in your absence. So, I repeat. Please knock before you enter".

"The only thing I'm going to knock is somebody's bloody block off, if I don't get some answers".

The Chief Superintendent stood up quickly as Inspector Rupert approached his desk.

"Have you gone completely crazy, Rupert? That's a dismissible offence, threatening any senior officer like that. "

"I'll take my chances, sir, it's your word against mine, and let me say this, that if you make any move to reach for the emergency button, you'll be joining the gaggle of geese that have just flown by your window".

Inspector Rupert showed his anger by clenching his fists.

"Now tell me the real reason, Skinner? Why was I sent to Blackpool on a wild goose chase? Knowing that I hadn't a hope in hell of getting anywhere. The nearest I got to the circus was when I attended an afternoon show. Even their caravans and trailers were guarded by security gorillas and Rottweilers"

The Chief Superintendent sat down. "Take a seat, Rupert, I can tell you so much, the rest you'll have to get from the Commissioner himself".

Inspector Rupert sat down to listen and calmed down before he did or said any more.

"The Russian State Circus and drugs are not the issue, Rupert. We know that there are secret Russian agents operating in the north of England, and to draw them out into the open, we decided to send you, knowing your obstinacy, for disobeying the rules, and of course, your inquisitive nature. That's all there is to it, Rupert, that's all I know, so make an appointment to see the Commissioner".

Inspector Rupert stood up; the C.S. moved uneasily in his chair, not knowing what to expect.

"I don't need an appointment, Skinner. You crowd put me at risk, hanging me out to dry with no thought for my safety or well-being. You make me sick". He shook his head.

"I'm going upstairs, I'll start with the Assistant Commissioner, and please do not inform him by picking up the telephone, that would make me angrier than I am at the moment, and if you do inform them, then you better lock your door and scarper like you all did before, realising I would be unhappiest about the appointment in Blackpool". He walked to the door and turned to face the ashen-faced Chief Superintendent.

"Let's see what these lying bastards upstairs have got to say, because believe me, I'm one step away from being arrested for murder".

Inspector Rupert climbed the stairs to the fifth floor. The Assistant Commissioner's door was locked. He walked along the corridor to the secretary's desk.

"When will the Assistant Commissioner be back in his office"?

The question was asked tersely.

The secretary continued typing and, without looking up, said quickly, "Friday, he won't be back until Friday".

Inspector Rupert walked to the Commissioner's office door before the secretary could get out of her seat to protest. He entered, then closed the door and locked it.

" I called to see you before I was shunted off to Blackpool Commissioner, unfortunately I found your door locked, you and the rest of your cronies had flown the nest before I got the chance to say what I would've said then, but did not get the opportunity to say it, however I've my chance now, but before I begin, I demand to know why I was sent to Blackpool to flush out some Russian State circus accused of drug smuggling, without any warning as to what could have happened to my wellbeing, something which over the years I've been particularly careful about, and yet, as I approach retirement, I'm pitched head first into a ring of bloody spies and drug smuggling " He paused. "I think you have some explaining to do, Commissioner, because right now I'm not a happy bunny".

The Commissioner remained calm". There was absolutely no question of you being put at risk, Rupert; you were simply a courier, transporting false aircraft components on microfilm. We knew the Russian State circus was never involved or dealings with drugs, but there was something much more important on the agenda. There was an element of risk, certainly, but nothing like the way you have described it".

He unclasped his hands. "Take a seat Inspector and I'll give you the gist of the trip to Blackpool, which I understand you made the most of, but I'm not about to hold it against you, because you have succeeded in flushing out a very important operative who was under suspicion for some time, she certainly swallowed the plot, hook line, and sinker". He paused.

"An Inspector from Scotland Yard carrying a microfilm was ideal to get Olga Romanovsky out in the open. She was using the cover of the Russian state circus, but she was in real life a Russian spy who worked with the circus under false pretences as a trapeze artist, which I have to say she was very good at. Being there for the summer season, she took a room in the Metropole hotel. We placed you in a room close to hers to give her every opportunity to search your room. So, over a period, she had access to your room. If you think about it, you'll find that your room had been searched, your hand cream container tampered with, because that's where the fake microfilm was placed by an MI. 5 agent who accessed your apartment in Mayfair before you left for Blackpool. I knew how you would react to the orders given by Chief Inspector Skinner, who has now been promoted to Chief Superintendent".

He gave a slight smile.

"That's why we left in a hurry. This left you seething in your car until your curiosity got the better of you. Officers watched you smarting from a cleaning cupboard window. Then you made the decision to head north to Blackpool".

The Commissioner hid his delight. "So, all's well that ends well, Inspector".

When the crocodile's smile appeared, Inspector Rupert felt uneasy. He wondered if the smile came with the job, the higher up the greasy pole you progressed, with promotion.

"Surely that would've been a job for the Secret Service, sir. They're much more experienced at that kind of subterfuge than me".

"Exactly, Rupert, Olga Kosnofsky's handler, who is very adept, would've smelled a rat, and been very reluctant to expose his agent who has given him more false information over a period of time". He paused.

"We were happy to feed the spy false information; we had our suspicions, but we needed to know for sure who her handler was". He hesitated before revealing other information.

"From a political view, documents of importance were photographed and passed on, without any of the military people who attended these conferences being aware that the secret documents were photographed and then replaced". He smiled that crocodile smile.

"That's when MI5 decided to make a move, feeding her a lot of useless information, knowing that the aircraft components were highly sought after by her Russian handler. So, they concocted this plan". The Commissioner clasped his hands.

"You'll be pleased to know that the operation was a complete success. Comrade Olga passed on the fake microfilm and will continue to pass on other useless information until M.I.5 has no further use for her; it is then, she and her handler will be arrested". He stood up quickly. It was an indication that the meeting was over.

"That's a feather in your cap, Rupert. It's never too late to gain promotion before you retire. You have the option to sign on for another five years, which is worth considering, but let's face it, you still have another few years to serve, so why are you talking about retirement?".

Inspector Rupert stood up. "I take it that's what you've decided I should do, sir"?

He saw the scowl on the Commissioner's face.

"I'll just go back to do what I'm good at for the present there will be plenty of time for decisions, if I last that long, sir". He walked to the door and unlocked it.

He had already made up his mind about the future, and it did not include signing on with the Metropolitan Police for another five years. He stopped at the secretary's desk.

"Really, Lucy, who would've thought you were like that"?

Her face went red. "What do you mean, Rupert? What has he been saying about me"?

Inspector Rupert just rubbed his nose. "Don't worry, your secret is safe with me. "

He left her in a quandary as he walked down the stairs laughing. Now it was time to get back to police business.

His first thought when he lifted his in-box pile was the Julie Linton case. He wondered if a trial date had been set; it was something he would check on. There was still the nagging question of doubt: who had carried out the murder? he knew one participant would blame the other. It would certainly make a difference when it came to the judge passing sentence.

Inspector Rupert thought there would be repercussions over the way he had spoken to a senior officer. He had overstepped the mark by threatening to throw the 'Chief Inspector Skinner' out the window. Not that he would've done it, but it certainly must have put the frighteners on him, because time had passed and nothing more was said about the incident.

Inspector Rupert carried on solving menial crimes that the woolly suits could have handled, but it got him out of the office occasionally.

Spring had moved to Summer. He was getting bored with his menial tasks.

He was thankful he had holidays coming up, which were long overdue. He sat in his office staring at the empty in-tray. What would he do, perhaps take another Irish holiday?

One thing did cross his mind as the summer date drew closer. The 23rd of May, when the masked ball at Dentary Manor would take place.

He knew the very shop in Oxford Street where he could hire a costume and mask.

Without hesitation, he made his way along the busy streets until he spied the shop with an inflatable of Jimmy Cricket taking up most of the window space. He peered through the glass before making his entrance. The bell above the door rang. "Ho-Ho-Ho, don't just stand there, come in and buy something". Amadeus looked at the vibrating illuminated figure of the Mad Hatter, who continued the rhetoric until he stepped away towards the counter.

"I wish to hire a costume for an elaborate party, also a face mask. Can you fit me out with something"? He said to an overenthusiastic assistant who produced a measuring tape from around his neck.

"What kind of costume do you require, sir"? he asked while taking measurements. "If you give me a clue as to what the party is about, is it a birthday party? A fancy dress parade or what"?

"None of these, it's a costume ball," Amadeus said quickly.

"Ah, yes, I think I know exactly what you are looking for, sir". The shop assistant started to take more measurements, then disappeared into the back shop. He put his head from behind the curtain.

"Come through, sir, we have different costumes for your choice". He pulled out a rack of colourful attire. "I chose this one for you, which is popular with masquerade balls. I would suggest you make up your mind quickly if the function is close, because we usually get a last-minute rush for such items". He paused. "When is this masquerade ball to take place, sir"?

"The 23rd of May". Amadeus said without thinking.

"Mm, that's strange, we normally get a warning of such an event. Is it to be held in or near London"?

"An estate in Essex, actually, now I'm in a bit of a hurry, it being my lunch break".

"I do apologise, sir; I'll just take down a few details while you go into the dressing room and try it on". Amadeus appeared from the dressing room dressed in the masquerade ball attire.

"Perfect, if I may say so, sir, now I think a red and black cape, silk stockings and buckled black shoes should answer all your requirements. The other garments and shoes were tried on before Amadeus said. "Just the mask, and that's me sorted". He smiled.

"Indeed, sir, and I have one that I'm sure will fit your needs for such an occasion".

The assistant appeared with three masks that were grotesque to look at. He thrust one towards Amadeus, who accepted it without question.

When everything was fitted on him, he gazed at himself in the mirror.

"I think this outfit and mask will turn a few heads at the ball, Mr. Rupert. All we must do now is ascertain how long you wish to hire the costume, and then we can agree on a price. However, I do insist that the costume and mask, etc, are returned to us in the condition you took them from the shop; otherwise, you can keep them, and you'll be charged for the attire, of course". He paused. "If you fail to return the hired outfit on the date agreed, you'll be charged with a penalty, and there is a deposit to pay, which is all listed in the contract of hire".

He produced a contract from his pocket like some magician pulling a rabbit from a hat.

Everything was signed and sealed. He carried the large box back to Scotland Yard, not escaping the looks from the sergeant on desk duty.

He was delighted with the costume and mask he had selected. Now all he had to do was inform those in the secretarial department that he would be away over the weekend, then wait for the days to pass before heading to Chelmsford, where he booked a room at the Albion hotel.

He had already decided to use a taxi to transport him the thirteen miles to Dentary Manor for the masquerade ball.

Detective Inspector Amadeus Rupert tried to keep a low profile, keeping his head below the parapet in case he got it 'shot off,' was the common saying at the Yard. The last thing he wanted was his weekend to be cancelled if some unsavoury case should appear out of the blue.

His fears were unfounded as he packed an overnight bag containing his outfit.

After he finished his shift, he drove out of London along the busy A12 to Chelmsford, where he settled into a comfortable room, he had pre-booked in the Albion hotel.

The next morning, he took time to roam around the town, taking care to avoid the central police station and pretended to look in shop windows when policemen and women patrolled the beat in his direction.

In the afternoon, he decided to take a nap because it could be a long night at the ball.

He didn't enjoy the bland food served at the hotel and left the dining room earlier than planned. After relaxing and carrying out ablutions and a shave, he removed the costume and mask from the overnight bag. After giving it a rub over with the travel iron, he began to dress for the ball.

He then telephoned reception to order a taxi. He was glad when it arrived and was waiting at the front door. He didn't put on the mask until the taxi was well out of the illumination of the town's streetlights. The darkness came swiftly when the taxi left the town of Chelmsford behind. The taxi driver handed him a hip flask.

"For a new customer on such a grand occasion, the best of brandy, sir". Amadeus accepted the drink without question just glad he was on his way.

In between polite conversation with the driver, he watched the starlight sky go by.

The journey to Dentary Manor seemed to take forever. He wondered if the taxi driver had taken the longer route, intent on charging the stranger in the grotesque mask the tourist fare price. Eventually, the taxi driver informed him they were leaving the main road, approaching the country lane that would take him the eight miles off the beaten track towards Dentary Manor.

"There is one thing you can do for me, driver". He paused. I want you to come back for me just before midnight. I might be delayed for a short time. However, I'll make your wait worthwhile when you return to collect me. Take this for the fare and a deposit for later. A big thanks for getting me here".

Amadeus handed the taxi driver a sweetener of one hundred pounds.

"There's no need to be so extravagant, sir. Fifty would have covered it quite adequately". The driver said, still holding the wad of cash tightly in his hand.

"I need to be sure you'll come back to collect me, Bert, so think of it as a little bonus".

The driver stuck the payment hastily into his waistcoat.

There was a glow in the distance. "Nearly there, sir, so I'll be waiting just before midnight. I'll wait for two hours after that. I'll assume you've picked up a lumber and will be staying the night. However, I can come back tomorrow morning if you wish".

"No, Bert, I think I can safely say be here at midnight".

The taxi pulled up at the flood-lit, large iron gates entrance.

Amadeus jumped enthusiastically from the taxi and watched it pull away into the night.

CHAPTER

Six

He stood for a moment, admiring the large gate posts with security cameras moving constantly in timely sweeps, observing the new arrival, before the large gates swung open.

"Good evening, sir. May I see your ticket"? The tall, broad gateman asked, dressed in what looked like Tower of London warders' attire. Amadeus had to think quickly on his feet.

"Dash it all, I've left it in my jacket pocket in my hotel room, how stupid of me". He said in a posh accent.

"Put your mind at rest, sir, we are equipped to deal with such trivialities". He reached into his red coat and produced a gold-embossed card.

"Take this, you'll need it to gain entry to the Manor and the ball". He handed Amadeus the card.

"I noticed you came alone by taxi, sir. Any particular reason for that"?

"Problems with the car, so my wife refused to take a taxi, still, she's the one who is missing all the fun. What, what"?

"Indeed, she is, sir". He snapped his fingers. A French Citroen car appeared almost immediately. "This is just another perk we lay on for our guests who arrive with a problem. Our driver will drive you the remaining three miles to the Manor, sir. Enjoy your evening".

The gatekeeper ushered him into the back seat, bowed, then closed the door.

Amadeus tried to make polite conversation with the black chauffer driver, who said nothing as he drove slowly towards the Manor. The route was lined with pillars of grotesque faces, and flaming torchlight illuminated the narrow approach lane.

They finally reached Dentary Manor, which looked magnificent in the floodlights that made the marble pillars and steps sparkle.

The driver got out quickly and opened the rear door of the car. He bowed in silence as Amadeus stepped out onto the chalk white gravel.

He stood in admiration of the magnificent building. However, his attention was caught by the modes of transport that were parked in a semicircle in front of the manor.

A Silver Ghost Rolls-Royce was among many. Bentleys and sports cars of the highest quality, names.

The flickering of the blazing torches brought him back to the present. He climbed the thirteen steps before turning to look at the flaming pillars that shone for some distance down the approach lane.

He was relieved to see other vehicles arrive, which meant he could join them in their entrance. It also indicated that he was not late in arriving. He began to feel quite excited as the others joined him at the main door entrance.

One of the other groups pressed the doorbell, and the large door was opened to reveal a spacious vestibule area, and a marble staircase led up to the other floors.

A tall, slim, well-dressed gentleman welcomed them as they entered the Manor. He stood erect. His heels clicked together as he bowed slightly to shake the guests' hands. His greying hair was immaculately cut and combed straight back above his ears. His light-brown skin shone in the crystal chandelier light. Amadeus assumed he was a foreign gentleman from some foreign land.

The lady, standing beside him, was also immaculately dressed in a long purple evening gown, and a string of pearls was trapped in her beautiful cleavage that left nothing to the imagination.

When she gave a slight courtesy, she then offered her long, white, gloved hand to be kissed. Her ears displayed diamond earrings that sparkled, and the diamond tiara on her head fascinated Amadeus. There was a moment of rapture when she squeezed each guest's hand, wishing them a warm welcome.

One thing that Amadeus noticed was that the immaculately dressed pair wore no masks, and their dress code told him that they were very well groomed, perhaps from some rich European Royal family? But that was only a wild guess.

After the handshakes, they made their way to the large doors, opened by two doormen in seventeenth-century attire and wigs. This was obliviously the dining room where other masked guests stood talking, eating, and holding glasses of different alcohol beverages. A servant approached and handed him a flute of champagne. He was told to help himself to the food on the long buffet table.

There was the occasional sound of music when other double doors opened to what he thought was the ballroom, then faded as the doors were closed again by the footmen.

However, he was more interested in the masked people who stood in conversation, sipping their drinks through straws, with masks that were askew on their heads to allow food and drinks to be taken. But the masks were hastily replaced when each couple finished and made their way to the ballroom for the evening entertainment.

Everything seemed perfectly normal when they excused themselves, shaking their hands, bringing an end to the polite conversations.

One thing Amadeus did notice was the lack of names. No one introduced themselves formally.

No hint as to what their employment was, which at times was a normal topic of introduction and conversation. But everything had gone well so far with him gaining entrance to the masked ball, so he dismissed it as being omitted unintentionally.

He helped himself to food from the buffet, as his champagne flute was taken from him and a freshly filled glass placed in his hand. He was beginning to feel slightly dizzy.

Wiping his lips and fingers, he replaced the mask and made his way to the ballroom.

He looked casually at his watch, which told him he had been in the Manor for over an hour. A waiter approached to ask what his preference was from the cocktail bar.

"I think I'll stick to the champers for now. "He said innocently. The waiter lifted his hand and snapped his fingers. A tray of champagne was brought promptly by another waiter.

Amadeus thanked the waiters and turned to listen to the orchestra that was playing different tunes. Vienna waltzes, foxtrots, tangos, every dance was catered for.

Amadeus stood agog at the fantastic sounds that seemed to echo into the rafters and corridors above, where other guests looked down on the dancers that filled the dancefloor.

Again, he began to feel a little dizzy as he stood alone, enjoying the music. Another replenished Champagne flute was put into his hand. He wanted to refuse, but the words would not come out. He looked up towards the fuzzy balcony that now appeared to be empty of people.

He tried to take another sip of champagne, but he could not lift the glass. He felt a hand slip beneath his cape.

"Let's get rid of this, sir; it should have been taken off before you began to eat". It was his host.

He felt her gloved hand remove the cape. "You should not be alone on such a night. I will get you a partner who will help prepare you for what is to come".

Amadeus was swaying but managed to turn and face the perfumed lady, who seemed to sparkle.

"I think I've had too much champagne, and I must get some fresh air". He slurred softly.

"Nonsense," the beautiful lady said as she lifted and waved her hand at a group of women.

"This is Contesa, she will take care of your needs for the rest of the evening".

Amadeus noted, despite his drunken state, that a name had been mentioned for the first time.

But his mind was telling him he was not complimented on his state after drinking so many flutes of champagne. How many had he been offered? He was confused.

"I really must be getting back to my wife; she will be…" he couldn't finish the sentence.

The memory of Deborah, his ex-wife, penetrated his memory as his pleading was interrupted and went unnoticed. The masked woman with bare breasts took his hand and led him from the ballroom. He lethargically climbed the stairs, and the feather-plumed woman with a cockerel mask led him into a bedroom. She began to undress him. All resistance by him had practically disappeared. He stood naked, facing the woman who removed her G-string and stood naked in front of him. They embraced before falling onto the king-size bed, where he was completely under her spell. That thought twigged something. "Spell, spell". He said loudly as she came on top of him and guided his erect penis into her.

He had no idea of time. He had no idea of how many times he had ejaculated into her. The next thing he remembered was being taken back downstairs to the ballroom. Dressed in a white robe. He watched in amazement as the busy ballroom dancers, now naked on the floor, took sexual pleasure from each other.

The tall, slim brunette held him by the hand and disrobed him. They fell to the floor in wild abandon. She was fantastic. The drug, whatever it was, had begun to wear off slightly.

He was still totally captivated by this woman. There was something about her that stirred his loins. The brown eyes that seemed to look right through him. The windows to the soul blinked behind her mask. He couldn't think straight. Where had he seen those eyes before? Was he imagining it? The brain was trying hard to remember, but nothing came to him. The tall, slim brunette helped him put on his robe before she walked away.

The loud beating of the two kettle drums came to an abrupt halt. Those who were still having sex on the floor ceased immediately, standing up quickly to put on their white robes.

Amadeus looked around the crowded ballroom for his partner, but there was no sign of her.

Suddenly, there was strange music from behind a draped curtain. It sounded like a cello, with other stringed instruments filling the gap. The drumbeat started to fall into rhythmic time again. The beat got steadily louder until everything became silent.

Amadeus, who had become aware and realized where he was, but couldn't believe what was happening. The sombre masked guests swayed gently with their arms linked to each other before dropping to their knees and bending forward like Muslims in a Mosque, paying tribute to their great Prophet. Their hands touched the floor before coming back to the crouching position. The mumbo jumbo they were chanting meant nothing to him.

Suddenly, a Pyrotechnic of flames erupted on the stage. A figure in a red cloak stepped from behind the fireworks display. Wearing a grotesque goat's mask that portrayed the Devil. The so-called image of the Devil was handed a live cockerel; he cut its throat. The throng of guests gasped as the head lifted the blood-filled chalice above his head, then offered the goblet to his robed assistant, who drank the warm blood quickly. The black roasted turnips were then put into the chalice and moved around in a circular movement.

Amadeus was coming to his senses and had a suspicion he was witnessing a High Black Mass.

The turnip cuttings were thrown into the assembly, which fought and tried to obtain a piece. The ones closest to the stage were the lucky ones, each taking their turnip pieces into their mouths with joy. A young virgin was placed on the altar, and the Devil had his way with her.

Another Pyrotechnic flashed, and the throng gasped, falling forward again to pay homage to the Devil who disappeared behind the velvet purple curtain. The chanting began again as the weird music started up. The High Priest stood behind the altar and raised his hands. The crowded ballroom fell silent except for the drumbeat and music that got louder, then became silent again.

Amadeus was pulled roughly to his feet and was held by two muscular black servants acting as security men. Held tightly between them, he listened to the High Priest.

"Fellow members of the Satanic Circle, we have among us an imposter who thought he could infiltrate our meeting tonight. This imposter will know the wrath of our Master, Satan".

The High Priest pointed at Amadeus, who stood trembling in his flimsy robe. He felt the warm urine run down his leg and disperse on the floor.

"However, fellow Satanists, a request has been put forward by a member of our order for this intruder's life to be spared". The crowd gasped. "However, for this request to be carried out according to our ancient Satanic Laws, a price must be paid. The person who has made the request must forfeit their life for his".

He pointed to the balcony where a tall brunette figure in a cockerel mask appeared, held firmly by two Satanists.

"Our Satanic member has put herself forward to protect this imbecile; therefore, he must be set free and without harm, escorted to the outside steps where he will be offered transport".

The High Priest pointed to the balcony. "Take her to the execution room where she will be dealt with". There were loud gasps, then cheers that filled the ballroom.

Amadeus had come completely out of his drugged stupor, although his head felt as if it were about to explode. He was now witnessing the nightmare that was unfolding before him as the chanting started up again in time to the drumbeat and music.

He felt a grip on both his shoulders and was turned around to face the well-groomed man who, three hours ago, had welcomed him into Dentary Manor. The host loosened his grip.

"You fool, Inspector Amadeus Rupert, to think you could arrive by taxi, when I'm sure you spotted the modes of transport parked outside. Then, without a ticket, without a partner, claiming your wife would not belittle herself travelling by taxi, when in fact we both know you are divorced, and your ex-wife has now remarried and is living in Florida, where her husband is an aircraft engineer with Boeing International. And how stupid of you to fail to give or take part in the earlier, simple signs and rituals, which made you look like a fish out of water. We knew of your intentions to infiltrate this grand masqueraded ball before you even visited the blind occultist, then went ahead to purchase your mask and attire from the party dress shop in Oxford Street". He paused

"You can consider yourself fortunate that when you are dressed, you will be free to leave because a Satanist member has given up her life for yours, but hear this and take heed, Inspector Amadeus Rupert. Before you are released, you must swear an oath on the pearl of your life, and your family's lives, that should you ever reveal the whereabouts and what you have witnessed here tonight, then woe betide you, your children, and your grandchildren who will suffer an untimely, horrific death".

The warning was given in a cold and calculating sentence from the host.

Amadeus could hardly get the promise out. "I swear on my mother's grave that nothing will be said about tonight's masquerade ball and what took place here at Dentary Manor".

The host took a step back. "Dress him and take him to the main gate".

The host turned and walked quickly away.

Amadeus, now dressed, was thrown down the marble steps where he was roughly manhandled and thrown into the backseat of a car, then driven swiftly to the illuminated gates, where he was dragged from the car and left lying on the road as the gates slammed shut.

He looked at his watch, which showed 00:30 am. There was no sign of the taxi. He stared into the darkness, afraid to move, when the hum of an engine with headlights on full beam turned the corner. "Thank God," he whimpered as the black cab drew up beside him.

"Back to the hotel, Bert and don't spare the horses". He said with relief in his voice.

"I sat waiting for you at midnight, Mr. Rupert, but I was told in no uncertain terms to clear off. I turned the cab at a lay-by and then parked in the lane. I did this twice more before my cab was attacked with an iron bar. This was going to be my last attempt, Mr. Rupert. They're not very nice people, those friends of yours. Who needs enemies when you have friends like that"?

Amadeus said nothing and fell into a troubled sleep on the journey back to the Chelmsford hotel.

He was gently awakened by the taxi driver, who helped him out of the cab.

"It's a bit late to start working out the fare, sir, so I'll call round in the morning, and you can square things up".

Amadeus thanked him and said, "Hang on, my cape, it must be in the taxi".

"No cape, sir, you must have left it at the ball". The taxi driver said, concerned.

Amadeus nodded and made his way into the hotel. He fell asleep without another thought of the masquerade ball; he was thoroughly exhausted by the night's events. He woke up with a throbbing headache. He went over in his mind what he had witnessed last night. Not very much came back to him, except the tall, slim brunette with piercing brown eyes. He had seen them somewhere before he embarked on his quest to find out what went on at Dentary Manor. He hoped the lapse in memory would come back to him, which might answer some unanswered questions.

He cursed his memory, then cursed at leaving the ball without his cape.

After a shower, shave, and ablutions followed by a full English breakfast, he made the journey back to London, where he spent the next day relaxing before returning to work at the Yard.

He took the items of dress back to the party dress shop without the cape. He was advised about the contract and the loss of his deposit. The other masquerade dress items were carefully scrutinised before the shop assistant accepted them back.

"We'll overlook the lost cape for a small price. Should you come across the cape, sir, and it's in good condition, we will make a full deposit payment to you, although I must be frank, sir. Lost Items are seldom found, and most are stolen. However, please call again for any future masquerade engagements".

The shop assistant folded the items to be dry cleaned and placed the mask to one side to be disinfected before being put back on display.

"I don't think I'll be attending any more masquerade balls in the future," Amadeus said in response.

"I take it you did not enjoy the evening. What a pity".

The shop attendant paused. "Where was this masquerade ball held, as I said earlier, we normally get notification of large events but received nothing".

"I'd rather not discuss the night in question, so please return what money I'm due, and I'll be off back to work".

"You certainly must be kept busy, Inspector, with all the prostitution and drug-related crime in the city. Amadeus took the money due to him. Then thought about what this roly-poly.

The monocled man had said. Amadeus had never at any time during the transaction ever revealed his employment as a policeman, let alone an Inspector. He was about to put on his policeman's helmet and start asking questions; however, that could wait, because he had other things on his mind. The cape left at Dentary Manor would give him the excuse to pay the Manor a visit, despite the severe warning put to him on the night of the masquerade ball.

He had never been afraid of anything in his life and was not about to start now. But then he remembered him urinating in fear when discovered. That played heavy on his mind. There was also the threat to his family to consider.

He left the shop quickly and made his way back to Scotland Yard.

There was another epidemic in the city. Bank raids had now taken up the time of the serious crime squad. The younger hood had begun to get ambitious just as Harry, the ageing crime boss, had prophesied. A more dangerous, hardened brood of thugs that were attempting to take over the city rackets from the crime bosses, which meant trouble, big trouble like a gang war in the not-too-distant future.

Inspector Rupert was torn between his work and his personal life. Work always came first in the past, but now things had changed and not for the better.

His mind couldn't escape, wouldn't let him escape from the terrifying night spent at the masquerade ball. The party shop assistant called him Inspector, when no mention of his rank or surname was ever made.

That's when he made the decision to take a drive into the Essex countryside and pay a visit to Dentary Manor. Only this time it would be in an official capacity. He considered taking a couple of uniformed officers along. That usually put the frighteners on anything anybody had in mind.

However, he thought better of it at this stage, just to keep it low-key until he found out more.

The winter winds were blowing sleet and snowflakes by the time he had a space in his work commitment.

The A12 was slow-moving, even at that time of the morning, and he was glad to bypass Chelmsford and continue the eight miles along the country road until he spotted the large iron gates that hung loosely off their hinges as if they were about to fall. He stopped the police car and got out. The cream gate posts were flaking and blown away by the wind.

He walked through the rattling gates to look for the security portacabin. There was no hint as to a security cabin having ever been there.

He stepped out onto the entrance and looked up at the security cameras. Nothing, not even any brackets or fixings that would have supported them.

He scratched his head, then rubbed his chin while taking in the surroundings. The large Azealia bushes and the Elm trees on each side of the entrance driveway were still inside the gates. That gave him the confidence that he was in the right place, although the large, brightly lit board with The Dentary Manor name had disappeared. He drove along the drive for a short distance.

There was no sign of the gargoyle plinths that held the flaming torches the night he was driven towards the Manor. He got out of the car and walked along the driveway searching the grass verges, which were now overgrown. Looking for some evidence that a flaming torch plinth had been there. Once again, there was no hint of burning grass or concrete bases where the heavy plinth would have stood. He drove slowly along the three miles to the Manor, looking for some indication of the burning torches that had lined the route.

He eventually arrived at the Manor, only to find that it was in a bad state of deterioration.

Like the gateposts, the paint was flaking from the stonework.

There was something else that was different about the Manor.

He remembered when he arrived on the 23rd of May, that there were thirteen marble steps that led up to the front door. He had counted them, but now, there were entrances to the main door by side steps on either side of the flaking balustrade. He looked up at the building.

Inspector Rupert was confused. He knew the English weather could be atrocious at times, but the long, hot summer would not have allowed the Manor to deteriorate to its present state so quickly. Even the gravel where the Rolls-Royces and Bentleys were parked that night showed signs of weed growth. The Nymphs' fountain no longer threw water into the air, and a green, slimy Algy weed grew in the bowl. But it came to him that there was no fountain on his arrival that night. He knew it would have stood out like a sore thumb. He stood for a moment before a coarse voice asked, "What are you doing here? This is private property, clear off or I'll call the police". Inspector Rupert turned to face the bearded man in tattered clothes. "I am the police, and you are"? He said, walking towards the long-haired character. "I'm Doddy the gardener. What is your business here"?

"To be frank, Doddy, I was at a masquerade ball back in May. I stupidly left my cape here and have come to retrieve it, in order that I can receive my deposit from the outfitters. You know how it is with them. So, I thought I'd kill two birds with one stone because there have been several break-ins in the area, and I want to give the owner some advice, how to protect the family silver".

"Whatever are you talking about, Inspector? There hasn't been a party held here since young Belinda Clement died, then her parents became virtual recluses. Now show me your warrant card if you please". There was that rank mentioned again when he hadn't mentioned it. He showed the unkempt gardener the card. "Somebody is trying to hide something, Doddy, and that makes me suspicious. One other thing is the fact I'm not quite ga-ga yet despite my age, and I can state quite categorically I was at a ball in this very Manor on the 23rd May this year.

So, I think while I'm here, I'll have a word with the owner. "Please yourself, Inspector Rupert, but you'll find Mr. and Mrs Gardiner as ga-ga as you are". He made his way up the side steps and pressed the doorbell. Standing in the cold winter blast of the November wind. He went through in his mind how all this had started.

He remembered talking to W.P.C. Cartland about the discovery of witches using the old church and burial ground two miles from the village of Tringford.

How villagers, including the barber and farmer, had lied about its use. However, after spying on the witch's initiation ceremony, with the coven dancing around the bonfire, he also had more than enough proof that witchcraft was being practiced. Then there was the conversation between Amanda Chapman, the Priestess and the initiated coven member discussing the masquerade ball on the 23rd of May.

Getting no answer, he knocked on the door rapturously, before going back to his thoughts.

It wasn't Amanda Chapman who mentioned Dentary Manor, but W.P.C. Cartland had suggested to him that Dentary Manor had been used for Devil worship in the past and had an evil reputation. It was she who warned him to steer clear of it.

There were people he could interview when he drove back to Chelmsford. Starting with the taxi company and driver. W.P.C. Cartland must be spoken to.

He would then drive over to Tringford village and speak to Amanda Chapman. He would also pay the barber a visit. Tommy Stanton knew much more than he had said, lying about the Royalist annual celebrations.

The large Oak door finally creaked open. An old, grey-haired man with a stoop, wearing a duffle coat with a hood. Gloved hands, a bowtie and a V-neck jumper that was too big for him stood in faded green corduroys.

"It's the surveyor, Emma darling; I'll attend to him". He said in a croaking posh voice.

"Sorry, sir, I should have introduced myself sooner".

Inspector Rupert withdrew the warrant card from his wallet.

"Inspector Rupert Scotland Yard, sir, if I could have a few words about protecting your silver, etc., apparently, break-ins in the area". He stepped into the Manor without an invitation.

"Sorry, darling, some geezer selling silverware". He closed the door and instructed the stranger to follow him.

Inspector Rupert wondered if it would be warmer holding the conversation outside because inside the Manor was bloody freezing.

He put the warrant card back into his wallet, keeping his hands in his pockets for some kind of warmth. Their breath gave out a vapour of condensation as they walked towards a large door.

Inspector Rupert stopped suddenly while taking in the surroundings. The main stairway was of oak with figured decoration. Not the marble staircase he had witnessed. No crystal chandeliers in the entrance ceilings. He pointed. "The ballroom doors, sir, have the entrance to the hall been altered or renovated"?

"You're the expert, Mr?... sorry, I've forgotten your name. You're the surveyor, you tell me".

Inspector Rupert shook his head. He had no wish to get into conversation with this old aristocrat. After studying the entrance layout, he followed the old man through the large door marked morning room.

This was much better; a log and coal fire blazed in the largely decorated fireplace. An old, grey-haired woman sat knitting.

"Emma, darling, the surveyor has arrived to advise us about the leaking roofs".

Inspector Rupert showed his warrant card.

She put down the knitting and got up with a struggle. "I apologise for Desmond Inspector, I could hear you introduce yourself when you were talking to Doddy the gardener, and when you came into the entrance hall. Please pull a chair over to the fire and explain why you're here".

She sat down and spoke. "Desmond darling, make yourself useful and make us some tea".

Inspector Rupert held up both hands. "Not for me, Mrs. Clement, I have a busy day ahead; however, what I need to know won't take long".

She gave a smile that showed black and missing teeth.

"So, your visit has nothing to do with break-ins, not that it would make much difference because we have nothing valuable to steal".

Inspector Rupert was aware that this old woman had her wits about her.

"To be truthful, Mrs Clement, my reason for this visit is to do with a dress cape I left here while attending a masquerade ball in May this year".

"I'm afraid you're barking up the wrong tree, Inspector. We haven't held a celebration at the Manor since our daughter was killed in a drowning accident in Spain some fifteen years ago.

We can't afford such an extravaganza, Inspector. This house and estate haemorrhage money, as you can see by the outside paintwork and leaking roofs, which Desmond does his best to repair, bless him".

She gave a sigh.

"Let me get this straight, Mrs. Clement. Doddy has confirmed that this is Dentary Manor, so I'll ask you to confirm that this is indeed Dentary Manor listed on the atlas map in the county of Essex".

"What can I say, Inspector, except Dentary Manor has been in our family for over three hundred years, how much longer remains to be seen"? She threw a log onto the fire.

Desmond Clement came shuffling in with the tea trolley. "Have you agreed with the surveyor, what should be done with the main roof, darling"?

"I'm truly sorry, Mrs. Clement, I seem to have wasted your time, so I'll take my leave and let you enjoy your tea". He got up quickly and nodded his appreciation to both before letting himself out. He stood in the cold wind, rubbing his chin. He couldn't understand what was going on. He remembered that the driver of the Citroen that brought him to the house had said, from the gates to the Manor was three miles. He checked the odometer on the dashboard and set off, back down the overgrown driveway to the country lane.

When he reached the broken gates that blew in the strong wind, he looked at the odometer. He had covered only two miles. But the Oak trees shook in the wind, and the Azealia bushes still gave off a scented odour. However, those landmarks could be just a coincidence, something that he didn't like. Now was the time to drive first to Chelmsford, then to Tringford village. There were a lot of questions that needed to be asked to satisfy his curiosity. "Why am I doing this"? He asked himself, looking in the rear-view mirror.

His first stop was at the Chelmsford police station, where he was warmly greeted.

"Two things, Sergeant. I need the address of the Hackney taxi company in the town, then I need to speak to W.P.C. Cartland if she's available, or I can go to her home".

"I can give you two taxi firms' addresses, sir, but regarding your second request, I'm unable to help with it, because W.P.C. Cartland left the force surrounded by a cloud of mystery. She was six months pregnant; she never revealed who the father was, then right out of the blue, she emigrated to Canada, leaving no forwarding address or telephone contact".

Inspector Rupert rubbed his chin in disappointment.

After receiving the taxi firm's addresses, he made his way to Aberdour Street. I need to speak to Bert, one of your drivers. Can you get him on the radio and bring him in"? He showed his warrant card. The girl behind the glass screen pulled a face. "Bert? We don't have a Bert working for us. A Brian, and two Bobs, but no Bert".

You obviously keep a record for tax and accountancy purposes, I need to know if there was a hire from the Albion hotel to a Manor house in the country on the 23rd May this year". She "asked" then retrieved a ledger from below the counter. She turned over the pages. "Yes, it's what we call a no-show. The driver arrived to pick up the passenger, only to be informed that the passenger had left in another taxi".

He thanked her and drove to Regency Lane. Asking the same questions and getting the same answers. The only difference was that the firm had no Brian, or Bobs, and certainly no Berts.

"Are there any other private cabs, run by single operators in the town, or around this area"?

"Not to our Knowledge". The controller said with a smile. "Besides, the boss does not tolerate anybody starting up without a hackney licence, or an individual encroaching on our patch".

Inspector Rupert understood the gist and walked away. Three down with nothing to show for his efforts. The decision was made to travel to Tringford to question Amanda Chapman and Tommy the barber. Two people he knew were involved in witchcraft.

He remembered the journey well from the days he travelled to the village and carried out an investigation, which he solved. Tractors, flocks of sheep are blocking the road. It was a bloody nightmare as he sat waiting for a herd of cattle to be moved from one field to another.

Finally, he reached his destination. Starting with the barbers' shop, which was closed, and the shutters pulled down. He asked a passing pedestrian. "When does Tommy open? I need a trim". He added this quickly, knowing that the villagers were not cooperative before.

"Tommy died about five months ago, found drowned in some pond up by the old church". The pedestrian carried on walking. The next port of call was the vicarage, where he got some surprising news. Amanda Chapman had received a three-year prison sentence, and her husband, the vicar, had been replaced. The

The new vicar or his wife knew nothing of the circumstances surrounding Amanda Chapman's witchcraft activities.

While he was in the village, he might as well pay Angela Farlow a courtesy visit, perhaps a small refreshment. He parked outside the hotel and made his way to the reception.

A well-dressed man appeared. "Can I help you, sir"? He asked politely.

Amadeus took off his policeman's helmet. "The co-owners of the hotel, Angela and Jack Farlow, are old friends, and since I'm in the village decided to pay them a call".

"If you're an old friend, then you're a bit out of touch, chum. I bought the hotel from the 'Farlows', then what do you know. Jack Farlow fucked off with my wife, and Angela Farlow went off with the shepherd". The owner hesitated. "You don't know of Jack Farlow's whereabouts. I'd pay plenty if you knew, and I would set about to kill them both".

Amadeus held up his hand before the owner could express his rantings any further.

"Sorry, I've been in London for some time and as you say, a bit out of touch". He made his way quickly out to the car and started the drive back to London.

As he drove along the A12, he realized that the day had been a complete waste of time, except for the fact that some unknown taxi had picked him up. He had fallen asleep on the way out to the masquerade ball. He had dozed off on the return from the masquerade ball, after his run-in with the Satanists. He suddenly realized that he could have been taken further than what the bogus taxi driver had said. In fact, the drive he had just made today was less than half an hour out to Dentary Manor, and the journey back was similar. Things were just not adding up.

When he parked the police car in the Scotland Yard compound, he went into his office drawer and took out a protractor. He averaged that with an hourly drive at approximately forty miles per hour, he radius would be forty miles, so he placed the pointed protractor at Chelmsford and drew a forty-mile circle. Now he could check out how many Mansions and Manor house estates were within the radius circle. He walked to the detailed wall maps that listed four surrounding counties. Taking notes of them, he suddenly came across Tilsberry Manor Estate in Hertfordshire, where he had a previous run-in with the Hesketh Aristocratic family. He would leave that until last on his list. There was no need to upset the applecart if he found the mysterious Manor where the masquerade ball had taken place. He checked his work rota and discovered he had three free weekends to investigate where whereabouts of the grand English houses, only this time he would use his own Rover and spend his own time driving from county to county. There was a total of four Manor estates and three mansions.

The next morning, there was a summons to the fifth floor awaiting him. The Commissioner wanted to speak to him immediately.

He took the lift and was advised by the secretary to wait a moment. She lifted the phone.

"Inspector Rupert, sir," she said softly. The office door opened almost immediately.

"Rupert, come in". The voice didn't sound threatening, but that was how the Commissioner carried out his interviews, lulling the victim into a false sense of security before tenderizing him before taking him down for a delicious lunch.

"Take a seat, Rupert and straighten your tie". That was the opener.

"We were looking for you yesterday, but you seemed to have vanished off the face of the earth. Would you care to tell me what you were up to"?

"Witchcraft and devil-worship, sir, something I'm sure you would hate, if it spread any further into London. I can add that it is rife in Essex and probably common among some other counties throughout England".

"Are you off your head, Rupert. Do you mean to tell me you went off on a wild-goose chase, a Witch hunt without my express authorization? And I suppose you used a police car to carry out this ludicrous, futile game".

"Oh, believe me, sir, it is not a game, far from it".

Inspector Rupert did not tell the Commissioner about the Satanic masquerade ball.

"It was drawn to my attention when we were carrying out the Tringford murder, sir. I never mentioned it because I had no proof that a coven initiation ceremony ever took place, but after doing a bit of sleuthing, I now have all the answers I need and can point the finger at witches who took part in the coven's initiation ceremony".

The Commissioner shook his head. "I sometimes wonder what the Metropolitan Police pay you for Rupert. How long until your retirement?

Inspector Rupert ignored the question. "What do you want me to do, sir? Shall I continue digging a little deeper"? He knew he had every intention of doing that, regardless of what the Commissioner said.

"No, Rupert, we have much more serious business to attend to, which should have started yesterday, but the bird had flown the nest".

He laid his hand flat on his desk.

"We have something serious which has been brought to our attention, both from border patrol and the civil service". He paused. "A pornographic industry has sprung up in the capital. Pornographic film videos for the black-market are being filmed in the capital, then put into video cassettes and sold in pubs and street corners". The Commissioner clasped his hands in the usual fashion as if in prayer when he was worried about something serious.

"You know the Soho area and the girls that work the streets, see if you can get them talking."

"Yes, I know a lot of prostitutes who work in that area, so I'll start with them". He hesitated.

"Don't forget my family is coming home for Christmas, and my shift rota shows I'm off Christmas Eve, Christmas Day, plus Boxing Day. I won't allow anything to come between their happiness, sir".

"You'll do what you're told, Rupert". He stood up. "So, the sooner you do a little sleuthing, the quicker you'll be able to enjoy Christmas". He gave the crocodile smile as he showed the Inspector to the door.

Over the three-weekend approaching Christmas, Inspector Rupert paid little attention to the girls who were commonly known as call girls. They would always be there, in their cosy apartments or rented hotel rooms. So, he adopted a softly, softly approach, questioning some girls standing frozen on the street corners. A fiver and a cardboard cup of coffee usually got them singing like canaries.

Driving around the counties, crossing out the mansions and Manors he had listed proved to be more difficult than he had imagined.

However, he got lucky on his fifth visit. He drove up and parked outside the large cream pillars that supported the large iron gates. The video security cameras were still suspended above the posts, but motionless. He looked at the name on the map.

"Powder-hall Manor" in the county of Kent. He looked through the gates. The security building was there, but it looked abandoned. The Oak trees and Azealia bushes were in place where he remembered them. There was no large advertising board that had portrayed the false name 'Dentary Manor' on the night he arrived for the ball. The gates were chained and padlocked, so he took out his bunch of keys and L-shaped feelers that he had been taught to use by an old safe cracker in London. He fiddled with the padlock until he heard it click open. Withdrawing the chain, he opened both gates, then drove inside, getting out of the car to close them over and suspend the padlock and chain. Now he drove up the driveway, stopping occasionally to look at the grotesque faces on the pillars that had once held the burning torches. He drove slowly up towards the Mansion that stood brightly decorated, three miles from the gates. He got out of the car, now convinced he had found the place where the masquerade ball had taken place. He climbed the thirteen steps leading up to the large Oak door. It was obvious to him that there was nobody at the Manor; every window at the front had the shutters closed. However, he pressed the bell and knocked on the door loudly, repeating it several times. There was no sign of life, so he wandered round to the rear of the building. The outhouse doors were locked, and the windows boarded up. The back door, known as the staff and tradesman's entrance, was also locked, and all windows at the rear shuttered.

The letterbox was also jammed shut, so he was unable to call through the letterbox as was the normal procedure. He toyed with the idea of trying to pick the locks, but that would be classed as breaking and entering without the owners' permission if someone should suddenly appear. He scrutinized every window of the three-floored manor. He had an uneasy feeling that someone was watching him but dismissed it as paranoia.

He walked back to the centre of the large courtyard at the front. Looking up to each floor and the roof of the Manor.

That strange sensation came over him again, that someone was watching him. He scanned each shuttered window carefully, then checked the walled garden and greenhouses before walking back to the front steps.

He found it strange that such a fine building was left unattended. He tried knocking on the front door again. Pressing the bell several times, with no response, he turned and walked down the thirteen steps to his Rover car.

Something hit him like a bolt of lightning out of the blue. He began to shake as the memory of the eyes behind the cockerel mask began to attack his memory. The tall, slim, naked brunette who had been given to him that night by the diamond-studded lady, whom he assumed was the joint owner when he had first entered the Manor. The beautiful, shaped body he had sex with several times, the Satanist who dressed him in the gown before taking part in the Satanic worship ceremony, and who stood looking down at him from the balcony that fateful night, before she was taken off to be sacrificed for his freedom. "W.P.C. Rosalyn Cartland". He said in alarm as he remembered the sergeant telling him that she had left the force after falling pregnant. He was shaken to his foundation as parts of that night entered his memory.

He hung onto the door of the Rover, afraid to let go, in case he fell to the gravel.

He turned quickly around when that feeling came over him again, that someone was watching him. He sat in the car looking up at the beautiful English treasure, still suffering from the shock, now he knew who the Satanist was that saved him that night.

Much as the Manor looked magnificent, there was something about it that gave him the creeps. He shuddered at the thought of entering the manor that night.

He started up the engine and drove quickly down to the gates.

It had occurred to him that Rosalyn Cartland's sacrifice had not taken place because the sergeant had said she left the force and emigrated to Canada. "Was the sergeant lying"? That was the question he asked himself. It could easily be checked.

He assumed her so-called sacrifice was all part of the game, an attempt to scare him, and it worked to a certain degree.

After wrapping the chain around the gates, he padlocked them before looking up at the security cameras. He stood for a moment, hoping they would move, but they remained in their position, so he jumped into the car and drove back to London.

During the drive, he went over in his mind everything that he could remember. Everything had happened, from the time he mentioned how suspicious he was that the old church in Tringford was used for coven meetings, how W.P.C. Cartland had tried to dissuade him from carrying out another recce, to the minute he mentioned the Witchcraft ritual.

There was one thing sure in his mind. This discovery of the abandoned Manor gave him nothing to work on. He had made enquiries to the Kent County Council as to who the owner of the Manor was. The reply came back that it was owned by an Austrian millionaire who used it when in England on business trips. His name was Gustaf Meyerhof. It did not specify what business Meyerhof was in.

His wife was a co-owner. Her name was Jasmine-Constantine-Meyerhof, with Russian Royal blue blood in her veins.

He could visit Amanda Chapman in prison, question her about her involvement in Witchcraft and Devil worship. But then what? What he could do was wait for Halloween night or the 23rd of May next year. That was dangerous and playing with fire.

It was time to draw a line under the whole unsavoury affair. It was an experience he did not want to repeat. The thought of having sex with a colleague disgusted him.

Tired and depressed, he made his way home to Mayfair.

He spotted it immediately as he stepped out of the lift. A twig in the shape of an inverted V had a dead raven attached to it. Hanging on the door handle, the raven's blood had trickled down the door and congealed. He removed it, giving it little thought for this prank. Was this a warning? Mrs Dobson, the housekeeper, assured him it wasn't on the door handle when she came in for house duties at 07:00 am. "What is it all about, Mr. Rupert"? she asked pensively.

"A prank, Mrs Dobson, nothing more".

After cleaning the blood, he took the dead raven and the cloth down to the rubbish in the basement. As he placed it in a dustbin, a sudden state of fear came over him. It made him turn around quickly, which recalled something he should have done after his encounter with the Satanists. He phoned Señor Philippe de Santos and explained every detail that had occurred that night at the ball. He told him of his discovery of 'Powder-hall Manor' in Kent. The dilapidated state of Dentary Manor in Essex, whose name had been falsely portrayed at the entrance to 'Powder Hall.' "I think you have got off very lightly, Mr. Rupert. I don't think you witnessed the whole black mass as an intruder; if so, you would be dead regardless of the woman who sacrificed herself for you, being shown mercy by the Satanists, which I think would be extremely rare. She, on the other hand, would have suffered at the hands of her brethren and the order of the High Priest. Although I personally think she would've been severely dealt with, perhaps told to leave the coven, even leave the country, where she would be watched closely by other Satanists". Amadeus told him about W.P.C. Rosalyn Cartland, who had apparently emigrated so quickly to Canada. "Yes, I can see the logic of getting rid of her". The Occultist paused. "Let me warn you again, Mr. Rupert, you are out of your depth with those people. You have played a dangerous game that could have cost you your life, so here is the bottom line, Inspector. Forget what you witnessed that night at the masquerade ball. Forget the lost cape. Forget the mysterious 'Powder-hall Manor' in Kent. Forget the Meyerhof family in Austria. Forget the mystery taxi driver who so conveniently arrived with excuses.

Forget your ex-colleague who has emigrated. Forget any future dates that are linked to Witchcraft and Devil worship".

He paused. "However, I don't want you to disregard the warning placed on your door, keep that in the back of your mind forever, because that was the Devils' sign of death and the Satanists will kill you, should you ever reveal what you witnessed that night, they probably know about you tracking them from 'Dentary Manor' to 'Powder-hall Manor.' How could you be so stupid as to continue with this, after they gave you a verbal warning? Mark my words, Mr. Rupert, don't mess with those people; they will kill you, and if they can't get to you, then your family is in great danger. Heed my final warning".

Amadeus ended the call to the Occultist.

He was tired, so he made his way into the lounge and poured a large stiff brandy with no diluter.

After a restless, sleepless night of dreams, he headed into work as normal.

CHAPTER

Seven

It was time to get started with the softly, softly approach concerning the city prostitutes, but with Christmas now on the horizon, there would not be much investigating done until the new year.

Daughter April and her family had phoned, confirming they would be arriving for Christmas, and how the years had flown by. The last time they celebrated Christmas together was when they were at boarding school. He dismissed the thought, just glad that they would be spending Christmas together.

There was always time for reminiscing over the Christmas mornings when he and his wife Deborah were wakened at the crack of dawn by the enthusiastic, but pensive children, eager to go into the living room and see what Santa had brought them, but afraid in case he was still there, the milk and cake had been devoured as had the carrot, left for Rudolph his leading reindeer, stockings still hanging on the fire guard that they had hung up empty the night before but were now bulging with fruit, chocolate, and pennies. The Christmas tree lights were switched on at 06.35 on Christmas morning, the carol singing on the radio, and later the church bells ringing. His favourite time was Christmas Eve, when the family went into the city and did their Christmas shopping, watching the toy train sets zipping round the shop window, the Salvation Army band playing favourite carols as the snow fell silently, laying a blanket of powdered snow on the pavements. A time of loving, a time of giving.

Inspector Rupert had to give himself a shake to lift himself out of the nostalgia that threatened to envelope him that reminding him of times gone by.

He was so glad that April and her husband Duncan, along with the three children, were travelling over from Oxford to be with him. His son Colin, now an Inspector with the Brighton and Hove police, was still single, Inspector Rupert wondered if it was a result of his own turbulent marriage that took place post war, when he was unable to make compromises after Deborah's affair with an American Air Force major, when she learned that he had been shot down, missing in action presumed dead. That affair was forgivable; however, it was her other affairs that he could not forgive. She had become the talk of the washhouse.

He understood that his ex-wife, Deborah, had nursed him through a very traumatic time in his life when he returned from the German prisoner of war camp. His mind drifted further into the past. Why did the festive season always bring back the sad memories?

A knock at his office door brought him back to the present. A tanned-faced, red-haired woman police constable entered.

"Sorry to disturb you, sir, but you're wanted in the incident room, something important apparently. "

"I'm busy at the moment, Constable. Tell them to get someone else from upstairs or wait until I'm free". The constable hovered nervously before uttering,

"The superintendent has asked specifically for you, sir, so will I tell him you're unavailable"?

"Relax, constable, and tell him I'll be through in a minute, after I've sorted out my in-tray". Inspector Rupert knew it must be important to have sent a messenger instead of lifting the phone. Perhaps he had already heard about the tantrums he had in the Commissioner's office. The secretary was bound to have heard the raised voices behind the locked door. She, in turn, would've phoned her friend in the typing department. Jungle drums would've beat out their message. He was in no hurry to oblige the superintendent's demand. He smiled as he recalled a favourite quotation.

"When the lord made time, he made plenty of it". That was told to the young police officers who had just graduated from the London Metropolitan Police College. They were keen to show what they could do, and sometimes ran about like chickens with no head, getting nowhere fast. Always keen to please the "High Hied Yins," who made his and his friend Colin Freeman's life a misery and at times still do with him.

He sorted out his tray, what was important that needed immediate attention, and the other crimes that could be handled by the woolly suits who plodded the streets of London.

These police officers knew more and were aware of what was happening in the capital, even more than the lord mayor himself.

Inspector Rupert closed the filing cabinet and locked the safe. He went to the canteen to fetch a mug of coffee before responding to the superintendent's demands and call to duty.

He understood it must be something important when Superintendent Angus MacAulay had summoned him to the incident room. Normally, Inspector Rupert would find out in the morning, but there did seem to be something important in the air, so he walked smartly into the busy incident room.

Inspector Rupert and the Superintendent were old friends and on first-name terms.

"Well, Angus, what is so important that I've had to drop everything"? He gave a smile.

The Superintendent smiled. "This is something that's right up your street, Amadeus. There has been a surge in drugs in the city, funded by illegal pornographic magazines and films. A very lucrative business which gets more lucrative by the day, that's why you've been transferred to the drugs and vice squad, you'll head the investigation into this illegal racket".

The Superintendent looked at the empty information board.

"As you can see, there is not a lot happening out there at the moment, probably too cold for the criminals to be wandering about in this sodding weather".

"That board won't stay like that forever, sir". Inspector Rupert gave him his proper ranking title as a young Detective Constable approached.

"This is D.C. Chloe Reynolds; she'll be working with you until we can break up this porn ring". He paused for a moment.

We've a lead on the director of those films, shot in various locations here in London, and along the south coast, where there is sea and sand, usually a favourite location when the weather is good. The director's name is Ricardo Bonetti, who attempted to catch a flight to Brazil, but apparently, he was on a standby ticket and couldn't get a seat on the flight. We believe he is holding up somewhere in London until next week's flight to Brazil, that's the time allocated to you before he attempts to skip the country".

"Does this mean I'll be away from home again, sir, and I'll say it now. I've no intention of flying to Brazil on a wild goose chase like I did three weeks ago, going to Blackpool on a ridiculous errand". He paused, "What became of the Russian spy handler and his accomplice, Olga Kosnofsky"?

The Superintendent gave a puzzled look. "Never heard of them, Inspector. What was that all about"?

"The 'High Heid Yins 'dreamed up a scheme to flush spies out into the open, and according to the Commissioner, it worked. Strange you never heard anything about it, surely with you and Sorley like peas in a pod, then something would've been said".

"Don't be ridiculous, Inspector, we don't exactly see eye to eye on certain matters".

Inspector Rupert could understand why.

"OK. Reynolds let's go and open a can of worms". He said to the eager young detective.

They sat in the car while D.C. Reynolds pulled a London A to Z street book from the glove compartment. "We'll start with the seedy hotels first, the places that rent a room by the hour, or afternoon". D.C. Reynolds giggled.

"Do you know of these places, sir"? The Inspector just gave her a look as he drove out of the compound onto the busy London street.

"The pornographic film crew must have a box van or something similar for transporting their equipment about, so we will give that to another officer to look into when we get back".

After they had visited some of the disreputable hotels, the Inspector thought it a waste of time to continue. "Those hotels would've been paid handsomely to keep their mouths shut,

Reynolds. The film crew would be given ample warning that we were on the doorstep; we need more officers to help cover the exits if we're to succeed. However, my belief is this: if the pornographic film industry is making a high-budget film, they'll not use such locations as these seedy hotels. I think the locations will be much more exotic, however, let's consider this". He paused", if it is a low-budget film, then they won't use professional actresses, and I know the very people that can give us the information we need".

They drove quickly across the city to Soho's red-light district. Inspector Rupert stopped the car close to the pavement.

"A word, Alison," he said calmly to a girl dressed in a red leather outfit, trying to find shelter in a doorway from the driving sleet, while still trying to ply her trade.

"Get into the car, Alison. I need some information. "He pulled a fiver from his wallet.

"Have you or any of the girls been offered any film work recently"? He turned to face the shivering girl. "We know there is a film crew in London offering girls work on a film set, only the films in question are pornographic and illegal, so I was hoping you could help us trace a film director called Ricardo Bonetti.

"Never heard of him, Rupert, and if you think a sky diver is going to get you that kind of information, you'd better grunt back to your pigsty where you came from. I heard you were back in town, can't stay away from us mature girls". She giggled,

"Besides, I'm not the one to ask". She lifted her greasy hair to reveal an earlobe that was missing and a scar that stretched across the side of her face, hidden by her shoulder-length hair. "Do you want to see the rest, Inspector, or perhaps your colleague would like to see the finished article"? She began to unbutton her blouse. "No need for that, Alison, you know the risks of being out on the street".

"Do I have an alternative, Inspector? It's this attractive career or starve"? D. C. Reynolds snatched the fiver from her hand, then held up a crisp ten-pound note. "Perhaps this will jog your memory, Alison. A name is all we require, and I can understand why you were never selected by the film director due to your scars, but I know you're hiding something. "The prostitute attempted to grab the note from D. C. Reynold's hand.

"When we have a name, Alison". The ten-pound note was waved in front of the prostitute.

"I'm not the one to talk to; Nadia Porteous is the one to talk to; she was propositioned to do a group sex film at the Swallow Hotel in Richmond. She has the looks and the figure; however, she is on a job now, so while we're waiting, why don't you, your friend, and I go round to the Amazon hotel and have some fun"? She laughed loudly as she stepped out into the driving sleet. A car drew up, and after a quick negotiation, Alison jumped in and closed the door.

D.C. Reynolds spoke softly. "Those poor girls, Inspector, what kind of life is that? A quick romp in a stranger's car".

Inspector Rupert interrupted her. "There's a lot worse than that that goes on in D.C. Reynolds, so let me give you some advice," He paused. "If you want to succeed as a detective, then you must learn quickly. We're not social workers; we fight crime and disassociate ourselves by showing a hardness, it's not that we don't care, but we must never get embroiled in political thinking and sympathy, otherwise it will be you, the men in white coats will be taking away".

The Inspector sat for a moment. "There is no telling when Nadia Porteous will return, besides if she is tucked up in a hotel, she is not going to advertise her wares in a wet and windy street, when the light is fading, so we'll go back and arrange some assistance for tomorrow, hopefully the weather will be a bit better, and Nadia Porteous will be back on the street, and that's where we'll make a break through".

They drove back to Scotland Yard; Inspector Rupert telephoned the Met. To arrange the backup for tomorrow morning. The day had gone quite quickly. he took the underground, then the bus to Mayfair, then decided to have a drink at the Queen Vic, before going home. He enjoyed the bar conversation about the football, especially when he mentioned Watford F.C. "Who"? Some smarty pants asked in a gesture to stir the conversation.

After a couple, he made his way back to his luxury apartment that Colin Freeman, his dead friend, had left him in his will, along with a substantial amount of money.

The housekeeper always had a hot meal ready for him. Mrs. Dobson was in many ways a Godsend, just like Mrs McGinty, his previous housekeeper, who had served his family well in the old days at the villa in Welwyn Garden City.

Now, circumstances had brought him back to London, a move he didn't regret, thinking that he could leave all the ghosts behind, but that did not happen. He knew the memory and ghost of his dear, dead friend, Squadron Leader Colin Freeman or Friedman, would haunt him forever. The good and bad times of his marriage to Deborah would always play tricks with his memory. He dismissed the thoughts and poured a large glass of wine to have with his steak dinner. He retired to the lounge and settled down to study unsolved cases.

Prostitution was a dirty business, having to go into the seedy part of the city, where the young and old alike were under threats of violence and mistreatment. The older prostitutes were more streetwise, always unwilling to co–cooperate with the police unless a few pound notes were slipped into their cold hands. He understood that the information he needed was not going to come cheap; that was the name of the game in the alleyways and back streets.

The incident room was buzzing. A young prostitute's body had been pulled from the River Thames. Superintendent Angus MacAulay was already in attendance at the scene.

"We need a name. "He said bluntly, looking at Inspector Rupert. After the pathologist and the forensics arrived, they made their way back to the Yard and entered the incident room.

The superintendent pointed at the board.

"This is another one in a week, Inspector. Do those girls have no common sense? "It was a futile moan that went unheeded.

"This one had half her ear bitten off, and her young body slashed a dozen times. "He shook his head.

Inspector Rupert spoke softly. "Her name is Alison Jones from Pontypridd in Wales, sir. She hasn't been on the streets all that long. She appeared on our radar shortly after I arrived back in the city from the Tringford murder case, so not that long. I spoke to Alison yesterday and had hoped to have another word with her today after I had spoken to another prostitute called Nadia Porteous".

"In the city long enough to get her murdered, Rupert, so get onto it". The Superintendent said loudly.

Inspector Rupert took out his notebook. "I got information about a car that picked her up, sir, a black Ford Consul. I also got the registration number from a prostitute at a price. I've got that on my desk, so we can put a call out on the car radios to see if we can trace it. "

So, you spoke to this girl, Inspector? Did she appear scared or upset? They normally are after a job".

"All those girls are scared, sir. Just because somebody drives up in a posh car doesn't mean he's going to treat them well; there is not a day that goes by that one of them is assaulted or not paid; it's the hazard of their trade, sir".

Inspector Rupert saw the glare that young D.C. Reynolds gave him.

"The question is, sir, did this girl get murdered because she spoke to us about a contact called Nadia Porteous, who could be involved in the pornographic film industry, or is it just another assault that got out of hand"? He paused, "Nadia Porteous is the line of inquiry we should follow, sir".

"No, Rupert, you handle it, to see if it has any bearing on your present investigation with the pornographic industry. You know, those girls, Rupert, they respect you, so get out there and question those who work the red-light district; they just might come up with something. "

"I doubt it, sir, unless you're prepared to pay," he smiled. "Come on, Detective Constable Reynolds, it's time you learned how the other half live in this beautiful city of ours".

They walked quickly out of the incident room.

The day was a mixture of sunshine and sleet showers, although there was a hint of heavy grey snow clouds in the sky. D.C. Reynolds took the wheel, driving carefully, while Inspector Rupert put out a call for the type, colour, and registration of the car that had picked up Alison Jones yesterday.

They arrived in Soho just as the morning rush hour was abating. She pulled the car close to the kerb and awaited instructions. The Inspector sat quietly for a time, then made his move. He sprinted across the street, dodging the traffic, and ran down a lane in pursuit of Nadia Porteous. He caught up with her, threatening her with arrest if she didn't obey his warning.

"You bastard Rupert, you fucking pigs are all the same, you should have stayed in Welwyn, you're an arsehole".

Inspector Rupert laughed. "Come now, Nadia, that's no way for a lady to talk or behave".

"Fuck you, Rupert," was her response. She was taken back to the police car.

D.C. Reynolds got out of the car and opened the door when she saw them coming. She held Nadia's head down to avoid her getting hurt as she was bundled into the back of the car. "Okay, Nadia, we can do this here or at the station, it's your choice".

The prostitute said nothing, "I just need some information, because I know you have been doing pornographic films to earn a bit of extra cash". He lied; he didn't know for sure that Nadia Porteous was involved in any porn.

"I've the director's name, Nadia, a Mr. Bonetti, who is holed up somewhere in London, and I need to find him. I also want you to tell me where the locations are where the filming is done, what hotels they use, and the names of any other participants in the film industry. Now that's not a lot to ask, is it, Nadia"? She sat stubbornly silent for a moment with her arms folded, then spoke.

"My clients won't wait while you interrogate me, arsehole. How long is this going to take"?

The Inspector smiled. "That depends on you, Nadi. A quick answer to my questions will stop whoever is keeping tabs on you girls. Is it a pimp or a crime boss? That's the big question."

He paused for a second. "Did you know that Alison Jones was pulled from the River Thames in the early hours of the morning, Nadia"? He watched her reaction before going on.

"Apparently badly beaten, then strangled, poor kid has had a life of it. Slashed to her severe disfigurement. I hope she finds eternal rest in the next world, because she sure as hell didn't find much of it in this one".

He changed his aggressive attitude. "A black Ford Consul, registration number KLT 43, picked her up off the street yesterday afternoon. Any ideas who that car might belong to"?

Nadia shook her head, "Take a look at the wall in the lane where you accosted me. Sometimes the girls write down a registration if it's a weirdo looking for business extras. If it's serious, they'll put a name beside it, albeit the name is probably fake".

She unfolded her arms. "Listen, Inspector, I know most of the vehicles that patrol this area looking for fresh young girls, who are practically giving it away for free with green stamps. They are the ones most at risk, many just trying to find a better life for themselves, but we know that's not how it works". She lit a cigarette.

"I'll put the word about anyway, one of the girls might have been picked up in this mystery vehicle. Now, back to the question of pornographic films. I've done three but got dropped because I refused to entertain a foursome. Don't get me wrong, you get paid well and treated well for these shoots, except when Bonetti is directing. The big money is in photography, for porno magazines that pay a fortune for decent exposure of the body, you're given a top hotel room, usually in an exotic location. If you come up trumps, it could be the Seychelles or the Bahamas, that's my dream, Inspector". She inhaled deeply, then continued.

"Ricardo Bonetti is not a kind director. He is good at his job, except he has been known to knock the girls about if they don't give him a freebee, and that could cost them a place in the film if their body and faces are marked, but there are plenty more beautiful models ready to replace them and take their clothes off for sex". she hesitated.

"The last I heard, he was down in Kingston on Thames, holed up with a twenty-year-old film extra, and her young sister. That should keep him happy; he likes them young".

Nadia tweaked her finger and thumb together. "My time and expenses must be considered, Inspector. I've given you Bonetti's location, but for a crisp fifty, I could give you the hotels they use, not just in London but all over England, and abroad. What's wrong, Inspector? You look surprised". She laughed loudly.

"Ah, I get it, you think the porn industry doesn't exist outside this beautiful city, well, more fool you. It's big and growing, Inspector Rupert, it's what people want, so don't try to hold back the tide".

She reached for the door handle. Inspector Rupert took out his wallet.

"Twenty-five now, Nadia, and the rest when we confirm what you're about to disclose to Detective Constable Reynolds, who will take down your hotel list".

He withdrew twenty-five pounds and held it up in front of her. She tried to snatch it. "Uh, uh, Nadia, information first".

"You don't trust me, you're a moron". She began to disclose the information.

"For an extra ton, I can give you names and addresses of participants, names that would make your eyes water. Do you think it's only prostitutes and girls of low self-esteem that take part in the pornographic industry? Well, I could tell you different, Inspector. You could not be more wrong. A lonely housewife looking for a bit of excitement to spice up her dull married life". She smiled. "You would be surprised if you came up with the readies".

After she had finished, the Inspector handed her the money. "Don't go buying drugs, Nadia, and I'll come calling for these names, so stay safe until we meet again".

The Inspector reached over and opened the door.

"Goodbye, Inspector, you pervert, if you ever need a blow job, stay clear of me, I might be tempted to bite it off".

She slammed the rear door hard and disappeared into the crowd. They drove to the first hotel on the list, The Exeter was certainly not seedy, at least not from the outside; it looked perfectly respectable, freshly decorated, and as they walked into the foyer, it was the same. Inspector Rupert and Reynolds showed their warrant cards. "Is the manager available"? he asked with authority.

The receptionist lifted the phone. She listened for a time, then replaced the receiver, "I'm sorry, Mr. Arlington is busy. Can you make an appointment"? Inspector Rupert walked to the manager's door with D.C. Reynolds hard on his heels. He didn't knock; he walked straight in. "Sorry, Arlington, I don't have time for appointments".

The manager sprang to his feet. "I must protest most strongly to this intrusion. What exactly is it you want, Inspector? I'm a busy man". He sat back down, "Make it quick, I've a staff meeting in ten minutes".,

"Just a few questions, sir. It should not take long if you cooperate". He looked at D.C. Reynolds, who took the hint and produced a notebook and pencil. She stood at the ready to take notes. "I believe you had a film crew booked into this hotel recently. I was wondering how many rooms they used. How long did they stay? How many girls were involved in the film shoot? Did it take time with an overnight stay? And finally, who made the reservation booking, who paid the bill, and was it paid in cash or by cheque? I suspect by cash".

D.C. Reynolds could not resist a smile.

"There, you have all the questions in one sentence, so take your time, and D.C. Reynolds will write down what you have to say". He watched the manager's reaction.

"I have not the slightest idea what you're talking about Inspector, film crews, girls, overnight stays, I'm sorry but we don't rent out rooms for that purpose, meetings in the foyer yes, even in the dining room, but not the bedrooms, we're a respectable hotel, and are far too busy with that kind of thing". The manager was nervous.

"What kind of thing, Mr. Arlington? I never said what kind of film it was, yet you seem to be making out that it is something sordid. Tell me, why are you lying to me"? He paused.

"Film companies use bedrooms in the best of pictures, so why are you so reluctant to say that you let several rooms to a film crew, unless you have something to hide? Do you have something to hide, Arlington? "The Inspector changed tack and dropped the politeness.

"I'll tell you why you're reluctant to say, because the film crew was shooting a pornographic movie. There were several girls involved, several men involved, a director called Ricardo Bonetti, so how can you sit there and lie to me"? He paused.

"We've a witness who took part in the porno movie industry". Inspector Rupert changed tactics again.

"Listen, Mr. Arlington, I'm not interested in how you rent your rooms; it's a tough old business the hotel game, I know how hard it must be keeping it afloat".

That seemed to do the trick; the manager's face lit up.

"I'm glad someone understands my position, Inspector," he hesitated. "The film crew has used the hotel on numerous occasions; how else could we afford to decorate the hotel the way we have done? You do understand, Inspector".

"Of course, I do Mr Arlington, however I'll need the names of the guests who stayed in the hotel, including the person that paid the bills, you must have a record, and just in case you have a fire, you can give us the dates of the times the film crew were staying right now".

The manager got out of his chair and walked to the door. He came back shortly and handed the Inspector the ledgers that had the names of the girls, the men and the pornographic film crew, along with Ricardo Bonetti's signature, for a cash payment. Inspector Rupert couldn't believe the amount that was paid for each bill.

"You've been very helpful, Arlington, that will go in your favour when you appear in court. You're under arrest for running a hotel of ill repute, allowing pornographic films to be filmed in the property, the vice and fraud squad will probably want to examine your accounts, but for now, you don't have to say anything, but anything you do say will be written down and may be used in evidence against you".

Arlington was handcuffed and taken out to the police car. There were still several hotels that would have to go through the same procedure. Inspector Rupert was delighted at the progress they had made this morning.

The sleet and snow had started again, and the dark grey clouds signalled it was going to be a white Christmas. Everybody seemed to be in a joyous mood, except Inspector Amadeus Rupert. The family was due at the end of the week, but the Inspector had received orders that he would be the senior officer working with D.C. Reynolds over the Christmas and the New Year period.

He tried everything to change the "High Heid Yins "minds, explaining again that he had family coming to stay over the festive season, but that fell on deaf ears. He tried a shift swap, but nobody was prepared to work the festive season. He could always phone in sick, but that would be unfair to the other officer who would be called in to cover him.

The pornography case had practically ground to a halt, despite visitations to the other six hotels which were on the list given by Nadia Porteous. It was the same old Mother Hubbard story.

Cash paid, false signatures, and the failure to arrest Ricardo Bonetti before he skipped the country. All the directors would be charged with making pornographic films, and slapping the girls would be another matter and very hard to prove. He would probably get a fine and a slap on the wrist, but that was immaterial now, since he was probably sunning himself on the Copacabana beach in Brazil.

The focus had turned to the murdered girl, Alison Jones, who had been pulled from the River Thames.

Inspector Rupert and D.C. Reynolds made their way to the city mortuary; he wanted a full report on the dead girl before things closed for the festive season.

As usual, the traffic was horrendous, and the snowfall had made things worse. "Where are the bloody snow ploughs? We pay taxes for them to clear the roads."

The moan was futile and ignored. D.C. Reynolds was concentrating on her driving as the wipers were not clearing the windscreen. It took them an hour for a journey that should have taken twenty minutes. Finally reaching the mortuary before midday. The pathologist pulled the body of Alison Jones from the freezer, then removed the white cover.

"The bruises on her neck are where a tie was used. The reason I know this is because there were tiny fragments of the tie's texture. The bruises on her arms are where she had been taken from a vehicle and thrown into the Thames from a height that broke her neck in the fall. There were signs of sexual contact".

He slid the corpse back into the freezer. "Follow me, please, and I'll show you what was taken from her pockets". He walked in front of the two officers. Opening a drawer marked. With the freezer number and the date of her autopsy, he took out several items. Money that had dried and stuck together. The Inspector lifted the bundle. "There's a lot of money here, Mr. Bottomley, how much"?

"We counted it when she was brought in, and it totalled five hundred pounds. This is her expensive watch, and a twenty-two-carat gold bracelet. Her hair had been cut and styled just hours before she was murdered. Hair cuttings were discovered on her clothes, so I assume it was styled just before her death. Another interesting fact is that her toenails and fingernails had been manicured and painted professionally," he paused. "One more thing, Inspector". He placed a crumpled receipt on the table.

"Look at the label, Saville Row, she had obviously bought somebody a suit, as you can see, a very expensive suit, one that we could not afford".

He started to put the bagged items back into the drawer. Inspector Rupert stopped him.

"Hold on a minute, I'll keep hold of the receipt if you don't mind. We can trace the outlet where the suit was purchased. "He gave the pathologist a smile.

After leaving the mortuary, they made their way to Saville Row. The shop was filled with seasonal decorations and holly. They found the gent's department on the third floor. They stood waiting until the sales assistant was finished serving a customer. Inspector Rupert produced the crumpled receipt from his pocket, along with his warrant card.

"You should have a record of this purchase, the date is a bit obscure; However, there is a number that hopefully you can trace and give us a name and address".

The sales assistant was about to ask a question.

"Just get on with it, we've other places to visit after this". The sales assistant huffed.

"We all have places to go," he said with ire as he opened a drawer and took out a ledger.

He traced the number.

He wrote it down with haste, "Here we are, Inspector, purchased by a Miss Alison Jones, flat 342, at 29 Abbey Grove Mansions, Knightsbridge.

There was a light hint of frustration in his voice. He shut the ledger and put it back in the sales counter drawer.

"Is there anything else, Inspector"? The sales assistant had his eye on a potential customer.

"No, that will be all. You have been very helpful".

They walked out into the bitter wind and hurried back to the car in haste. There was a parking ticket placed on the windscreen. Inspector Rupert rolled it into a ball and threw it into the waste basket attached to the lamppost.

"Right, Reynolds, next stop Knightsbridge, let's see what kind of property young Alison was living in".

The Inspector had become optimistic.

"I think Alison Jones and her boyfriend were in some way mixed up in the pornography business, who was doing what will eventually become clear". He paused.

"However, there is more to it than just posing for a camera, I think there is somebody big, somebody important who was protecting Alison at first, and then had her murdered, why? Well, that's another big question. D.C. Reynolds.

"So, you don't think the person who picked Alison up in the car that day is the actual killer"?

Reynolds drummed her fingers on the steering wheel while waiting for the traffic lights to change to green. "I had my mind fixed on that person being the killer, "

"Never let your mind be fixed on anything, Reynolds. Weigh up the evidence and keep your options open. The three most important questions you must remind yourself of are motive, opportunity and location. There are plenty more questions you must ask yourself, but that will come with experience. Okay, the lights have changed, Detective Constable".

He suppressed a smile.

The light was beginning to fade in the wintery afternoon. They drew up at 29 Abbey Grove Mansions and were gobsmacked at the building that confronted them. Inspector Rupert compared it to his own mansion block.

"We're here, so we might as well look around," he said, getting out of the car.

They showed their warrant cards through the smoke glass door to the security guard, who looked at them suspiciously before allowing them entry.

"Do you have a pass key to Alison Jones' apartment? "Inspector Rupert asked indignantly.

He watched the security guard unhook a key from the board.

"Third floor, 342 is on the left". Inspector Rupert took the key graciously.

"How long has Alison Jones been gone from her apartment"? The Inspector watched as the security looked at his resident's book that listed who came in and who went out.

"October 31st. She was going to a Halloween party with two friends".

"Do you know where that was or who she was with"? He watched the security shake his head.

"If they don't say, I don't ask". The security guard closed the book. "Besides, the two men were wearing face masks". Inspector Rupert was intrigued.

There was mention of two men again. Inspector Rupert remembered immediately about Alison's abduction from the city centre, during her shopping trip and her encounter with the Morris family.

"One more question, did she have any visitors or persons who perhaps stayed over with her before, or after the night she went to the Halloween party? A young man, for instance? "

"We start at seven in the morning and finish at seven in the evening; what goes on in between times is anyone's guess, although we do check the C.C.T.V. monitor when we come in".

The Inspector looked at the security cameras," You keep saying we, is there someone else on duty, someone we could talk to, and is it possible to see your C.C.T.V. footage"?

"Yes, I've a female colleague who is doing her rounds at the moment, and no, the footage gets wiped clean every morning".

It was short and to the point. "Tell your colleague I wish to speak to her after we've checked out the apartment".

"Don't forget we finish at 19:00 pm, Inspector". The guard said with authority.

"Well, she'll just have to bloody wait until we're finished upstairs". The Inspector retorted angrily as they walked to the lift. "They sit cosy in this palace while we freeze our arses off; there is no justice in this world."

He knew his outburst was futile and uncalled for. Reynolds ignored him and pressed the third-floor button. They stepped out into a carpeted corridor.

He opened the door of apartment 342, and they were confronted with an upturned apartment. A search that had gone horribly wrong. Tables and chairs had been overturned and the drawers emptied onto the floor; The apartment was like a bomb site.

"We need to get forensics in here, Reynolds. See to that, please, and put on your forensic gloves when making the phone call, and touch nothing else".

The order was received loud and clear.

A dark-skinned woman appeared at the door. "Don't enter, I'll come out," the Inspector said quickly, not wanting to disturb the crime scene.

"Thanks for coming up, as you can see, we're going to be here a while".

The Inspector asked the same questions as he had done with the security guard in the foyer. After he was satisfied that the woman could not give him any further information, he thanked her. "Just one thing, Donalda, the forensic team will be arriving shortly, just make sure they're allowed entry". He watched her walk away. Inspector Rupert had a good look around. Nothing was obvious in the mess except a photograph of Alison and a young man. He removed it from the frame and looked at the back.

"Ronny and I in Blackpool" was the inscription. D.C. Reynolds took the proffered photograph. "Is this the mystery driver whom she bought the suit for"? She studied the handsome young faces.

"That is possible, Reynolds, but let's not jump to conclusions just yet". He paused.

"Do you know; I was thinking about another conundrum? Did Alison Jones have a pimp? Girls in her situation often do, and it is most likely she had one. Detection, arrest, and conviction, just three tenets of what we were talking about earlier. "

There was a commotion in the corridor as the forensic team carried their equipment to the door.

The photographer greeted the Inspector with a smile. "Afternoon, sir, struth, what a mess".

He stepped over the items and then loaded his camera with a flash bulb. The rest of the team had dressed in their forensic overshoes and suits.

"No bodies then, Inspector."

"Correct, Stanford, no bodies just yet anyway. Just make sure you go over this apartment with a fine-tooth comb, and the report comes direct to me. I don't want anyone else getting hold of the final report until I study it first, understand".

The team leader nodded.

It was a dull grey day; thankfully, the snow had stopped falling. The Inspector threw the results of the forensic tests onto his desk. It proved inconclusive except for two things. Money and lots of it, hidden below the floorboards of the wardrobe. There were fingerprints that would have to be checked through the national police system.

There was one item in a forensic bag that interested him. A partly torn film reel bag, the markings on it were foreign; however, it was conclusive proof that filming had taken place in the apartment. He was in no doubt that it would've been pornographic.

The security, who had said there was one on duty while the other did their rounds, that was fine, but the security guard had said they checked the C.C.T.V. recordings before erasing them every morning, which meant they were lying and hiding something.

He looked at his watch. He made the decision to go back to the apartment of Alison Jones and, while there, interview both security guards at length.

The two officers spoke in the car as they made the journey to Knightsbridge.

"You interview the woman, Reynolds; I'll take the male guard".

Inspector Rupert knocked on the door of the apartment block loudly. It was the female guard who looked out through the glass before recognising who it was. The two officers stood shivering as the guard unlocked the door. "Where is your compatriot, Donalda"?

The DI asked, appreciating the heat of the foyer.

"He is doing his morning rounds, Inspector". She said timidly.

"Get him on your two-way radio now". He commanded in an authoritative voice.

"In the meantime, you'll take Detective Constable Reynolds somewhere quiet where she can interview you without interruptions".

He watched the uncertainty in the female guard's face. Eventually, the male guard appeared from the stairs. "What is it now, Inspector? I'm busy in the mornings with the older residents, so make it snappy. "He walked towards his desk.

Inspector Rupert removed himself from the warm radiator. "Certainly, Reg, I'll make it snappy when you start telling me the truth. "He paused.

"You told me that you checked the video recordings each morning, but you failed to say that there were a lot of comings and goings on after your shifts had finished. That's when I became suspicious, Reg. So, we'll start again, shall we"? He put his face close to the security guard. "We have it that a lot of filming went on in this building, and I'm not talking Michael Mouse cartoons, Reg, but pornographic movies which are illegal in this country, so perhaps you can enlighten me as to what was going on, and why you failed to tell me about it".

He waited patiently.

"I don't have the slightest idea what you're talking about, Inspector". The guard said defiantly.

"Alright Reg, I've tried to be patient, but now I've lost it, so get your coat, we can do this at the police station where you'll be formally charged with trying to pervert the course of justice, and wasting police time, and that my friend can carry a maximum jail term of five years".

He watched the guard wipe his forehead to remove the beads of sweat.

"Alright, keep your hair on, Inspector". He hesitated, "Yes, there was a film crew who came here on several occasions, but all I was asked to do was make sure that the C.C.T.V. cameras were switched off from the time we went off shift until we came in the next morning".

He hesitated, "That's the truth".

Inspector Rupert thought for a moment and rubbed his chin.

"I'm sorry, Reg, I think you're holding something back," he said angrily.

Reg. got up quickly and walked into the back office. He unlocked a drawer, then removed three video cassettes.

"The film crowd got careless after a few visits, so I never switched the cameras off on those occasions. I just wanted some form of protection, so I kept them as insurance, just in case their heavies came calling". He handed over the videotapes. "That's all, Inspector", he looked pale and frightened at the prospect of being taken to a police station and charged.

"What would my wife say if that happened, Inspector"? He wiped the sweat from his brow and tears from his eyes as Inspector Rupert nodded,

"How much were you paid for your services, Reg"? He asked softly.

"I got twenty pounds a time, Donalda got fifty pounds because she stayed back to let them in, she also made sure the apartment was aired, and all cigarettes and cigars were safely put out after they had gone. She also made a little extra serving of drinks and coffee during the night, which was left on the corridor floor outside the apartment door".

The Inspector rubbed his chin again.

"Alright, Reg. I'm prepared to accept your story; however, if I find that you or Donalda has held anything back, your feet won't touch the ground "He waited until D.C. Reynolds appeared with the female security guard.

Donalda spoke first. "I know what you are going to ask, Inspector, but I can say quite categorically I never paid any attention to the faces of the film crew, actors or actresses. I was kept in the cupboard on the first floor when they arrived and again until everyone had gone, then I proceeded to tidy and clean things up, stripping the soiled bed, etc. However, after a week had gone by, there were two men who claimed to be insurance agents. I thought they looked a bit suspicious, so I checked with Alison

Jones, who confirmed that they were giving her an estimate on oil paintings, so I allowed them entry".

Reg. Interrupted. "I was doing my usual rounds when I passed them in the corridor but thought nothing of it when Alison gave them a hug and invited them into the apartment".

"Have those characters been caught on the security video? "He asked in hope.

"Sorry, Inspector, those security videos taken on our daily shift are wiped clean and a fresh tape inserted; it is standard procedure carried out by the two of us, besides those two so-called insurance agents, probably impostors, arrived a week after the film crew had gone".

Inspector Rupert nodded. "Clients, and film extras no doubt". He looked at the guards.

"Okay, I want to have a look around the apartment again on my own, before Alison Jones parents arrive, So, when I'm finished, you two can begin to sort out the mess and tidy the place up a bit, one of you can also assist in the packing if required, and I don't want you helping yourselves to her possessions and ornaments, because we've taken an inventory of her things that are valuable and important".

D.C. Reynolds looked like the cat that got the cream. She waited until the Inspector was ready to go upstairs before following him.

"Donalda has been very helpful, sir; however, I'll wait until we get into the apartment before revealing what she has told me".

This drew a frown from Inspector Rupert.

"Okay, then you can start knocking on doors; somebody must have seen or heard something".

He slipped the key into the Yale lock and entered.

"Some neighbours have already been questioned with a negative outcome from those that cared to answer the door, so just knock on their doors again, see if you have better luck".

He walked into the spacious living room. "Somebody has been looking for something, judging by the mess. The forensics team checked the king-size bedroom and found traces of semen, but I think the film crew were very careful when they were doing the action shots of the porn stars on the bed". He rubbed his chin.

"I live in an apartment similar to this, and I'm aware that the soundproofing is excellent; you hear nothing of what is going on above or below you, so I imagine there would've been a lot of groans and moans as the participants reached their climax".

D.C. Reynolds ignored the small talk, "Do you know that Alison Jones worked in a department store when she came to London and went on the game, sir"? She paused. "I've just realized that that is the store we visited concerning the suit purchase. Is it possible it has a bearing and a connection to this crime"? Inspector Rupert scowled at her.

"You must know D.C. Reynolds, that this is a severe misjudgement by you". He was trying to keep calm as he thought about it.

"I suppose it only gave Alison Jones the knowledge of where to purchase such an expensive item, but who in the store had conferred with Alison Jones? Perhaps on a tea or lunch break". He was still trying very hard not to reprimand the young Detective Constable.

"She has done much more than that, sir. During a conversation with Alison Jones, Donalda found out that the young prostitute was doing favours for store clients in the past; she had used it as a springboard to earn cash before she needed a bit extra on the side. That's when she parachuted herself into the so-called glamour world of a call-girl with expensive clients and a mediocre apartment for entertaining".

D.C. Reynolds pulled back the net curtain. "Furthermore, sir, Alison Jones was involved in a scam of human trafficking. Bringing girls in from abroad to be sold into the sex slave market, that's how she got the money to buy an apartment like this". She closed the net curtain. "Interesting, wouldn't you agree, sir"?

Inspector Rupert exploded. "Why in heaven's name did you not tell me all this before, Reynolds"?

D.C. Reynolds kept her composure but spoke sternly.

"I only found out about all this downstairs a few minutes ago, when I questioned Donalda. That is what took me so long. Is that a revelation or not, sir"?

"It certainly is D.C. Reynolds, perhaps Alison Jones, and the Essex hotel manager were involved in the illegal trafficking scam. That's why the manager and his wife went abroad so often. An ideal way of trafficking from the holiday resorts of southeastern Spain. You could earn brownie points for what you have just discovered, D.C. Reynolds".

He rubbed his chin. "That's why the manager was very lax with the truth; it is possible that the hotel staff also knew what was going on. I'm beginning to wonder if the hotel staff are made up of illegal foreigners. A way of hiding them while preparing them for other sexual activities. However, we can go back there to question the manager when things quieten down, and we solve this murder".

He paced the lounge. "There is another anomaly that is annoying me, and that is why we've not heard back from the driving licensing agency when we put in a request for the registration number, road tax application, and logbook duplicate regarding the mystery car KLT 43. That should have come back almost immediately". He held up his finger.

"Not unless it has come back, perhaps somebody is blocking it, if the request was ever sent in the first place, so that's something you can check when you've finished here".

He walked around the apartment as D.C. Reynolds went to knock on doors.

She returned in time to greet the parents, along with an entourage of relations. The family cursed when they saw the mess. The two police officers were careful not to step on any ornaments that were lying on the floor as they made their way to the door. Glad he had given instructions to the security guards to help tidy the place up. After the introductions and handshakes, D.C. Reynolds took him aside. "I think all hell is about to break loose here, sir, a bit like Pandora's box, so might I suggest we go over to Alison's bungalow to see what forensics are up to. What is seen and heard here does not concern us, sir. They look like a crowd of bloody vultures and parasites to me, just here for what they can get."

"You're learning, Constable; my motto has always been the three wise monkeys. See no evil, hear no evil, speak no evil. That always prevents you from getting involved in domestic disputes," He smiled. "Let's get out of here," he whispered amid the fracas that was going on in the lounge.

They made their way over to the bungalow where Alison Jones had lived, away from the apartment that took her away from the call-girl, prostitution, and filming activities, perhaps trying to lead a normal suburban life.

CHAPTER

Eight

The Metropolitan Police Commissioner stood with his hands behind his back as he addressed the superintendent. "Well, MacAulay, we're not hearing much from Rupert or Reynolds. Have they been transferred or what? I've checked with the Assistant Commissioner and Chief Superintendent Skinner, after his untimely promotion. They have heard nothing, so perhaps you can tell me what is happening since you and Inspector Rupert are thick as thieves".

The Commissioner's voice did not conceal his displeasure.

"The Inspector and his young protégé are extremely busy, sir. Don't forget, he went from one difficult murder case straight into another, although at the time he was withdrawn from the illegal pornographic filmmaking, linked to prostitution cases in the city, sir. That was your decision, sir".

"Nevertheless, Superintendent, he should be making regular reports to you, who in turn should pass it on to the Chief Superintendent Skinner, who then passes it on to my Assistant. It is then I who decides whether the case is worth pursuing. It's called the chain of command, Superintendent".

He sat down and clasped his hands". How long has Rupert been working on this present murder case, MacAulay"?

He drummed his fingers on the desk. I'll check, sir, but at a guess, two to three weeks; however, I'll speak to him personally, expressing your concern, sir".

The Commissioner nodded. "Sooner rather than later, MacAulay, that will be all for the present".

The Superintendent left the room quickly. "Prat, "he said under his breath as he left the office. It was true, however, that it had been a while since he had heard from Inspector Amadeus Rupert. Rupert would need to be informed immediately about the Commissioner's order.

He himself did not want to incur the wrath of the fifth floor when he was told on other occasions not to rock the boat.

Even though he and Amadeus Rupert were friends, there was always his own promotion to consider. Hopefully, that would be forthcoming shortly, so Inspector Rupert would have to obey orders.

The Inspector was exhausted when he entered the Scotland Yard incident room. Superintendent MacAulay approached him immediately.

"Inspector, I need to have a word with you; the top brass is going ballistic regarding the lack of reports on the murdered girl, so for God's sake, put pen to paper, in order that I can take it to the top brass".

Inspector Rupert acknowledged it was a genuine plea for obedience from Superintendent MacAulay, not the usual barked-out orders that came from the "High Heid Yins" on the top floor, clinging on desperately for their pensions.

"Fine, Angus, but you must do something for me. I need to know if we got word back from the vehicle licensing centre. I also need to know if Alison Jones' parents have been to the mortuary to identify the body. We know it is her lying in the mortuary, but a positive ID is necessary. I put that request upstairs the day her body was dragged from the Thames, and now the family are currently picking and choosing her belongings at her apartment. They have requested that we finish the forensic tests at the bungalow so the family can start there. And another thing, Angus, I should have been given a list of all new prostitutes who are not on our computer yet, so speed things along, because I feel as if I'm being blocked every time I turn. It is not the first time I've experienced this, Angus". He paused.

"Just one more thing, I want to put Reynolds forward for promotion to Detective Sergeant, because in time she will become an asset to the force. Speaking of promotion, when did that parasite Skinner climb the greasy pole, bypassing you to D.C.S.?

He stood waiting for the Superintendent's response when a sergeant approached.

"Sorry to interrupt, sir, but the car we've been looking for has been found abandoned and burnt out on the Leyton estate, in northeast London, "he paused

"Charred body remains have been found on what is left of the back seat. "

"Okay, Sergeant, get the pathologist Bottomley and our forensics team mobilized. Then you can join D.C. Reynolds and me at the crime scene".

He turned to the Superintendent. "Sorry, sir, duty calls".

He went out of the incident room to put a call out for Reynolds, who was preparing to tuck into a prawn salad lunch.

"Bugger", she said loudly as Inspector Rupert approached.

The burnt body in the car sparked a memory, a ghost from the past that would never leave him. He was thinking of his dear friend Colin Freeman, killed in 1940, roasted alive when his Spitfire exploded due to overheating, because he was up in the air and down on the ground for re-armament and fuel all morning, ignoring the advice of the ground crew and mechanics, and for that, he paid the price with his life.

"Are you alright, sir? Is it something I've said"? D.C. Reynolds looked sheepishly at the Inspector.

"No, nothing you've said, Constable, I'll tell you about it someday".

They made their way out to Leyton in northeast London.

When they arrived at the crime scene, Inspector Rupert investigated the back of the burnt-out car. The charred remains were huddled up in the back as if in a sleeping position.

"You don't have to see this, Reynolds. I want you to get through to the licensing centre now that we have a positive number plate, KLT 43. It seems Nadia Porteous was telling the truth after all."

He stood for a moment at the burnt-out car while the pathologist did tests in the cramped surroundings that still held the smell of petrol and burnt flesh.

"Two weeks Rupert, maybe more, I need to get the young man back to the mortuary to carry out further tests, but definitely male, I'm afraid that's all I can tell you for the moment except there is nothing left of any identification marks or indeed paperwork, everything has been destroyed in the fire, except his teeth, which you might be able to get a trace as to who he actually is". The pathologist took off his protective clothes.

"I think I'll be able to give you a name before the end of play today, Bottomley. I'm waiting on word back from the vehicle registration centre, so that should speed things up a bit".

The pathologist nodded his approval, then ordered the removal of the charred remains from the back seat of the burnt-out Ford Consul car.

Word had come through about the registration of the vehicle, which belonged to Ivor Rigsby of 26 Redcar Quadrant, Woolwich, London. That was where they headed after the pathologist had left.

"This will be a bit sensitive, Reynolds, so, if need be, you take the wife, mother, whoever into the kitchen to make tea".

They arrived shortly after 18:00 pm. The bungalow was well-lit. Inspector Rupert tapped the door lightly, then rang the doorbell. A tall man answered. "None today, thanks" He was about to close the door.

"I'm sorry, sir, police. Is it possible I can have a word"?

The resident looked surprised. After checking their warrant cards, they were shown into the sitting room while Mr. Rigsby shouted to his wife. Mandy Rigsby was summoned harshly. "Come through a minute, the police are here and have something to tell us, bad news by the sound of it, so brace yourself".

The woman stood erect with her hands behind her back,

"I take it you and Mandy are husband and wife who own a Ford Consul registration number.

K L T 43" The husband nodded, "Yes, Inspector, that's our vehicle".

"Was it your son who was driving the vehicle two weeks ago and perhaps more recently"?

The wife gave a short laugh, "We have three daughters, because he hasn't the manhood or balls to produce boys".

The Inspector stood unmoved. "So, if you have no boys, who was driving your car, was it close family, or a friend"?

It was the husband's turn to laugh. "I'll let you answer that one, Mandy".

She stood silent with her arms folded.

Derek Rigsby spoke with contempt in his voice. We've friendly neighbours called Mr. and Mrs Morris, who live four bungalows up the Quadrant. Their son, who is a regular visitor, borrows the car from time to time, especially to take my wife shopping, or when I'm at work. Is that not right, Mandy"?

"The name of this young man"? Inspector Rupert asked quickly, "Ronny Morris, our neighbour's son, is a local stud. Mandy can give you details about him".

Inspector Rupert started to make his way to the door. "I'm sorry we've got our wires crossed, but thanks for your help".

He signalled to D.C. Reynolds; it was time to leave.

"My car, Inspector, what has happened to my car"? Mr. Rigsby asked pensively.

"I'll leave Detective Constable Reynolds to explain". He made his way quickly to the door.

He waited for the D. C. to come out of the bungalow to the police car.

"Thanks for that, sir. Now there's a bloody storm brewing in there, might I suggest we move up to the Morris's bungalow? What we don't speak, see or hear is not our problem. "

"You're learning, Reynolds. Three wise monkeys are my motto. See no evil, speak no evil, hear no evil. Remember, it is always a good excuse to prevent you from becoming involved in domestic arguments and quarrels, which usually end up with the husband and wife joining forces and attacking you". He started the car and drove up to the Morris's bungalow.

After gaining entry and expressing his deepest sympathy at their loss, D.C. Reynolds helped the wife to make a strong pot of tea.

"Tell me, Mr. Morris, did your son Ronny ever talk about what he was doing with the Rigby's Ford Consul? It is evident he borrowed it on several occasions, sometimes for a while, so do you have any hints that could help catch your son's killer? We know he had a girlfriend who was a prostitute and a pornographic actress, with plenty of cash to spend; however, we're not throwing accusations towards your son, who might be an innocent party in all this. I'm just interested in the times he drove Alison Jones to filming appointments. It is our prime aim to catch the killer or killers who have murdered two young people. Did he ever mention the girl's name, Alison Jones from Wales to you or your wife"?

Mr. Morris shook his head, close to tears. "When can I see my boy"? The question was asked softly.

"I don't think that will be possible until after a post-mortem. The pathologist will have Ronny's body examined and placed in a sealed coffin. Then you'll be able to visit the chapel of rest at the mortuary. Formal identification is out of the question due to the severity of the charred remains".

The tea and biscuits arrived. It was obvious Reynolds had used her female intuition and touch to help soften the blow before the Inspector went to work on questioning her.

"I've spoken to your husband, Mrs. Morris; however, I must ask the same questions regarding your son Ronny. I'm fully aware of how hard this must be, but as I explained to your husband, the more information we get, the quicker we can find your son's killer. So, I need you to confirm the name of Ronny's girlfriend. Did he ever bring her home? Was there ever any talk about what she did, or what she got up to? What did Ronny do? Did he ever discuss his work with you"?

He took the photograph from his pocket and showed both parents the one he had taken from Alison's apartment.

"Take a good look, was she ever invited home by Ronny? If so, did she ever talk about her other friends or her employer? The woman just shook her head.

"A very pretty girl, I would love to meet her".

"That will not be possible, Mrs. Morris, because she was murdered as well, and we believe that Ronny's death and hers are linked because of what she was".

"What did she do, Inspector"? Mrs. Morris asked quietly.

Inspector Rupert smiled. "If you don't mind, Mrs. Morris, I'll ask the questions".

He said it in a soft tone, realising they had just lost their only son. He remembered how Mr. and Mrs Freeman had reacted when they lost their only son, Colin, killed back in 1940 during the Battle of Britain. He was convinced they died of broken hearts.

He handed Mr. Morris a card.

"If you think of anything, no matter how trivial, call this number". "Just a minute, Inspector, let me see that photograph again". Mr. Morris studied it, then handed it to his wife. "We've seen that girl before, Maureen. Remember when Ronny took us into central London on a shopping spree, he dropped us in Oxford Street, and this girl in the photograph knocked on the passenger door window and waved, yes, that's her, Inspector, I'm sure of it".

His wife agreed. "Yes, I remember, two men pulled her away quite hard. The girl looked quite frightened, and that's when our Ronny sped away without an explanation". She paused.

"That was so uncharacteristic of Ronny," she hesitated.

"I thought she was being arrested, Inspector. The tall, broad man was in what looked like some kind of uniform under his trench coat. I remember it quite clearly now. They were police uniforms. Ronny usually gives us a hug, but when we got out of the car further along the street, he couldn't wait to get away. I remember looking back, and that is the same girl who was bundled into a car, but not a police car. After that, we went shopping, and I forgot all about it". She handed the Photograph back to the Inspector.

"Would you recognize those two men, Mrs. Morris? Perhaps you could give D.C. Reynolds a description".

He put the photograph back into his pocket. "I'll leave D.C. Reynolds to take down the description. I need to go to the car for something". He took his leave quickly.

The information he had now gathered was crucial to the case.

Eventually, the D.C. walked down the path to the car. "I've been thinking, sir," she hesitated. "There is a possibility that Rigsby could be involved in all this. Ronny Morris was having an affair with his wife, and let's not forget, it is Rigsby's car that Ronny Morris was found dead in," she paused. "A jealous husband, with a grudge to bear, murders have been carried out for less".

The Inspector nodded. "How long did it take you to come up with that, Reynolds? I've already thought of that; however, I don't think Mr. Rigsby has the balls to commit murder". He gave a wry smile. D.C. Reynolds was not put off by his remark.

"Okay, Inspector, what about Mandy Rigsby? Hell knows no wrath as a woman scorned". The D.C. pressed the point.

"Much as I appreciate your enthusiasm, Reynolds, however, let's keep it within the bounds of reality. We need to concentrate on those two men, who I think are the same two who paid Alison

Jones a visit at her apartment from time to time, then took her for a joy ride and killed her".

He rubbed his chin. "I also believe that Ronny Morris witnessed something, and that's why he got out of his girlfriend's car quickly, but most boyfriends would've got out of the car and gone to his girlfriend's aid, but he didn't. I think you'll find in your notes the description of the two men who were trying to persuade her to stop whatever it was she was doing, and I don't mean her being on the game. The money in her flat is also a key factor; was she blackmailing the two men? I think she knew them personally, professional men, possibly the same two who abducted her from the street. I think they had sex with her, and I also think they watched her perform with other men, although not given a part in the pornographic films because of her body scars, but they in fact were part of the production, putting money into the project rather than being actual participants". He paused. "I also think that those two men are part of a criminal gang in the city, who are involved in prostitution and people trafficking". He started the engine after he had studied the descriptions of the two men in her notebook.

"We need to get a look at the videotapes and hope it gives us something to go on".

The car skidded as he drove around the Quadrant turning circle.

"I want you to pay the two security guards another visit, just to let them know they're not out of the woods just yet. Get a look at today's video; you never know what it might reveal".

The snow was falling thick and fast as he got out of the car at Scotland Yard.

"When you've finished at 29 Abbey Grove mansion, then pay Mr. Arlington a visit at the Exeter hotel, give him a description of the two men who visited Alison's flat. Is it possible this was the same two in the Halloween masks who were on their way to a party with Alison Jones? And ask him if the two men ever visited the hotel again with Alison. Show him the photo of the young couple. I think now we have their names and a photograph; it might jog his memory of the young couple who might have spent a night together in the hotel. You can drop a hint about his frequent visits abroad and Alison Jones being involved in people trafficking".

D.C. Reynolds drove off, looking at her watch constantly. She had a date that night, and she did not want to disappoint. The visit to Abbey Grove mansion produced nothing. She cursed at having to drive across London at this time of day. It was the law as the streets became practically impassable due to the earlier snowfall. She eventually arrived at the Exeter hotel.

She looked at her watch again. "There goes another chance of romance, "she said to herself, slamming the car door.

She walked up the steps and into the foyer. "Is Arlington about"? She asked bluntly. "Tell him I'm not a happy bunny, and I want to see him now. "

The receptionist smiled. "I'm sorry to disappoint you, but Mr. Arlington has gone home for the day. Can I help"?

D.C. Reynolds cursed under her breath. A wasted journey, a waste of precious time. She took the photocopy of the photograph from her coat pocket. "Have you ever seen this pair before? She thrust the photograph at the receptionist. The receptionist looked upset.

"Sorry, it's been one of those days. "She gestured an apology. "I need to know if those two spent a night here within the last three to four weeks"?

The receptionist screwed up her face. "She did, but not him. She was with two men, one tall and slim, the other tall and broad. I remember them well because the housemaids complained about the mess they left, wine bottles, and used contraceptives. I think the maid said there was a hint of cocaine on the dressing table".

"Can I speak to her? It's very important," the receptionist said, taking out a duty roster. "Sorry, Annie is on days off and won't be in until Saturday". D.C. Reynolds cursed under her breath again.

"Can you give me their arrival and departure dates? That would help".

The receptionist bent down to retrieve the registration ledger. She smiled,

"Most of our clients use false names". She looked carefully at the register.

"Here you are, the 31st of October. They arrived, then left with Alison. Another thing I remember about that night was that the two men were wearing face masks". She paused.

"I was just going off duty and paid little attention, with it being Halloween. The next morning, I was on the same shift as I am now when they checked out. I was in the back office when one of them signed the register quickly, then disappeared after leaving an envelope with the payment and a little bonus for the staff".

She was about to replace the ledger. "If I could take the ledger with the signature of whoever paid the bill. I suppose it was paid in cash with a false signature"? The receptionist was hesitant.

"I'm not sure Mr. Arlington would like any paperwork getting removed from the hotel". She kept a firm grip on the ledger.

"You leave Mr. Arlington to me". She looked at her watch. "Thanks for your help, Dianne. Tell your boss we'll be back tomorrow after my boss has seen it". The receptionist smiled

"Is it that grumpy bugger that was with you on your last visit? "The question was asked with civility.

"The very same Dianne, so now you have a customer arriving, it's time for me to go".

She took the ledger and made her way to the car that sparkled with frost.

Inspector Rupert was delighted as his protégé handed him a photocopy of the signature from the ledger. "I'll give you a tip, Reynolds. Always have a search warrant before you remove anything from property or have somebody with you so it cannot be construed that you took it by force or without the owner's consent, but well done, it will help us build the case when we arrest the perpetrators".

"Have you anybody particular in mind, sir"?

She watched the clever Inspector rub his chin and give a slight nod.

"I have my suspicions, Reynolds, but we need proof before we can act, so I want you to go back to the Exeter hotel and return the ledger with thanks, see if you can get a word with the chambermaid's upstairs, you know how things get spoken about on their tea or lunch break. Just see if any of them speak with a foreign accent".

He paused. "Speak to Arlington, because I still think he's holding something back. He knows much more than he is letting on".

Inspector Rupert went upstairs to deliver his late report from last month.

Things were starting to move, but not as quickly as he would've liked. He sat waiting patiently for the Commissioner's meeting with his understudy to end. Eventually, the Assistant Commissioner came out with a smile on his face. "Your turn, Rupert".

It wasn't a friendly gesture, as he and the Assistant never got on well. No appointment was necessary, according to the advice he had been given by Superintendent Angus MacAulay.

He breezed into the commissioner's office.

"Come in, Rupert, take a seat "The Commissioner seemed in a jovial mood.

"I've just received the crime figures for the past year, and it makes good reading, that's what makes our job so worthwhile, wouldn't you agree, Rupert"? He paused and smiled.

"Okay, Rupert, fill me in with your late monthly report, and I hope it makes for better reading than last month, which was also late".

"Not really, sir, but the Alison Jones murder case has taken a turn for the better,"

He took out a page from his notes and handed it across the desk to the Commissioner, who snatched it from his hand.

"The young man who was found in the burned-out Ford Consul in northeast London was her pimp, called Ronny Morris". He paused. "Now we thought Ronny Morris was Alison's boyfriend, but in fact he was her drug-pushing pimp, who had her working the streets for him. However, we now know it was he who picked Alison up on the day she was murdered, but let me stress, he was not her killer. It would be senseless for him to kill somebody who was earning money for him". He paused.

"I believe that Ronny Morris was blackmailing somebody at the top of the heap, perhaps a crime boss, who had him burned alive in the Ford Consul, which belongs to a couple called the Rigsby's, who, apart from owning the car, have no connection to the case".

"Not a good way to go, sir, burnt alive". He added. "We haven't had a chance to go back to Soho to interview the prostitutes, but we will have that done by the end of the week, starting this afternoon".

"You keep saying 'We, ' Rupert. Who is this "We" you keep referring to?

"Young D, C. Reynolds, sir, a good young detective who has a bright future ahead of her. I've spoken to Superintendent MacAulay, indicating she is ready for promotion to Sergeant, and he agrees, so you should get a request document across your desk shortly".

"We'd better keep her well clear of you, then Rupert, we don't want her picking up any of your bad habits at a young age".

"I don't know what you mean, sir. I don't have any bad habits worth mentioning".

"What about this luxury apartment block Alison Jones was using as a place for her expensive clients? Have you come up with anything positive? Is there any forensics we can count on"?

"Nothing except a stash of cash, sir, £93,000 to be precise. We did find paper wrapping made in Holland; the film is wrapped in that paper and then boxed for export around the world. It tells us that pornographic filming was carried out in the apartment over a period. Another place they filmed was at the Exeter hotel in Soho, but so far, nothing else has turned up. D.C. Reynolds is over there as we speak, tidying up loose ends".

The Commissioner drummed his fingers on his desk. "I thought I told you to drop the prostitution case, Rupert. It's a waste of good resources, and now you tell me there is pornographic filming taking place in the city, understand this, Rupert, drop it until we have the resources to proceed further".

Inspector Rupert could not believe the order that had come from the Commissioner.

"I'm sorry, sir, but during our murder investigation, it has drawn us into the pornographic film industry, which in turn uses prostitutes, hence the connection with all three murders. We need to continue our investigation if we're to get anywhere, sir. The investigations can't be dropped, sir, just like that. "

The Commissioner was about to speak. Inspector Rupert interrupted him.

"There is one more important factor in all this," he paused ", The two men who visited Alison Jones at her apartment were the same two men who also took her to the Exeter hotel on

Halloween night. We'll bring in the forensics team to the hotel when they've finished at Alison Jones' bungalow. We need to see if there are any clues left, which I doubt due to constant cleaning by the housemaids". He paused, wondering if he should share his discovery with the Commissioner. Inspector Rupert decided to cast a line into the pool, hoping for a bite.

"Finally, sir, the two men mentioned were the ones who abducted Alison Jones from Oxford Street on the day she was murdered. They are policemen, or impostors dressed in police uniforms. We have witnesses who will testify to this and have given us a positive ID which matches the statement given by the Exeter hotel receptionist.

"This is a serious accusation you're making, Rupert. However, keep me informed. Meanwhile, I have an important meeting," he looked at his watch. "My word is that the time"?

After a brief pause, Inspector Rupert got up and made his way down to the incident room. He studied the board again. There was something missing from the jigsaw that would bring this case to a close. He rubbed his chin several times, staring at the board when he heard the news that every bona fide police officer hates to hear.

"Code red, officer down. Exeter Hotel, Blenheim Street, Soho".

Inspector Amadeus Rupert rocked on his feet and grabbed the table for support. His blood ran cold until he finally came to his senses. He hurried to the vehicle output and demanded that a driver take him to Soho.

They sped through the city with headlights on full beam. The blue light flashing and the siren wailing. They reached the Exeter hotel just as the ambulance was leaving for St. Thomas's hospital with his injured colleague.

It was ascertained that D.C. Chloe Reynolds had been fatally shot.

"Why, why, why"? He said, choking back the tears as the snow began to fall, helping to cover the blood-stained steps of the hotel.

"It was a simple task she was carrying out; there was no need for this to happen". He gave himself a shake before entering the hotel to start the enquiries.

"Nobody goes in or out of this place until my inquiry is over. I want statements from every member of staff and residents, starting with the manager".

All the police officers were allocated their tasks; he then made his way to the hospital.

Inspector Rupert sat waiting patiently. He did not like hospitals and knew that they also did things in a methodical fashion. He was shown into a side room and given a mug of tea. However, he was wise enough to know that things did not look good; no matter how kind the hospital staff were, there was always that nagging doubt of how things would pan out.

The most important thing was that Chloe Reynolds pulled through this ordeal.

There was always the offer of more tea, which he politely turned down.

He said softly, "I'll be peeing all the way back to the Yard". It was said as a defence mechanism, not meaning any offence.

A doctor appeared after a while.

"I'll be perfectly frank with you, Inspector, Chloe Reynold's chances of survival are extremely slim; all we can do now is wait," He paused. "We've removed the bullet from her skull, but the extreme trauma to her brain cells is causing some concern. The swelling left by the bullet infiltration has caused severe swelling; we can only hope for the time being that the swelling goes down. Chloe has been taken into the intensive care unit, where she will be monitored twenty-four hours a day".

Inspector Rupert nodded, then asked, "Would it be possible for me to see her doctor? It would mean a lot to me".

The doctor stood for a minute in thought. "Two minutes only, Inspector, the first two hours are critical, and you'll have to put on a gown, head cover and overshoes before entering the intensive care unit". He paused.

"Wait here, I'll arrange for an orderly to take you to the fourth floor, where you'll be kitted out for entry". Inspector Rupert nodded his appreciation.

"After your visit, Inspector, I suggest you go home and rest because there is nothing more we can do for the moment".

Inspector Rupert shook his head. "I'm going back to work, doctor, to find the bastard that done this, and when I do, you'll find you're called upon to carry out another operation, because I'll make the perpetrator suffer".

The doctor ignored the angry outburst and walked out of the quiet room. An orderly appeared a short time later. "Follow me, please, sir," it was said in a monotonous tone, something the hospital orderly probably said several times a day.

Inspector Rupert followed him like a little lamb trailing behind the ewe.

After he was kitted out, he was shown into the intensive care area by a nursing sister.

"Two minutes, Inspector", she said with authority.

He stood looking through the glass window, watching the monitors rise to an apex before levelling out. Chloe lay motionless, with wires and tubes attached to her body. Her head was swathed in bandages, and an oxygen mask was placed on her face; it reminded the Inspector of his time with Bomber Command when he flew Lancaster bombers over Germany. He touched the glass in a futile attempt to communicate. It was a nurse who touched his arm gently.

"That can't be two minutes already, nurse, surely not". His pleadings were in vain.

She touched his arm gently again. "Time to go, sir," was all she said softly.

Inspector Rupert thanked her profusely.

"You'll take good care of my colleague, won't you"?

He was led out of the intensive care unit, and back to the changing room where he dispersed of the protective clothing into a collection swing bin. He walked sombrely out of the hospital, then decided to return to the Exeter hotel, Superintendent MacAulay met him in the foyer.

"Have Lisa's parents been informed"? He asked his superior softly. "Yes, all that has been taken care of, Amadeus; however, we must move on with this. The Commissioner is having kittens as we speak".

"Was it a routine enquiry she was carrying out or what"? Superintendent MacAulay asked sternly.

Inspector Rupert spoke calmly, but inside his stomach was in knots.

"Of course, sir, do you think I would've sent an officer on her own if I thought otherwise. Chloe was returning a ledger with a signature that was important. We have a photocopy of the pages with the signature, and it was checked for prints, which turned up nothing".

The Superintendent gave a wry smile. "No, of course not, Rupert, that's not what I meant. I'm concerned that this might be some crime boss trying to get even with us. What do you think Rupert? You and the mob go back a long way. Over time, you've sent a few down. Perhaps they have been tailing you. In your current investigation, it just seems like something out of a movie".

"That's exactly what it's like, sir, just like the Chicago twenties and thirties, but I don't think this is a crime boss's revenge, it could be a hired hit, somebody that does not want our investigation to go on, I think an assassin's bullet is more like it". He paused.

"All we can do now is continue to question the staff and the manager in Arlington because I think he is holding something back".

"He has his solicitor with him, so tread lightly, don't go throwing false allegations at him until we're sure he has some involvement in your investigation". The Superintendent pointed at a vacant warehouse on the other side of the street.

"When the forensics team are finished in room 142, then get them to check out that building, although I think Chloe was shot from a passing car, or a pedestrian whose tracks were covered by the snowfall. The team can give us angles of the bullet entry when Chloe is fit enough to be interviewed". The late afternoon passed quickly. Arlington and his staff had been interviewed thoroughly for two hours. The manager was hesitant to answer questions and looked at his lawyer for advice, with a nod or a shake of the solicitor's head. Arlington spoke softly.

"There is one thing I can tell you, Inspector, and that is the broad, tall man who accompanied Miss Jones on Halloween night had very large feet, and walked like a duck, according to Fiona the chambermaid who was on duty that night. She said the shoes were removed by the night porter for polishing, just a little extra for our guests".

The Superintendent spoke. "This maid, is she on duty"? The manager lifted the phone. "Dianne, tell Fiona to come down to the office; the police want to talk to her". He replaced the black telephone in its cradle.

"Any word on the young Detective Constable's condition"? He asked politely.

"Critical", came the reply from the Inspector.

"You told me that one of the men paid cash; surely the receptionist would've got a good look at them".

The manager shook his head. The money was in an envelope and put in the safe, the threesome left by the emergency exit at the back, which opens out into the wasteland we use as a car park," Inspector Rupert challenged him "Indeed, Mr. Arlington, then please tell the Superintendent how we have in our possession a signature from your accounts ledger".

His lawyer looked at his client and shook his head vigorously.

Inspector Rupert gave a tired smile. "Don't worry, Mr. Arlington, we have a photocopy just in case your ledger disappears. We also know your receptionist was busy in the back office when one of them checked out, leaving an envelope with the bill payment. I don't suppose you still have that envelope"?

The manager shook his head as the office door opened slowly, and the young chambermaid appeared.

"This is very important, Fiona. What colour were the shoes? Were they lace-ups or slip-ons?

The maid stood for a moment.

"Brown brogues, with laces, I remember the night because the porter was cursing because he had to go down to the cellar to fetch the brown polish. There is another thing that springs to mind, Inspector, whoever it was that took the shoes into the room in the morning, wore a string vest and had a strawberry mark on his left shoulder".

She looked at the police officers with suspicion. "Is that all? I still have a lot of beds to do before nightfall". The Superintendent looked at Rupert, who just nodded.

"Thank you, Fiona you have been most helpful".

"There is another thing," she paused, "Forget it. It's not important".

Everything is important Fiona". Inspector Rupert said quickly.

"Earlier today, after the Detective Constable interviewed everyone upstairs, she made a telephone call from the public phone in the hall. She was on the line for quite a while. She sounded quite agitated when she finally hung up, but I had to help with the preparation for a party of guests arriving, so I never paid much attention, but I did notice she sat down to wait for somebody".

The maid turned and left. "Get onto the telephone exchange, sir, you'll carry more clout than me. I wonder if anyone else has used the phone today. If I dial the operator and explain, I might be lucky if they remember the number from here. Perhaps if I dial 1471, that will give me the last number dialled from here".

He raced out of the office. He was disappointed to see people waiting to use the phone.

And a resident is using the phone. He made his way upstairs to room 142, where the forensics team were busy dusting for prints.

"When you've finished here, Brian, take a couple of the lads across the road to the ruined building opposite, get a look around, it's possible that is where the shot was fired from, although I don't hold much hope of finding anything, but you never know".

The snow had completely covered the blood on the steps. A voice spoke out of the darkness, smoking a cigarette. "Can I clear the snow from the steps now, Inspector? I was told to leave it earlier while the forensic team looked for clues, but now, as you can see, the blood has been completely covered".

"Yes, that's fine, there is nothing more we can do here now". The Inspector looked at the man. "Are you the night porter at the hotel? "He asked bluntly.

"Yes, general dogs' body, that's me,"

Inspector Rupert asked quickly. "So, you were on duty the night the guisers came here for a bit of rumpy pump, two men in masks and a girl".

The porter thought. "Yes, a noisy bloody lot they were too, I had to tell them to keep the noise down on a couple of occasions,"

Inspector Rupert asked quickly, "Ah, so you would've seen one of the men"?

The porter shook his head. "They never came to the door, but I remember the voice, scratchy, squeaky, then a laugh like a donkey, heehaw, heehaw". The porter laughed at his own imitation.

Inspector Rupert went back inside to get the Superintendent. They discussed the day's sad event. After the description the night porter had given him, he was convinced he knew the identity of one of the two men.

Inspector Rupert had withheld the information he already had, but now was the time to inform Superintendent MacAulay of his fresh evidence and plot their attack on the two suspects.

"Fancy a snifter, Rupert?". It was an invitation for a drink.

"No, I'll give it a miss tonight sir, until I hear how D.C. Reynolds is doing, so I'll go back to the Yard before I head home; besides, it's been a long day".

He dropped the Superintendent at the Wellington pub in Richmond. "Goodnight, sir, see you in the morning," was the departing sentence from the worn-out Inspector.

"Not if I see you first, Rupert".

There was a slight guffaw as Superintendent Angus MacAulay walked away from the car into the falling snow.

Inspector Rupert knew it was a form of pressure release that Superintendent MacAulay was showing.

The days that passed brought fresh hope to Chloe Reynold's recovery. She had been kept in the intensive care recovery room. Inspector Rupert visited the hospital, sometimes twice during the day and then again at night.

He met with her parents at the hospital on several occasions; their daughter was still in a coma, and under supervision every minute of the day. The waiting was the worst part, waiting for news of her recovery. It was the doctor whom he had spoken to when Chloe was first brought in.

"I need to be honest with you, Inspector Rupert. Chloe Reynolds will never be the same again. The trauma that has been inflicted on her, as I said before, will leave her paralysed, from the neck down, the bullet entered her just below the neckline, then travelled up through her mouth and into her brain".

He removed the bullet from a plastic bag.

"You'll need this for future reference Inspector, and if I can just add that Chloe is not out of the woods yet, in fact, we're thinking of doing some more surgery to help reduce the swelling, which is a cause for concern. Her parents have been informed of how delicate an operation it will be, with no guarantees; however, if she doesn't have it, she will die. I'm sorry, I must be so explicit Inspector".

Inspector Rupert thanked him for his frankness and honesty. The news was bad; he thought that as the days passed, Chloe would recover, but that was a hammer blow; to know she was not recovering due to the swelling in her brain.

The Inspector sat in his office and got the information he had been waiting so desperately for.

Superintendent Angus MacAulay had been brought into Inspector Rupert's confidence. Everything was in place to make an arrest.

Inspector Rupert received the sad news as he put things in place. While sitting in his office, he received a call that D.C. Chloe Reynolds had passed away at 06:23 am that morning. She never survived the second operation that was needed to decrease the swelling in her brain and died without regaining consciousness.

He sat for a long time with tears appearing, each time he asked himself, "Why"? Going over again in his mind what had happened. He slammed his fist on the desk.

"Now it's another double murder, I'm going to kill you bastards".

With so many things on his mind, he had forgotten that his daughter April, her husband, and the children were arriving that afternoon from Oxford. His son Colin would be arriving later that afternoon at Paddington station from Brighton and Hove.

It was all go; the pathologist would have to carry out an autopsy, and there would have to be a coroner's inquest. He attended to his work commitment first, before offering his condolences to the Reynold family. He still awaited important information that he had requested. Things, however, would not be resolved quickly; there were not enough hours in the day to get everything attended to, much as he would've liked things to move quicker. However, he did leave a message with the Bar officer that he was to be informed immediately of any new developments.

CHAPTER
Nine

It had been a race against time, and he reached Euston Station minutes before the train arrived with his daughter. There was still time to deposit April at the Mayfair apartment before heading into the city again to collect his son Colin from Paddington station.

Typical, the train from Brighton and Hove had been delayed. The excuse they gave out over the Tannoy was "Heavy snow was causing disruption to services".

"Bollocks," Amadeus said to a ticket collector, "How can one service run on time and yet, a few miles apart in the same country, the other service is delayed"?

He could tell the ticket collector at the barrier was not interested, so he kept his mouth shut.

The Brighton and Hove Express pulled in an hour and twenty minutes late. After several cups of coffee in the refreshment area, Amadeus waved enthusiastically as his son walked tall and erect along the platform to the ticket collector.

They gave each other a hug. Amadeus refrained from asking how his journey was; there would be plenty of time for small talk in the car.

"I hear one of the constables in the Met was shot dead. Any arrest developments underway"? Colin asked quietly. "Still a couple of reports to come in before things become clear, but I have my suspicions".

Amadeus changed the subject, "I'm still on standby as senior officer, over the festive period, but the desk will inform me of any new developments. Besides, Christmas is at the weekend, which is officially my day off, so let's hope and pray that no other crime intrudes on our family Christmas reunion".

Amadeus took off his policeman's helmet and reminisced about times gone by, how he and his wife Deborah would take the children into central London at Christmas.

It was the tradition. They took the children to a film afternoon matinee showing Snow White and the Seven Dwarfs. They did some last-minute Christmas shopping while stopping to listen and donate to the Salvation Army brass band playing the usual traditional Christmas carols. The light flurries of snow added to the theme. They would then take the children to see the live Pantomime 'Cinderella' at the London Palladium. Both parents wondered who in the theatre was enjoying the Pantomime the most, the adults or the children.

When the show ended, he recalled how the hoarse family stood by the brazier, awaiting their turn for roasted chestnuts and marshmallows. Then it was back to the apartment in Mayfair to hang up their stocking, just in case Santa arrived early. They were sound asleep by 22:00 pm. That's when they went to work, filling the children's stockings hanging on the fireplace guard.

After a couple of stiff brandies, they would retire knowing it would be an early morning call from the children.

Amadeus was brought back to the present. There wasn't much preparation or cooking to be done. The housekeeper, Mrs. Dobson, had it all arranged before she went off on her Christmas jollies. "Just stick the cooked Turkey in the oven and heat the home-made broth," was her instruction to April, even though the Christmas pudding was ready to ignite, and it was April who showed her appreciation most by donating one of her shopping vouchers she had received from her college chums. Amadeus said that he had already contributed a money bonus and a present to Mrs Dobson's Christmas.

It was bedlam as expected on Christmas morning; Amadeus was up first. The presents were passed around and opened. There was a lot of thanks and hugs as the gifts were unwrapped. The tree lights were switched on as April opened the last square of the festivity calendar to pull out a chocolate. Drinks were served before dinner as the family sat down to listen as the young Queen_Elizabeth 2nd made her speech at 15:00 pm after which April served the Christmas Turkey dinner while Colin topped up the wine glasses.

Amadeus sat listening attentively for the phone to ring. It was his son Colin who wisely said, "Relax, Dad. They know where to find you if you're needed". He lifted his glass.

"A very merry Christmas to all present and those no longer with us". He said it with sincerity, meaning his mother, who was now in the United States.

They listened to the rest of the Royal family pass on their Christmas message to the United Kingdom and the British Empire. Amadeus thought again of the good times when they sat and watched television or listened to the radio, while the children amused themselves with their new toys. This Christmas Day seemed to be over in a flash.

The three men were about to slink off to the Old Queen Vic. for a sherbet or two, but they had been ordered into the kitchen to clear and wash the dinner pots and plates by April.

"You're not leaving this for me, or Mrs Dobson to clear, so get mobile, one clears the dining room, one wash, one dry, and I'll stack them away, then you can be on your way to the pub, you can put the rubbish down the chute and take the empty wine bottles to the bin area". The orders were given in a friendly tone, but April meant them all the same.

After much complaining, it was done. The kitchen and dining room sparkled once again. April's husband was only too eager to please.

Amadeus, Colin and Duncan went off to the old Vic pub for an evening session.

Amadeus was astounded at the friendship within the pub, like the fountain bar in Welwyn Garden City. They sat in comfort at a roaring log fire; it was small talk, discussing events that happened in Brighton and Hove and April and Duncan's Oxford college. "What about your dad? You seem to be holding ace cards close to your chest". Colin finished his pint and went for another round. They made their way home at closing time. Linked arms in arms singing. "Oh, come all ye faithful".

The new year was brought in with the same merriment, as Amadeus tried to sing "Auld Lang Syne" badly.

A song he had learned in Scotland while serving with Coastal Command during the early years of the Second World War, before joining Bomber Command.

They all agreed that the festive season had been a success. There were hugs and kisses as the family vacated the apartment. April and Duncan headed back to Oxford, and his son Colin went back to Brighton and Hove.

Colin's departing shot was, "I'm thinking of a transfer to the Met. Dad, so you might be seeing more of me in the future".

Amadeus hugged him. "You could do worse, son, but it's a bit different from a coastal station or town, just bear that in mind and you'll go far". They all jumped into the car and were driven to each of their railway stations for departure. Amadeus and Colin helped April and Duncan with the luggage. After a tearful farewell, he dropped his son at Paddington railway station, then he drove to Scotland Yard, just to check if there were any new developments, but still gripped in the festive season mood, things were much the same, very little was happening. He went home to a quiet, empty apartment.

However, although his mind was frequently with Chloe Reynolds' demise, he wasn't despondent. The family visit had certainly cheered him up.

The next morning, he decided to visit one of the crime lords in the city. They spoke candidly about things that were happening in the metropolis.

"Times are changing, Rupert, you and I are becoming dinosaurs of our time. It's the younger hoods who are running things while trying to take over this city. We try to advise them, but that's not the reason for your visit, is it, Rupert"?

"No, Harry, it's not. There is a manhunt going on for the killer of a policewoman recently, a fine young girl with a promising future. There are also two other murders, which are linked, and I need to add Harry, that I believe this crime could be connected to a city crime lord".

The old gangster shook his head. "This was not a hit by any crime family Rupert. You're barking up the wrong tree. We in the syndicate talked about the murdered policewoman among ourselves, because the last thing we want is you lot breathing down our necks, however it is the general consensus, among us that there is a new kid on the block, and we would be more than grateful if you crowd at the Yard can find him for us because whoever it is, nearly caused a gang war in the city". He paused. "You scratch my back, and I'll scratch yours Rupert".

"Yeah, Harry, we'll do the groundwork for you," He paused, "You know the script, you put the word about that this is a major investigation, and a lot of toes will be trampled on, and crushed if it's not solved soon".

Inspector Rupert said no more; he just wanted to be sure of the facts that none of the four crime bosses who controlled their parts of the city were in any way involved.

Now it was time for some real action. The Oxford hotel manager was arrested for running a house of ill repute.

Several prostitutes were taken in for more in-depth questioning. The telephone exchange had traced the fatal call that cost D.C. Reynolds her life. The bank accounts of the deceased, Jones and Morris, were seized, and the pathologist's report was crucial to the outcome of the case.

Chloe Reynolds had been shot with an old Smith and Weston magnum handgun; Inspector Rupert held the deadly bullet that had been removed from Chloe Reynolds' head in his wall safe at home. She was shot at close range, which would've left scorch marks on the clothing of the assassin, who was left-handed, and certainly used his left hand to carry out the killing.

After attending Chloe Reynolds' funeral in York, Inspector Rupert wanted to get back to London and the Yard as quickly as possible in preparation for the right time to pounce and make an arrest.

He made a phone call when he arrived at Euston railway station in London. "That's right sir, I'm ready to make an arrest tomorrow morning, so if you follow my instructions, then it should go without a hitch".

There was a moment's pause. "Yes, that's correct sir, so until tomorrow".

He contemplated going to the old Vic but decided against it. He must have a clear head for the task ahead. However, he had a couple of wine snifters while he got settled, concentrating his thoughts on the Times crossword.

The next morning, he was up with the proverbial lark, had a good hearty breakfast, a shower, a shave, and fresh clothes, and he set off enthusiastically for Scotland Yard.

He sat in his office and rolled the bullet around in his hand while waiting for the team to arrive.

Superintendent Angus MacAulay was the first to put his head around the door. "I'll be in the canteen Inspector, no breakfast".

He gave a short wave and then closed the door. The rest of the tea started to filter in one by one, and the three police officers from Welwyn Garden City gave him a hearty handshake.

He greeted them enthusiastically as the telephone engineer arrived.

"Excellent, now somebody go to the canteen and tell Superintendent MacAulay, we're ready to rock and roll. "He slammed his hands on the desk. "Now you already have your instructions. Okay, follow me".

There was no hesitation; each member knew exactly what to do as they walked past the gobsmacked secretary, and each followed their orders to the letter.

Inspector Victoria Buckingham of the Hertfordshire constabulary, following Inspector Rupert, walked into the Assistant Commissioners' office. Superintendent MacAulay and Sergeant

Godfrey entered the Chief Superintendent Skinner's office, placing handcuffs on him before he could reach into his desk drawer.

The telephone engineer began to dismantle the Chief Superintendent's phone, before moving into the office of the Assistant Commissioner then began to dismantle the telephone on the Assistant Commissioner's desk.

"What in hell's name are you playing at, Rupert? Have you gone completely insane"?

"Sometimes I wish that were the case, that way I could shoot you and your accomplice next door, then plead insanity".

He gave the Assistant Commissioner a look of disgust.

"Before I read you your rights Hadley, I want you to take off your uniform and dress with the suit you keep in your wardrobe, that way I'm not about to charge a scumbag, dressed in the uniform of a responsible person who has misused and abused his position of trust that's placed on you by the public of this city". The Assistant Commissioner refused to move.

Inspector Rupert stepped forward and ripped the crown insignias from the Assistant Commissioner's shoulders.

"Now you have a choice of dressing yourself in plain clothes or we'll do it for you".

He stepped nearer to the Assistant Commissioner again, who got up off his chair, then walked to his office wardrobe to change out of his damaged Police uniform.

"You'll pay for this, Rupert. You have just crossed the line, and I'll make sure you're thrown out of the force".

Inspector Rupert and Inspector Buckingham watched the Assistant Commissioner as he stepped out of his uniform and soiled shirt, then into his casual suit. He watched as Inspector Buckingham acknowledged the heart-shaped birthmark on Proctor Hardley's shoulder.

Inspector Rupert then forced open the desk drawer and removed the automatic pistol, carefully holding it with his forensic-gloved hand.

"I don't know yet whether it was you that killed D. C. Chloe Reynolds, or the other scum bag downstairs, but that will be made clear when we match the bullet taken from Chloe's head to this gun, or the gun that's in Skinner's office drawer. "

He paused, "One way or the other, both of you will be going away for a very long time, and I'll personally make sure the crime bosses in the city know where you and your henchman are imprisoned. I'm sure they will arrange a welcoming party, no matter where you're interning".

The Inspector waited until the Assistant Commissioner was dressed in his plain clothes before charging him. He wondered why the Commissioner had not appeared; the secretary was bound to have alerted him to the commotion going on. However, it appeared that the Commissioner was at a festive luncheon and would not be back in his office until tomorrow, so Inspector Rupert carried on.

"Proctor Hadley, I'm arresting you on suspicion of three counts of murder, also running brothels and prostitution rackets in the city of London, people trafficking, and illegal gambling casinos. Financing illegal pornographic films. There will be other charges to follow; however, you do have the right to remain silent, because anything you do say may harm your defence when you go to court". He paused, "I'll be holding you for further questioning and have arranged to have you formally charged on Friday, at 10 am. So, you need to appoint a solicitor, or we'll do it for you". He looked at the uniform piled up on the floor. "Take him away Inspector. "He watched as Proctor Hadley was led away in handcuffs.

He took a few minutes to gather himself before going downstairs to the Chief Superintendent's office. He went through the same procedure as he had done with Hadley.

The suspect was ordered to strip out of his uniform before being charged.

"I don't want you in your uniform, Skinner. It would pain me to charge someone in a uniform above my rank". Detective Inspector Rupert said, as the back-up team looked on.

"We have you banged to rights, Skinner. The thing that gets my back up is the fact that you killed one of your own. I just hope you and your accomplice are heading for the gallows, and a noose tied around your scrawny neck; however, I'm sure the judge will take into consideration the fact that you and Hardley murdered a colleague, a young police officer in her prime, and"

He paused. "Back in 1933, you were probably up to no good then, as you climbed the promotional ladder; however, a lengthy jail term will do for me, if you ever survive your sentence. You know what other prisoners think of corrupt policemen, and you can be sure they will be informed of who you are, and what rank you held".

He watched as Superintendent MacAulay pulled Skinner up from the chair by the scruff of his neck.

"Please be careful sir, we don't want to cheat the hangman, or the suspect claiming police brutality, then calling in the complaints division". Inspector Rupert said with a look of satisfaction spread across his face.

"I'll let you do the honours, Angus. It would leave a sour taste in my mouth to charge someone who had a promising career, who would've been the next Assistant Commissioner".

Detective Inspector Rupert shook his head. Here was a man totally stripped of integrity, who had let his wife and family down, to say nothing of the wasted years it had taken to elevate himself to the present rank; all his colleagues in the Metropolitan police would have a sour taste in their mouths later today when word leaked out about the arrests.

"Make sure you take his tie off, along with his brown brogue shoelaces, Angus. We don't want him escaping the law by attempting suicide".

Inspector Rupert watched as the suspect was dressed in his business suit, kept in his office wardrobe, that he used for casual functions.

The gun was removed from the desk drawer and placed in a forensic bag.

"You have the right to one phone call Skinner, so, if you want my advice, then I would not phone your own crooked lawyer".

He watched with satisfaction as Frank Skinner was led away in handcuffs.

"A good job well executed". He said loudly to the incident room, which had erupted into chatter between the officers, the gossip making the most of what had just taken place.

Inspector Rupert left them to converse with one another about what had happened upstairs.

He phoned the BBC press office to inform them of what had just taken place.

He telephoned the newspaper editors who deserved this story, which would hit the front pages of the morning newspapers.

He had just put on his hat, coat and scarf to go home when his office telephone rang.

It was the Commissioner who got wind of the occurrence.

"Rupert, I need to know if it is true what I've heard, that you have arrested two senior officers, without me being informed or present".

The voice was slurred because he was attending a festive function.

"Yes, sir, what you've heard is true. We arrested both suspects, who have been taken to Bow Street police station. They will be formally charged later in the week, then taken to a secure prison to await their court appearance. I'll explain when you're available, sir". He paused, "Enjoy your lunch sir". He replaced the phone onto its cradle before he got embroiled in technical jargon from the Metropolitan Police Commissioner.

It had been a very harrowing experience having to arrest two senior officers of the Metropolitan police force.

Inspector Rupert knew that Scotland Yard offices would now be buzzing with the news of the arrests concerning the Assistant Commissioner and his accomplice, Chief Superintendent Skinner. He had left the incident room, wondering what in hell's name was going on in the force these days. However, he relished in the satisfaction that he had brought to justice two officers who had let the force down badly.

He awaited the forensic results on the handguns. He had mug shots taken of the suspects, one in his string vest. That would be his revenge on the two scumbags, who had gunned down a young police officer in broad daylight while she was performing her duty at the Exeter hotel.

He had arranged to meet Inspector Victoria Buckingham and Superintendent Angus MacAulay for a late lunch. They were quite comfortable with what they had carried out in the name of justice. It seemed strange that D.I. Victoria Buckingham was now an officer of equal rank; her promotion had been achieved after the successful Aristocratic investigation, even his friend Superintendent Angus MacAulay outranked him, yet he was the one giving the orders when the arrests were made, and the preliminaries carried out. They talked openly about the morning's work; all they could do now was wait for forensics to match the bullet to the gun, and the clothing was tested for powder residue and scorch marks. The formal charges that would be made later that week would depend on the results.

D.I. Buckingham spoke gently. "This is surely the crowning glory of your career Inspector, perhaps promotion and a gong. Would be in order".

"I'm not interested in promotion any more Inspector, or a gong, because we were only doing our job; besides, I'd trade them all if I could bring young Chloe Reynolds back". He paused,

"She was like you, Victoria. Keen, inquisitive, sharp-minded, and determined to capture the villains".

"I had a good teacher Inspector Rupert". She said with a smile, then rose from the table.

"Time to go and face the journey back to Hertfordshire".

They gave each other a hug before parting company.

When she had gone, Superintendent Angus MacAulay spoke up.

"Imagine that: you really liked her, Amadeus; I didn't know you had any passion left in you".

"It's not passion Angus, it's knowing that the force is in good hands, while over the years I've moulded her into a fine police officer, who will go far, mark my words".

They finished their coffee, shook hands and went back to their separate departments.

Inspector Rupert went back to the Yard and was met by noisy reporters and media cameras.

He answered the questions that were fired at him.

"Yes, it's true that two senior officers have been arrested on suspicion of murder and other charges, however it would be unprofessional of me at this stage to comment or name them, before

I've spoken to the Commissioner, however you all know the drill, a media briefing will be arranged after the pair have been formally charged".

He turned and walked quickly into the revolving doors of the Yard, then he walked directly to the incident room to check on what was happening around the capital.

Things were relatively quiet, so he went back to his office,

The forensics had moved quickly in ascertaining which gun fired the lethal shot. It was as he had guessed, the gun taken from Skinner's office was fired recently and matched the bullet removed from Chloe Reynold's head. The scorch marks and residue were still traceable on his coat. It was confirmed that Frank Skinner had fired the fatal shot. Another factor was, his fingerprints were all over the weapon, including the trigger. There was more damning evidence that would hang the pair: the photographs, and what the chambermaid at the hotel Exeter hotel had said about the birthmark. The Morris couple, who identified themselves as the ones who abducted Alison Jones from a busy London Street. The security guard identified them as being the ones who visited Alison's flat, posing as art insurers.

Inspector Rupert gave a wry smile, now that he had all the evidence needed to send a report to the Crown Prosecution Service, who had been informed of what had taken place.

As the Inspector imagined, they were now asking questions, hoping to get some answers before things got out of hand and reached Government level. He received an urgent telephone call from their office.

"You'll have my report after the two suspects are formally charged. Meanwhile, I've to get charge sheets and witness statements typed up in preparation for Friday, so if you'll excuse me". He replaced the telephone, then took the paperwork up to the typing pool. Explaining that he needed duplicate copies for the suspect's lawyers.

Inspector Rupert had a clear head on his shoulders after a good night's sleep. He had a feeling that the meeting with the Commissioner would not be comprised of just the two of them present, and he was right.

He smiled at the receptionist, who lifted the phone. "Inspector Rupert, sir". She replaced the receiver, only this time she got off her seat and showed him to the door, opening it to allow him entry.

The Commissioner, and someone in a shiny tailored suit that looked as if it had been tailored in Saville Row. They sat talking and stopped abruptly when Inspector Rupert entered.

"This is Mr. Tompkins, from the Home Office. Rupert, take a seat and tell me what in the name of God is going on? And you better have a good excuse as to why I was kept in the dark about this sting operation". The Commissioner looked at the Home Office representative, who sat rigid and non-committal in the comfortable leather chair.

"The reason you were kept out of the investigation is simple, sir. I couldn't determine whether you were involved in it, and that's why I brought in trusted officers from another county and expressed my fears to a senior officer here at Scotland Yard, because there is far too much flummery going on in the Metropolitan Police. Fellow officers who are Freemasons, coercing with known criminals from their mother lodge, something that I think should be investigated and put a stop to".

Inspector Rupert was unsure if the Commissioner was a member of a Masonic Lodge. He had tested him on numerous occasions without getting a response. There was also the question of Mr. Tomkins: was he also a Freemason?

He himself had joined the brotherhood years ago and could still give a sign that a Freemason would recognise, then a word would follow, ending in the masonic handshake. He tried it again and got no response from either man.

"If I could give Superintendent Angus MacAulay a mention sir, with an opening that will come up for a Chief Superintendent's position, with him playing a major part in the apprehension of the suspects. A good down-to-earth officer, worth a mention sir".

"You're not a bloody mason as well Rupert"? The Commissioner smiled. "If so, are you not supposed to help each other in a time of need, charity and all that, which makes you a hypocrite if you are a mason, because Proctor Hardley and Frank Skinner are members of the Masonic Order here in London".

"There are good masons, and bad mason's sir, just like any other organization, good and bad, and it is up to the individual to uphold the tenets of freemasonry, and test Tweedle Doe, Tweedle Dee, and Tweedle Dum".

Inspector Rupert Hesitated". A figure of speech sir, please don't ask me to explain".

"Perhaps you're right Rupert, so where do we go from here"? It was a direct question. The Home Office representative was listening intently.

"Well, sir, I would wait before calling a press conference, at least until we've formally charged them, and the Crown Prosecution Service agree to push forward with the case, and with the evidence we've got, that will be a foregone conclusion. However, let the law determine the outcome of the accused".

He watched the civil servant move in his chair. "Well, if there is nothing else sir, I've a lot of paperwork to be getting on with. I'm afraid I'm now playing catch-up". He turned to the Commissioner. Will D.C. Reynolds get a commendation for bravery sir. Because she thoroughly deserves it. Shot in the line of duty, one newspaper editor put it. The Commissioner lifted his head at the mention of a newspaper editor.

"Leave it with me Rupert. I'll see what I can do" There was no commitment in his voice.

So, Inspector Rupert turned and walked out without a thank you or salute. He did stop at the secretary's desk. He smiled and rubbed his nose, reminding her of what he knew: her affair with the Commissioner. He heard her curse as the typewriter stopped, so he made his way quickly to the stairs, taking them two at a time until he reached the first floor. His new refurbished office was situated at the end of the corridor, with a view of the River Thames. But he bypassed it, continued down the stairs, and made his way home, stopping at the Old Queen Vic. for a refreshment.

He was glad that the meeting with the Commissioner was over and had gone well.

He tried to figure out why the man from Whitehall was there, and never said a word, which was typical of civil servants and members of Parliament, which he had experienced in the past, during his case in Hertfordshire before moving back to the Met. in London, accepting the demotion to Inspector.

Sometimes he wondered if he had done the right thing. Just a few years from retirement after eighteen years' service, he had considered signing on for another five years with the force he had once loved and adored. Now he was having second thoughts, after the downfall of two senior officers, knowing there would be more arrests to follow in the future.

CHAPTER

Inspector Rupert had been in the Yard since first light, having tea and scrambled eggs with toast. He studied all the relevant documents required for the interview. The recording machine had been loaded and was ready to record.

Proctor Hadley's solicitor joined him in the canteen. "Sorry to intrude on your breakfast, Inspector; however, I've a proposition to make". He paused. "My client is not the one who killed the Detective Constable and is prepared to turn Queen's evidence if we can come to some arrangement". He waited for a reply.

Inspector Rupert was in no hurry. He scooped up some scrambled egg onto the toast, took a bite, then washed it down with the tea. "What you're really asking, Danskin, is you want to make a deal, is that correct"?

The solicitor nodded hopefully. "Yes, that is correct, Inspector. My client might have been the ringleader, but it was Skinner who did the dirty work, and he enjoyed it".

"Listen Danskin, there are criminals I can do a deal with if it suits our end, but I won't discuss any deals, with those two scum bags, you'll hear when he is charged with the murders he took part in or committed, so, you can make that request to the Crown Prosecution Service, who in turn will hand it to the clerk of the court. You know the procedure; therefore, might I suggest you sell off in the direction of the door? But before you go, let me say this. After your client has been formally charged and taken away, then you'll know and I'll know it's out of my hands, so if you don't mind, I want to finish my breakfast in peace".

The solicitor looked disappointed and moved to another table.

Inspector Rupert continued with his breakfast while studying the statement papers.

When he walked into the interview room, the scene was set. The recording operator, the prisoner, and his lawyer, along with a W.P.S., who would act as a witness more than anything. The young constable guarding the door, and finally, Danskin the solicitor. He thanked everyone present before nodding to the recording operator, who switched the machine on. The Inspector introduced everyone present before starting to talk. This formal charge interview commences at 09.30 a.m. on Monday, 21st January 1951". He placed his palms on the table.

"Proctor Hadley, you have been arrested on suspicion of two counts of murder and participation in the murder of Detective Constable Chloe Reynolds. The other victims are Alison Jones and Ronny Morris. There are other charges, which I'll bring against you later in the proceedings. However, for the recording, I want you to answer "yes or no" clearly when asked a question, you have been read your rights in front of witnesses. You're now being formally charged; however, I must ask for the record that you understood those rights".

Proctor Hadley looked at his solicitor. "Yes", he spoke clearly with confidence.

"Good, so you were aware of what was said"? Inspector Rupert nodded, "Let me remind you that you are still under caution". Inspector Rupert moved the papers on the table. "Just confirm your name, your previous occupation, and address, please".

Proctor Hadley spoke softly in his scratchy voice, giving the recorder the information. At this point, Inspector Rupert handed the solicitor the statements taken from the hotel staff witnesses.

"For the record, I've just passed the witness statements to Mr. Hadley's solicitor; they clearly state that Mr. Hadley, with his Chief Inspector at that time, who held the rank of Chief Superintendent Skinner, before his arrest. They took a young prostitute, called Alison Jones, to the Exeter hotel on Halloween night last year; however, that was not the first or the last time you and Alison formed a threesome with Frank Skinner. "He paused. "Any comment to make regarding these sex trysts? "

The prisoner looked at his solicitor, who shook his head. "For the record, Mr. Procter's solicitor has advised his client not to answer; however, we know that Mr. Skinner and Mr. Hadley were at the hotel and the last to see the girl alive".

"What has Skinner been telling you, Rupert"? Gone was the self-assured attitude of Hadley.

"It was Frank Skinner who strangled her and dumped her into the Thames; I was a mere observer".

Inspector Rupert had him on the ropes. "What about the young pimp, Ronny Morris, who was blackmailing you? He knew what you were up to in the city, so you had him killed, setting fire to the car with him shot, but alive and bound in the back seat".

The Inspector threw a forensic bag onto the table. "For the record, this is the bullet removed from Ronny Morris's body, which matches the handgun removed from your office drawer Mr. Hadley".

Inspector Rupert threw another forensics bag onto the table. "This is the bullet removed from Alison Jones' body, which matches the same gun taken from your desk drawer".

Inspector Rupert inhaled deeply. "Therefore, Proctor Hadley, I charge you with committing the murders of Ronald Morris and Alison Jones. I also charge you with being an accomplice and accessory in the murder of Detective Constable Chloe Reynolds". He paused "Other charges will be made against you for running illegal brothels and prostitution rackets, also financing pornographic films. Those charges will be brought later, after a full investigation into your corrupt and illegal exploits can be carried out". Proctor Hadley was handcuffed and led away to await his court hearing.

The team sat in the canteen discussing the recent successful charges brought against Proctor Hadley; they didn't have much time before Frank Skinner was brought up from the cells. Inspector Rupert informed the team that this would be many of the same charges brought against Frank Skinner. Only this time, the much more serious charge of killing a police officer and an accomplice in the Murders of Alison Jones and Ronald Morris. The prostitution rackets and the running of illegal brothels.

"This will be a duplicate of the earlier interview except for the fact that it was Frank Skinner's gun that killed Lisa, it is also his tie and tissue fragments taken from below Alison Jones' nails, as she tried to protect herself. It is also a fact that the telephone call she made to me by Chloe Reynolds requesting assistance, bypassed the switchboard and was answered by Skinner, who took steps to assassinate her. He telephoned Hadley in a panic. I can only surmise that the order came from Hadley, because of the extortion, and what she knew would've brought both down".

Once again, the stage was set, and a new tape had been put into the recorder. They walked to the interview room, where the accused and his lawyer sat talking quietly.

The Inspector led the team in, and each took their seats, with the young constable taking up his position at the door, changing the sign from vacant to engaged.

"Thanks to everyone for being on time". He paused and turned to Frank Skinner's solicitor.

"I'm sorry we've not met or been introduced due to the time factor, so if you could give me your name and company name, so I can mention it when the recording machine is switched on, this is for future reference for the Crown Prosecution Service and the court".

"My name is Christine Chisholm, my company is Regency Associates of Putney, here to represent our client, Mr. Frank Skinner. Now, can we get underway"? Her voice was menacing before proceedings even started.

The company name twigged in his memory as he wrote down the details.

Inspector Rupert had heard of Regency associates. They sailed close to the wind on many occasions and were notorious for representing gangsters and the other lowlife that frequented the various London courtrooms".

"Before I begin, the charges, I want you, Frank Skinner, the accused, to speak clearly when answering the questions".

"I've the right to remain silent, Rupert. You can fire your questions at me, but don't forget, I've been sitting where you're sitting now, so don't expect any cooperation from me. I'll demand my right to remain silent".

"Indeed, you have that right, Mr. Skinner, which gives me the opportunity to remind you that you're still under caution".

Inspector Rupert ignored what was said and signalled for the recorder to be switched on.

"For the record, this interview has begun at 12:05 pm on Friday, 25th January 1953. He listed those present before turning to the accused. "For the record, please state your name and address, also your previous employment.?

The Inspector sat staring at the tight-lipped accused.

"The accused refuses to answer, so I will start to make the formal charges. "He handed the solicitor the witness's statements and charge sheets.

"Frank Skinner, you have been arrested on suspicion of several crimes, which include, the murder of Detective Constable Chloe Reynolds, running a prostitution racket, there is also a charge of owning and running illegal unlicensed casinos, there are public disorder charges, that you and your accomplice, called Proctor Hadley, tried to start a gang war, in order that you could rule parts of London under your own syndicate".

Inspector Rupert sipped his water before continuing.

"Today, I will charge you with the murder of Detective Constable Chloe Reynolds. Today I will charge you with being an accomplice in the murders of Alison Jones and Ronald Morris; the other charges will be brought later when a full investigation is conducted".

"You have been read your rights. I want you for the sake of the recording. Did you understand those rights, yes or no, please? "

The accused sat silent. "Alright, Mr. Skinner, I shall read those rights to you again in the presence of your lawyer so there is no misunderstanding or confusion". He paused.

"I've already listed what you're being formally charged with; however, you have the right to remain silent, but anything you do say may harm your defence. When used against you in court, do you understand what I've said"?

The accused sat with his arms folded. It was a form of hostility and defiance.

"I should at this point instruct Mr. Skinner's lawyer that for her client 's refusal to answer, this could be construed as guilt by the court".

The solicitor said nothing.

"Alright, let me show the solicitor what evidence we have that enabled us to arrest Mr. Frank Skinner. He bent down and held up a bag containing a telephone that had been converted for personal use. He explained exactly like before, the purpose of the wires being altered. He replaced it on the floor. Holding up another forensic bag.

"This is a revolver taken from Mr. Skinner's office desk. Forensics have concluded that the fingerprints on the gun are his, the same gun that shot and murdered his colleague, D.C. Chloe Reynolds, and the bullet that killed her is the same bullet belonging to the accused, Frank Skinner, which matches his gun. I repeat that this is the bullet taken from the head wound of D.C. Chloe Reynolds, resulting in her death. Have you any comment to make on that charge, Mr. Skinner"? He sat waiting for a response.

"Alright, if you refuse to answer, I will continue with another scenario. Forensics have matched your skin and blood type taken from the young prostitute called Alison Jones' fingernails, who was dragged from the River Thames. She obviously tried to defend herself; there were fibres taken from around her neck. They were also taken from a tie your accomplice owned Mr. Skinner, so it is our belief that after a sexual encounter, you assisted in murdering her in the room you and your accomplice used at the Exeter hotel, and with the help of your accomplice Hadley, moved her body to your car, which was parked in the vacant ground at the rear of the hotel, you drove her body to a bridge spanning the river Thames, where both of you disposed of her body from the bridge. The pathology department report concluded she fell from a height, which fractured her rib cage and broke her neck".

This brought an instant response from the accused.

"I've never been to this so-called hotel in my life, please tell me where it is, I might use it in future". The accused smirked with satisfaction. "Where is your proof, Rupert? You have none; all you're doing is clutching at straws. It's supposition, nothing more".

The accused gave a nervous laugh, "You have nothing, Rupert. You say you have witnesses. According to one witness, her statement says she saw me abduct a girl in broad daylight on a busy street. Well, let me tell you, she got it wrong. It wasn't me".

"Did I say the witness was a female Mr. Skinner? Did I say Alison Jones was abducted from a busy street in broad daylight"? He paused. "No, I did not".

Inspector Rupert now had Frank Skinner talking and sat for a moment before taking crucial evidence from a file holder. He passed the photographs to the silent solicitor.

"If you read the witness statements, you'll note that a man with very big feet put his shoes out for polishing. The bellboy and the chambermaid on duty that night can swear that those were size twelve". He was interrupted by the solicitor.

"How many people take a size twelve, Inspector? This would be dismissed and laughed out of court as circumstantial evidence". The solicitor waved the statements in the air.

"I couldn't agree more, but that's only for backup evidence; we have Mr. Skinner's fingerprints taken from each shoe". He passed a photograph to the accused.

"This was taken while you were changing into a fresh shirt and your suit, when you were first arrested Mr. Skinner, as you know it is standard procedure, when you're taken to the cells under caution, that a mug shot is taken, however, look very carefully, and remember that when they took your picture you were standing in your string vest, I don't know what excuse the photographer gave you, enticing you to remove your shirt. However, look at both pictures, which show quite clearly a strawberry mark shaped like a heart on your left shoulder. Now read the statement made by our two independent witnesses. I should add that the position of the strawberry mark and its shape are one in ten million, Mr. Skinner. So once again, I'm listening before I formally charge you with Detective Chloe Reynolds' murder, which I read out to you and your solicitor earlier".

He watched Skinner's expression change as he ripped up the statement documents, then ripped up the photographs, rolling the shredded pieces into a ball before throwing them across the desk like confetti at the Inspector. He sat watching the astounded solicitor, who strangely said nothing in defence of her client. Perhaps she was waiting for her day in court.

Inspector Rupert changed tactics, trying to confuse the suspect

"Please bear with me, Mr. Skinner and let's return to the murder of D.C. Chloe Reynolds. That is what you will be charged with today". He paused.

"As for the other charges, they will be carried out when we have made further investigations. Right now, I am more interested in the murder of D.C. Reynolds".

Frank Skinner was formally charged with the murder he had carried out on the steps of the Exeter hotel; now it was for the court to decide his fate.

"Before I close proceedings, you and your solicitor still have time together to confer as to whether you wish to make any comments, Mr. Skinner".

He waited for a moment, but there was no response from the accused or his solicitor.

"Okay, I bring this formal interview to its conclusion. Interview terminated at 14:37 pm".

He expected some backlash from Frank Skinner, the criminal enforcer sitting opposite him, but none came, so after Frank Skinner was handcuffed and taken away, it was a pleasure to sit in the quiet and stuffy interview room with his hands behind his head.

Inspector Rupert felt drained. He had brought the killers to justice; now it was up to the Crown Prosecution Service to do its job and bring the two murderers to court, hopefully a death sentence or a long prison sentence, which he doubted that they would serve if the mob bosses got their way.

The crime lords had patience but would still have their pound of flesh.

Inspector Rupert knew that they had just as much control and information about what was happening inside the prison walls, the governor of the prison had, just as they were informed about what was happening outside the prison in civvy street.

His warning to Proctor Hadley earlier that day was not meant as a joke; the prison showers and toilet blocks were favourite places for targeted prisoners to be ambushed, after being given orders and instructions from outside, to conduct their dastardly deeds, then melt away into the cell blocks and corridors of the prison.

Everything was ready for him to make his report to the Crown Prosecution Service; all the damning evidence against the two accused had been boxed and sealed, delivered by hand and a receipt obtained. Inspector Rupert trusted no one; there were flaws in the system, which had been proved when the two culprits had walked out of Bow Street police station in the early hours. He thought of pursuing that breach of professionalism, but decided to hand it to the complaints division, just to make them work for their wages, remembering the run-ins he had with them in the past. Was it sour grapes? Of course it was, something that had eaten away at his soul, like a cancer that had become malignant, and over the years had festered within him. He was glad to see the office staff busy preparing the photocopies of his report in preparation, ready to go upstairs to the fifth floor, now that the Commissioner had returned to the city, and demanded that Inspector Rupert bring the documentation up to his office personally.

Like so many times in the past, he climbed the stairs, only it took him a little longer, as time took its toll on the body; however, he was determined not to use the lift, because he always felt the exercise of climbing the stairs did him good.

He assumed his usual stance beside the ageing secretary, giving her a wink and rubbing the side of his nose; it was as good as a wink and nod to a blind horse.

He often wondered if Lucy had heeded his advice years before, when he was just a young and newly promoted Sergeant back in the 1930s. He also wondered if she and the Commissioner were still an item. He gave her a smile as she lifted the phone.

"Inspector Rupert sir," was all she said before replacing the receiver.

"Go right in Inspector. "She didn't bother getting up to open the door.

"Ah, Rupert, you have been a busy man in my absence, so give me your report in order that I can scrutinize it before it goes off to the Crown Prosecution Service. "

"No need for scrutiny sir, I can just give you the facts about the murders. Senior officers who turned out bad, both statements copies are practically the same except for a few slight differences, on who did what".

He passed the documentation across the desk.

"I've taken the liberty of sending the original copies with my report to the Crown Prosecution Service, with the formal charge reports sir. I know how busy you are going to be with press coverage; there are, of course, the TV cameras".

"You take too many liberties, Rupert. I should have read them first".

Inspector Rupert had to change the subject.

"There is something you should know sir". He paused. Both the accused were able to walk out of Bow Street police station after taking advantage of a young police officer. I've sent a copy of the report to the complaints division for them to investigate the breach. I can also state that the pair were quickly found and arrested".

"Concerning the complaints division, that was not your decision to make, Rupert; however, I'm prepared to overlook it, due to the fact". The Commissioner hesitated, "The fact that you have rid the force of two criminals". He shook his head.

"I still can't believe that Proctor Hadley would do such a thing. I trusted him implicitly. As for Frank Skinner, I've had my doubts regarding some of his arrest procedures and actions because he has always been heavy-handed, and he should have faced the complaints division long ago, which might have steered him in another direction. We also have what we call the resurrection school for officers, men and women of the force who step out of line. It helps those with attitude problems, helps them to adjust, because I'm sure you know, it's the last chance saloon, fail at the re-education school and you're out. It surprises me that you never attended that correction course Rupert. When I look at your record, the times in the past you've practically crossed that line".

"Am I here to listen to a character demolition on me, when the real subject up for discussion is the two criminals. Incidentally, I want you to authorize the criminal transport for today, because I want the two of them taken to a more secure place of imprisonment".

"Yes, I'll attend to that, Rupert; however, I've other things to consider".

The Commissioner was interrupted.

"I would rather you do that right now sir; otherwise, I'll take it upon myself to give the order".

The Commissioner shifted in his seat.

If looks could kill, Inspector Rupert thought, he would be dead already.

The Commissioner lifted the phone and dialled the prison services.

"Satisfied, Rupert," he said abruptly, while lifting the reports. "Yes, sir, now I'm satisfied".

There was a deathly hush while the Commissioner examined the witness statements, and then the accused documented report.

"I hope you have sent everything, and I mean everything, off to the Crown Prosecution Service, Rupert. You know how fussy they are before they make the decision, whether to go ahead with these cases "He threw the paperwork on the desk.

"Yes, sir, all that has been attended to, and I hope you don't mind me saying that I've covered my back in case anyone decides to have a pop at me. I've filed a copy of this report in my wall safe at home, with instructions to my son to release it to the media, in the event of my becoming another statistic, fitted out with a wooden overcoat". He paused.

"You can be damned sure, Commissioner, if there is any attempt at a cover-up or whitewash, I'll shout it from the highest mountain, do you understand, sir"?

The Commissioner was in a foul mood.

"Those papers you have taken are police property; you have removed them without my authorization, Rupert. You know the penalty for removing documents and disclosing secrets of what we do with arrests we have made, so I'm ordering you to bring those copies back into the Yard post-haste".

"I'm sorry, sir, I'll not carry out that order, simply because it is my insurance policy until those two criminals have been tried and sentenced".

"Get out, Rupert, until I decide what to do with you". His attitude changed.

"What has come over you? I remember you in the old days, you could be sitting where I am today; however, you failed in your career simply because you lacked discipline".

He slammed his palms on the desk. "Out". He yelled with froth appearing at the edge of his lips.

Inspector Rupert stood up and looked at his superior. He shook his head, then turned and walked out, ignoring the secretary, who continued typing. He made his way quickly downstairs. There was little else to do as he thumbed through his in tray. The meeting with the Commissioner should never have turned into a fencing match; it made him wonder just how deeply involved the Commissioner really was. His superior sounded as if the prosecution had no case to answer; however, time would prove him wrong.

Inspector Rupert gave a sigh of relief when two prison transport vans drew up and took each prisoner away.

The week had begun well enough but had slowly gone downhill. The rebuff from the Commissioner didn't help; he had a feeling that things were going to get worse before they got better, and he was right.

Apart from break-ins and assaults, his job had become a desk job, with more serious crime cases being handed out to other officers. This was not the way he intended to finish his police career. He made several attempts to have a word with the Commissioner; however, it was rejected each time, even though the newly promoted Chief Superintendent, Angus MacAulay, had made a request on Inspector Rupert's behalf and was told in no uncertain terms not to waste the Commissioner's time, as there were more important things that needed attention.

For Inspector Rupert, that was the final straw that broke the camel's back. Gone were the thoughts of being an Inspector who was at the beck and call of those higher ranks, who wouldn't know the difference between crime, law, and order if it jumped up and bit them on the arse. There was a time when he had been stuck behind a desk for nearly a year, a waste of policing resources, only being called in when other officers had failed to solve their serious crime cases. He felt he was reaching the apex of his career. After serving the police force so well in the past, he was now stuck behind a desk again, where the rank of Inspector carried little sway.

It was with a touch of sadness that he began to type out his letter of resignation, something he had considered before in his career. He wondered who was pulling his superior's strings. It all started to go pear-shaped when he solved the Aristocracy murders. He knew that somewhere in all this flummery, the Lord Lieutenant of Hertfordshire was involved, how deep he didn't know, and like it was back then, there was no way he could get at the higher aristocrats who were surrounded and protected by powerful friends and red tape of government circles. He also wondered again if the Commissioner knew about Proctor Hadley and Frank Skinner's activities.

When he finished typing the letter, he knew he was biting off his nose to spite his face. He was about to crumple it into a ball, setting it alight and disposing of it in the rubbish bucket.

Inspector Rupert held his temper in check. He had just over two years to serve before his pension, but it wasn't about the money. He was rich beyond his wildest dreams. Besides, what would he do with his life? That was the big question that filled him with dread.?

He would keep his letter of resignation until the time was right. He had a lot of private investigating to do, but he would grind it out until the oceans froze and the rivers ran dry.

He sat back and thought about his letter explaining why he had no affection for the force he once loved. The early days, when his dear dead friend, Squadron Leader Colin Freeman and himself, had joined the Metropolitan Police and passed out as qualified policemen together, before the declaration of war, Colin was a police constable based in Marylebone district, while he, Amadeus Rupert went on to join the Scotland Yard elite in the fraud squad, where his sharp brain and expertise talents were wasted, so he was moved into the serious crime squad, where his talents made the crime lords quiver.

Those were the good old days when comradeship was reliable. Back then, as a young man, he was quickly promoted to sergeant, then Inspector Rupert, a name that would become renowned for the way he was systematic in his approach to solving crimes, methodical and patient.

The days when he gave up a promising career for love, moving to Hertfordshire Constabulary, gaining promotion to Chief Inspector, then accepting demotion to Inspector, to assist his move back to the Metropolitan Police in London, and the city he loved.

"Those were the days". He sighed, then licked the envelope that contained the letter.

He didn't take it upstairs immediately but put it in the office safe for future reference. He remembered the time while serving with the Hertfordshire Constabulary when he had typed out a letter of resignation, which was refused and returned to him by the Chief Constable.

How the years had passed so quickly, and how things had changed within the force and the city of London?

After checking the empty in tray, he put on his hat, coat and scarf, then made his way home, calling into the Queen Vic for sustenance. He sat at the bar, reminiscing about how things had turned out. However, he was determined to put things right as soon as his twenty-five years' service was completed, which would come along just as things had done in the past.

The main concern for him, as he sat sipping his pint, was his son Colin. Now an Inspector with Brighton and Hove police. His move to the Metropolitan Police had been blocked. Amadeus always thought that his son, Colin Rupert would join the serious crime squad just like he had done. That's what Colin applied for, and under the wings of Chief Superintendent Angus MacAulay, he would be well looked after.

That was never going to happen. Someone with a high rank of importance informed the police board that he was not suitable for city work because he had spent his entire career with a seaside town police force.

Amadeus ordered another beer while thinking of his son. Was it the "High Heid Yins" that bore a grudge? Who it was became irrelevant; the damage had been done, but eventually he would find out who had blackballed his son from joining the Masonic Order.

He knew where all the skeletons were neatly stacked in the cupboards, both here in London and in Hertfordshire, and if push came to shove, "by George", he would bring the entire rotten structure tumbling to the ground.

He had peace of mind that the Commissioner knew this and would be foolish of him to target the son of Inspector Amadeus Rupert, but somebody did. He sat enjoying his beer.

There was a quiz night later, so he decided to leave before the pub got busy.

The January winds cut through him like a knife as he trudged head bowed, against the driving sleet.

It wasn't so bad when he reached the apartment block. The heat penetrated his body as he took the lift to the third floor.

He spent the night beside a log fire, doing the Times crossword, with a bottle of red wine breathing in the kitchen, ready for pouring.

He placed the Times newspaper on the couch and sat back. There was one thing that he had never lost, and that was the ability to smell a rat.

A gut feeling that something big was afoot. Whispers had been made in the canteen that the crime squad and immigration had failed in something big concerning the Met. and MI5.

Not his problem. No dirtier work would be carried out by him.

He finished the bottle of red wine and opened another before falling asleep on the couch.

He woke up with a stiff body and a throbbing head.

There was something he had to sort out in the office this morning, something important. He showered and felt the better for it, then dressed in fresh clothes and underwear, before heading across the city to Scotland Yard. On arrival, he was instructed by the desk sergeant to go immediately to the operations room.

He was greeted with a rapturous "Good morning, sir". He walked across the incident room, only to be informed by Detective Constable Wood that a meeting had been arranged with the Commissioner.

The Commissioner, who had side-lined him to a desk job, had apparently mellowed over time towards Inspector Rupert, who had arrested senior officers without his knowledge.

The Commissioner, who didn't have the courtesy to confront him with the problem now facing the London Metropolitan Police, leaving it to an officer of lower rank to carry the message of a pow-wow. It was another part of Inspector Rupert's knowledge, given to him many years ago. "Never shoot the messenger".

Nowadays, he takes the lift to the fifth floor. He approached the secretary's desk, expecting to confront Lucy, only to be told she had retired a year ago to be with her ailing mother.

He couldn't believe it had been that long since he had teased her about her affair with the Commissioner. The new middle-aged secretary still went through the same rigmarole. Lifting the telephone and saying softly. "Inspector Rupert sir". Before opening the office door.

Hardly anything had changed except that the Commissioner had aged somewhat. Inspector Rupert was offered a seat, which he accepted gladly.

"It's been a while, Rupert; I suppose you've heard Hadley and Skinner were hanged for the murders they committed".

"Indeed, sir, I attended both court cases as a Prosecution witness in the murder trials, then finally, when the other charges were brought against them".

Inspector Rupert tried to keep the conversation as brief as possible.

"Yes, I remember now". The Commissioner sounded tired.

"Before we begin, whatever it is I have been summoned to your office for, please answer me this". He paused for breath.

"Who was it that black-balled my son from joining the Metropolitan police"?

The Commissioner shook his head. "I've no idea what you are talking about, Rupert, now please let's move on".

"Not until I get an answer, Commissioner. You can't sit there and plead ignorance; all applications come across your desk".

"I can't give you the answer you want so badly, Rupert. If your son's application reached my desk, it would have been dealt with in the usual manner and passed to the police board for consideration and know this, Rupert, even if I did know who blocked your son's application, I would not tell you". The Commissioner leaned back in his chair.

"I have a job for you, Rupert, one that might resurrect your career. However, I need to know if you are ready to return to serious crime or remain where you are and see out your time sitting behind a desk".

"If you want the truth, Commissioner, I don't really care anymore. However, I'm always willing to listen and compromise". The Commissioner rose and walked lethargically to the window that looked down the River Thames to Tower Bridge.

"Two things are in the wind now, Rupert. Drugs in the capital have become epidemic; however, you will work with Superintendent MacAulay on that case".

He paused and turned to face the Inspector.

"The most important case is secret and must be kept that way". He paused

"It concerns people smuggling in a large way, hundreds being brought into England from the continent, much bigger than the people trafficking you managed to eradicate before. This is putting a massive strain on our social security and national health". He gave a wry smile.

"It also puts a strain on our housing, where students are now finding it hard to be accommodated". He gave another wry smile.

"You will liaise with MI. 5 and other government departments. It could also mean a promotion, Rupert. Solve this, and you could be elevated in rank very quickly".

"Too late for a so-called promotion for me, but just before you go any further, you say this is supposed to be top secret, yet I hear about it in the incident room".

Inspector Rupert laughed. "That is not top-secret, Commissioner".

"That is why I need you out there, Rupert. I know how good you are at getting to the root of a problem, and yes, there has been a leak somewhere in the early part of the operation".

"Alright, I accept this assignment on two conditions. One, my son is reconsidered for the Met. Two, I will have a contract drawn up and signed by you and M I 5 exonerating me from any downturns in the investigation. You know what those government agencies and officials are like. They tried to hang me out to dry before, and that is not going to happen again. They couldn't agree on the colour of shite".

Both appendices were agreed upon.

After the meeting, he descended the stairs to inform his colleagues of his decision, which was massive as far as his career was concerned. "What career"? He asked himself.

There were changes in the force, but nothing he couldn't handle. There was one important factor that Inspector Rupert was aware of, in all the years he had spent in the police, and that was people were not keen in involving the police, no matter how trivial, there was always that element of doubt in their minds, this was not a new thing in people's lives it was the same in the United States, and around the world, but they had Detective Agencies for generations, called gum shoes, however this was a new concept in England, and he considered becoming a part of it, but the thought was quickly dismissed as day dreaming. He still had the two years to serve of his original contract, and whether he would sign on for another five years when the time came would be another question.

There was still a lot of desire deep inside him to remain a policeman for some time to come, but another thought did cross his mind and often scared him.

"What would he do if he did retire or resign"?

He had to get out of the office and follow up on a case that was given to him by Chief Superintendent Angus MacAulay. Anything was better than investigating domestic abuse and housebreaking, which he had been lumbered with from the day he brought a prosecution against two senior officers. However, the drug epidemic was becoming more pressing as the crime rate soared in the city. The gun crime was getting more serious. Bank raids were an everyday occurrence in the city. However, the domestics could now be handled by the woolly suits. A friendly term used to describe officers of the lower ranks who wore the uniform. Most of the calls coming in were husbands and wives who would attack and assault each other after a night on the town. This had become of epidemic proportions, since fewer people were relying on the sanctity of marriage, living together as partners.

Each call was now put into categories of response, depending on how serious it was.

The police telephonist would take a note of the complaint, then pass it on to an adjudicator who listed it as a red mark that needed immediate response. It was almost always when the police officers who attended the incident found that the couple had made up or one of the pair had disappeared. No further action was required; however, he knew then, as he had found in the past, that most squabbles erupted when either partner was found to be having extra-marital affairs. There were always cases of the spouse emptying the shared bank account and salting it away in some other account. There was a growing number of cases where a woman suspected her husband of poisoning her. This was a case for Inspector Amadeus Rupert, a poisoning was right up his street, murder at its most foul.

Those were many of the cases Detective Inspector Rupert would handle, but he had so much on his plate and found it hard to become involved because of the government problem.

There was a touch of Spring in the air and a spring in his step as he walked out of Scotland Yard into the car compound. Another busy day ahead, policing the great metropolis of London, a side of the city tourists would never be allowed to see.

The End

www.ingramcontent.com/pod-product-compliance
Lightning Source LLC
Chambersburg PA
CBHW070918190726
48292CB00004B/1023